MW01612937

# Neravana

## Edited by

# Fred Towers

Herndon, Virginia

Herndon, VA

# Reprints

"Hardboiled," previously published in *Men Magazine* (April 2007) and the anthology *Sex by the Book* (2007)

"Hazard Pay-off," previously published in *Torso Magazine* (June 2008) and the anthology *Hard Hats* (2008)

# Acknowledgements

Thank you to all the talented contributors to *Nerdvana* whether your story is included or not. Keep writing and submitting.

Thank you to my husband, Mel, for supporting me and my writing. Love you.

Thank you to my junior editor, Boy Beaver, for reading and commenting on all the submissions for me first. All your work is greatly appreciated.

# Dedication

To my best bear friend, J. Michael Mills. I wish I had convinced you to submit your writing before you died, December 13, 2003, but thanks to your support and encouragement, I have succeeded in publishing my gay fiction.

# CONTENTS

INTRODUCTION ..........................................................................1

BOOK WORMS Wayne Mansfield ................................................3

ROBOT COCK Jay Starre ..........................................................19

THE WOOD WIZARD J. D Waters. ............................................35

FOUR-EYES AND EIGHT INCHES Rob Rosen.............................47

EXPOSED Bryl R. Tyne ............................................................59

    Chapter 1 – Waste of Time ................................................59

    Chapter 2 – Second Thoughts ...........................................63

    Chapter 3 – That's Life ......................................................67

    Chapter 4 – Just Cause .....................................................70

    Chapter 5 – Exposed ........................................................76

HAZARD PAY-OFF Landon Dixon ............................................83

GAN HAATZMAUT YERUSHALAYIM David Muller ....................93

A NIGHT IN MIDGAR Augusta Li ...........................................107

TREE HUGGER Jay Starre.......................................................129

HARDBOILED Landon Dixon ..................................................143

LUST CONSULTANT Dalton ....................................................153

BECOMING Jim Clark.............................................................165

THE GRAND DECEPTION Stephen Osborne ...........................175

ADVENTURES OF JAKE #1 Jeff Adams ...................................187

THE BULLY ON THE PLAYGROUND Helen E. H. Madden ..........209

AUTHORS .............................................................................235

EDITOR.................................................................................239

# INTRODUCTION

## *Brains are SEXY*

Figuring I'm not the only one who thinks so, I decided to edit an anthology highlighting the sexy side of the computer geeks, gamers, superhero freaks, and comic book fiends among us.

The nerd's creative mind can turn any activity into foreplay. I remember a hot time playing a strip version of a popular trivia game. I made up rules to convert it. Nothing hotter than being equally matched intellectually and slowly getting naked with each question. A race to see who exposes their treasured parts.

Or, political debates heating up the air getting the blood flowing – to hard cocks.

The torment between jocks and nerds is foreplay for the real attraction between them.

Underneath the glasses, sweater vest and too short pants lies a horny soul.

# BOOK WORMS
## Wayne Mansfield

Ike washed his hands and used the water on them to replaster his ginger hair to his head. He wiped the excess off on a paper towel, adjusted his black-rimmed glasses on his nose and pushed the door to the men's room open.

He immediately regretted his timing.

"Nerd alert! Nerd alert!"

It was Tony Warner, jock extraordinaire. Great teeth, great jaw line, great everything. Great pain in the ass, too.

Despite the fact that Ike had survived high school (by the skin of his teeth), it seemed that university wasn't going to be any easier. His type always seemed to attract the unwelcome attention of the sportier, better looking members of the particular learning institute he was attending. But worse than that, these cowards always travelled in packs. Tony was never far from at least one or two of his goons.

"Bug duster!" said Christopher, one of the guys flanking Tony.

Ike had never heard that one, but before he could ponder what it meant, Tony grabbed the back of his head and held it level with Christopher's ass. A great ripping sound issued forth, and soon Ike's nostrils were filled with the rank stench of a Grade A fart.

Tony pushed Ike's nose further into the cleft between Christopher's butt as the muscular track star expelled the last of the gas. "Careful you don't follow through," laughed Tony.

"Get ya nose out of my ass, ya faggot!" snarled Christopher when he had emptied his bowels. And, with one push he sent Ike staggering into the wall of the biology room before he joined the others as they continued down the corridor, roaring with laughter.

"Don't think ya got all the bugs, mate," Tony said patting his mate on the back.

"Next time," said Christopher. "Those little fuckers seem to always come back for more. They're like fuckin' cockroaches."

Ike glowered at the group of men, his nostrils flaring as he watched them disappear around a corner. He patted his hair down and picked up the books he had dropped, arranging them in order of size in the cradle of his arm.

"Don't worry, Ike. Guys like that always get theirs."

It was Craig. Ike and Craig had met at orientation and had instantly recognized in each other a kindred spirit. But whereas Ike was tall and lean, with ginger hair and freckles, Craig was more robust, stocky even, and had a mop of frizzy black hair and a moustache that threatened to grow in any day now. And while Ike's chest was flat and smooth, Craig was hirsute, the tuft of hair poking out over his top button never ceasing to catch Ike's attention.

"You want to come to the library and work on your research project?"

Ike nodded. "I was going there anyway. I mean, before I was ... attacked."

"Yeah, well like I said, they'll get theirs. I mean they might have the looks, but up top, shit man, it's like a void up there! We have our brains, man, and brains are what counts. Look at Bill Gates!"

Ike faced Craig, looking at him right in his big, brown eyes.

"You're not bad looking," he said, his voice cracking. "I mean, I'm not ... I mean ..."

Craig smiled. "I know mate. And thanks. Now let's get to the library before someone snaps up all the good reference books."

They arrived at the library, caught the elevator to the second floor to retrieve the books they needed and then went up to the third level. It was quieter there. Most people couldn't be bothered making the journey, so anyone who didn't want to be disturbed could quite easily find a table and get on with his work, completely undisturbed.

After half an hour of reading, Craig raised his head from between the pages of his book and looked at Ike taking notes. He smiled to himself as he watched Ike's tongue tracing the contour of his top lip as he wrote, too intently concentrating to notice he was being observed.

"What did you mean that I wasn't bad looking?" he asked after a while.

Ike looked up. "Hey?"

"I just wanted to know what you meant by saying that I wasn't bad looking."

Ike swallowed. His eyelids fluttered as he struggled to find an answer that wouldn't offend, or worse still, earn him a punch in the mouth.

"Well, you said that the jocks had looks and all we had were brains, but I just thought that perhaps you were quite good looking. You know, to the ladies."

"What about to the guys?"

Ike blushed. He felt his cheeks burn red and knew from the look on Craig's face that his new friend had seen it, too.

"Look what you've made me do," said Craig standing up.

Ike saw it immediately, the tent that formed in the front of Craig's cargo pants. He looked away immediately but couldn't help glancing back, especially since Craig seemed so proud of it.

"It looks so big," Ike commented.

"You wanna take a proper look at it?" asked Craig.

Ike swallowed hard again. His eyes flashed around the room. Was anybody watching this? He was already getting teased for being a nerd. If they saw him looking at the bulge in Craig's pants, they'd really let him have it.

5

"Come on, man. No one's looking," said Craig as his right hand came to rest on the zipper.

"Not here!" snapped Ike. "Someone might see."

Craig's face broke into a grin. "So you do want to see it? How about over there, behind the bookshelf?"

He moved away from the desk, the front of his trousers sticking out a good eight inches in front of him. Even when he was moving his cock remained in place due to the restrictions of the fabric. And then he stepped into the shadows of the massive wooden shelves. He walked a short way in and then turned. Ike's eyes were riveted on him. A wicked smile crept over Craig's face as his hands lowered his fly.

Ike hardly dared to draw breath. He wanted to see what was between Craig's legs almost as much as he wanted Craig to come back and stop all this messing around. What if they got caught? What if the university expelled them for lewd behavior? Oh God, then his parents would find out. He felt his heart race against his rib cage. A small sheen of perspiration suddenly appeared on his brow. It was also getting more and more difficult to breathe.

And there it was. Craig unleashed his huge member right out in front of the Psychology periodicals.

Ike gasped.

Craig's mouth still retained the smile of a rebel, perfect white teeth exposed as surely as the uncut monster between his legs was. But Craig hadn't finished his little display yet. He reached into his pants and brought out his great, hairy ball sac. They hung through the small opening of his fly, bulging beneath the cock that kept company with them.

Ike felt something unfurling within the elasticized fabric of his own underpants. He reached down and adjusted himself, giving the thickening prick a helping hand to free itself from the nest of red pubic hair it nested in. Within five seconds he was as hard as his friend behind the book shelves.

Then Ike felt his cheeks flush. Craig gestured for him to join him. He shook his head vigorously. He mouthed the word "No" and then nodded toward the main area of the library. Yet his friend was insistent. There was nothing for it. He scanned the room and found that the only three other people in it were nose-deep in books. He stood and scampered across to where Craig waited.

"Glad you could make it, buddy," he said, giving Ike a friendly slap on the back. "You wanted to see it so here it is. You can touch it if you like. Go ahead. Wrap your hand around it. Grip it!"

Ike wanted to feel Craig's cock more than anything he'd ever wanted before. The only cock he had ever touched had been his own and this one looked thicker, had more veins and was hairier. Every nerve in his body was firing sparks of electricity. He could almost hear it crackle in the air. Craig's cock looked so hard, so meaty and it gave off a slight aroma. Was it piss? Or something else? Pheromones? He'd read something about them in a magazine – the hormone of attraction – he'd just never experienced them before.

Finally, he touched it, his fingers closing around the firm, spongy girth. Suddenly, he felt alive. It was as if this one action had triggered something inside him. He stroked it, sliding his hand up and down once, twice, three times. All the time his eyes stayed glued to the swollen organ, its shiny, pink-purple head and the large, blue vein that wormed its way along the entire length sending a smaller tributary skirting around the shaft at the top before both tapered into nothingness. A small bead of precum appeared in Craig's piss slit. He smiled. It felt so electric to have another man's cock in his hand.

"Feels good, hey?" said Craig. "Wanna suck it?"

Ike removed his hand and looked about him as if some crime had already been committed. Every cell in his body wanted to further the experience, to feel another man's cock in his mouth and not just dream about it. He looked about him once more and

7

then peered through the shelves on either side before dropping to his knees.

"That's it mate," Craig said exhaling slowly. "Nice and gentle. Watch your teeth."

The throbbing cock tasted slightly salty. It wasn't a disagreeable flavor; in fact it was quite pleasant. He took more and more of it in his mouth trying to do it the way he had seen it done on the pornos he was in the habit of downloading. He gripped the root of the organ and fed the rest of it down his throat, sliding his mouth up and down the shaft until he found he was enjoying himself more than he suspected he would.

He felt Craig put a hand on the back of his head and push it deeper onto his pulsing prick. He gagged slightly but kept the momentum going. Soon he realized he was actually quite good at sucking cock. It slid down his throat with relative ease and Craig's hand on his head and the tiny slap, slap of his big hairy balls on the skin under his chin were all the encouragement he needed.

"You're a natural, mate," said Craig leaning his head back and closing his eyes. "How many times have you done this before?"

Ike took his mouth of the saliva-coated cock and swallowed the glob of spit and precum that accumulated at the back of his throat.

"This is the first time," he replied.

Craig's smile widened. He didn't believe his friend but didn't really care. He pushed Ike's head back onto his cock until he felt the head of it brush past the red-head's tonsils.

"That's it, Ike. Suck that fat cock and I'll give you your first taste of cock cream."

At that moment a librarian in a short-sleeved white shirt, an armful of books and a pen in a plastic holder around his neck appeared around the corner.

"Oh no!"

Craig's eyes turned into saucers and Ike nearly upended a whole shelf of books as he scrambled to his feet.

"It's n-n-not what it looks like," Ike stuttered.

The librarian looked at Craig's dripping erection and then up at Craig, who in turn raised his eyebrows at Ike's comment.

"You guys, er, shouldn't be doing that here," said the librarian shifting the books from one arm to another and back again.

Craig squinted to read the librarian's name badge as he stuffed his still hard cock into his trousers. "Listen Derek, no one needs to know about this, do they?"

Ike felt his body flood with adrenalin; his heart raced to distribute it. All he could think about was getting kicked out of university and his parent's finding out the reason. His breathing started getting deeper and deeper until he thought he might pass out.

"No one needs to find out at all," Derek replied. "If you come with me."

He turned and exited the aisle, depositing the armful of books on a nearby table.

"This way," he said, walking toward the toilets at the back of the room.

Ike had no idea what was going to happen to them. His mind was already concocting excuses for his parents. Someone had slipped him something. He had been bullied into doing it. They'd believe that one. Yet somehow, no matter what he came up with, it seemed a bit lame. His parents would see through his lies immediately.

Derek, as it turned out, didn't take them into the toilets but led them to a narrow door tucked between the edge of the toilet block and the window of the library.

"An old storage room," he said by way of explanation as his key found the lock. "No-one ever comes here."

He pushed the door open and ushered Craig and Ike in. Despite the corner being well-hidden by the rows of wooden shelves, thick with books, he still scouted the immediate area for any signs they were seen. Finding that they were still completely alone he pulled the door shut after him.

"I haven't got long guys, so we'd better get on with it," said Derek as he unbuttoned his shirt.

Ike looked at Craig, who shrugged and started removing his clothes. Soon all three of them were standing amongst the disused microfiche machines, outdated computer screens and piles of boxes full of old library cards and paperwork. Tall and gangly Ike, pale and freckled with his six-inches hanging semi-hard between his legs; stocky and hairy Craig with his cock still at full mast and massive hairy nuts hanging heavy between his thick thighs; and Derek with his lean, toned body, small patch of chest hair and thick seven-incher growing right before their eyes.

They stood together, arms around each other as they shared a three-way kiss. Tongues entwined, slipping over and around each other in an erotic dance. Lips sucked feverishly on other lips, on tongues, and small bursts of warm breath exploded on cheeks, on chins, before being inhaled.

Then Derek broke away from the kiss and dropped to his knees.

Craig and Ike continued to explore each other's mouths with close-eyed desire while Derek took their cocks into his mouth, sucking them simultaneously before concentrating first on one and then the other. He liked nothing more than having his mouth filled with as much cock as it could bear, and he was doing a good job of swallowing them both down as far as his taut lips and open throat would allow.

Craig reached up and took one of Ike's nipples between his thumb and forefinger and tweaked it, gently at first but pinching it harder and harder until Ike issued a muffled moan of protest. He felt Craig remove his fingers for a moment. "Sorry," he whispered, though it was still tender when his friend's fingers returned to gently twist the tiny buds of flesh. Further down, between his legs, he could feel the length of his cock squashed together against Craig's as Derek did his best to deep throat them both. He'd never felt such a buzz and was so excited that he felt the familiar feeling of an imminent ejaculation. But not yet. They had only just started. If he shot his load now, there was no telling what he might miss out on later. He pulled out of Derek's mouth and pinched the base of his cock-head to stop himself from coming, just like he had read you should.

Then Craig stopped the kiss and turned around. Derek's hands were at his hips, guiding him. Craig bent forward and spread his ass cheeks apart; his hole a reddish-pink and surrounded by a ring of thick black hair. There was something erotic about the colors and textures, about the way his thick sausage fingers were digging into the ample flesh of his ass cushions to keep that private orifice exposed. There was even something erotic about the way Derek leaned in and licked that hole, making it pucker and drawing a moan from its owner. He had tasted Craig's cock and now wanted to see what ass tasted like.

He took his glasses off, knelt down and joined Derek on the floor. He leaned forward, inviting himself to the feast. Derek moved his head just enough to allow Ike's tongue to find Craig's hairy pucker.

"Oh fuck yeah. Two guys. Lick it real good, guys. Fucking tongue that."

Ike's tongue pushed against the anal muscle and sampled just a hint of the soft, moist tissue that lay on the other side. Then it was joined by Derek's tongue and became part rim-job, part kiss. He closed his eyes and let his tongue explore whatever it found, let his nostrils breathe in the sweaty, musty aroma of ass hole, the hot breath of the librarian and the intoxicating perfume of someone's cock.

Derek brought a finger up to Craig's hole and wriggled it in through the puckered muscle. In and out it poked and invaded, sliding out, so they could both lick it, taste it and in doing so lubricate it. Then a second finger was introduced, and suddenly

11

there was no room for Ike's tongue. He watched as Derek pulled the reddened skin wide apart and opened it enough to create a small shadow. He leaned forward and tongued the small opening, and Ike noticed that Craig had begun to grind his ass against the slight pressure of the firm tongue invading his fuck-hole.

After only a minute or so Derek stood up.

"Give this a suck," he said looking directly at Ike.

Ike was on that hard prick like a seagull on a chip. He swallowed it immediately then slid his mouth back along the shaft, pausing at the large mushroom-shaped head to suck on it. His tongue wrapped itself around the smooth helmet, lingering at the piss slit to explore it and to lick off the small dribble of precum leaking out. Again, he took the cock down his throat, holding it there until he was red in the face and the smell of Derek's pubic bush was strong in his nostrils, before sliding back again. He gasped for air but kept the cock in his mouth, sucking it like a fuck machine until Derek tapped him on the shoulder.

"That's good work," Derek said withdrawing from Ike's eager lips.

The librarian spat on his hand and wiped the mucousy saliva along the length of Craig's hole. It only took one push and his cock was inside Craig; one more thrust and he was all the way up to his tangle of black public hair. His hips began to beat a constant tattoo against Craig's chubby cheeks, each collision sending almost invisible waves rippling across them and up toward his lower back.

Ike, who thought he had no option other than to stand watching and wanking, saw Derek look over his shoulder.

"You wanna do me?"

Ike felt his heartbeat suddenly pick up the pace. He pointed at Derek's ass.

"You mean ...?"

A frown flickered on Derek's forehead. "Yeah, of course. Get down there and get it wet."

Ike did as he was told, pulling the librarian's ass cheeks apart and pushing his face in between them. It smelt different to Craig's musty arse. This one was fresher and not as hairy. Only a few strands of dark brown hair straggled around a bright pink opening. He could feel Derek pushing it open around his tongue as he was probing. It felt a bit strange at first, he thought the guy was gonna take a dump in his mouth, but when he realized that wasn't the case, he relaxed and let himself enjoy the experience of rimming someone as they fucked.

"How's it going?" he asked. "Nice and wet?"

Ike nodded. "Yep."

"Well get your cock in there, matey."

Ike suddenly felt flustered. He rose to his feet and aimed his cock at Derek's ass hole. He pushed and pushed but kept missing the mark. It would be so much easier if Derek stopped thrusting. He tried again and missed. Obviously frustrated Derek reached around and guided the stiff poker into his hole, sighing as all six inches slid in.

Ike felt like such an idiot. Both Craig and Derek seemed to know exactly what they were doing. How had he got to eighteen and not experienced anything like this before? How was it that his experience of sex comprised of a drunken kiss and an unsuccessful fumble of Eileen Kerr's breasts at the high school graduation dance, and several years of masturbation?

But there was no time for reflection. Derek's hips slapped against Craig and in turn pretty much did all the work required to get Ike's cock throbbing. He gripped Derek's hips and pushed his cock deeper into the tight, warm chamber of Derek's fuck tunnel.

"That's it," said Derek, "Just pump my asshole full of cock."

Ike didn't need to be told. He had never felt anything so fucking wonderful in all his born days. Even the joy of his first successful wank didn't compare to the feeling of being buried inside someone's chute. The smell of sex was thick in the air. The skin of Derek's back was shiny with perspiration and soon it was forming small rivulets that snaked their way down to the place where their thighs met.

"Oh fuck," he heard himself utter, the exclamation seeming so natural. It had slipped from his lips as though he often had the opportunity to use it, which of course he didn't.

"Yeah, that feels good. Just keep doing what you're doing," moaned Derek.

From the front of their three-way fuck Ike could hear Craig moaning. "Fuck me deep. Ram that fucking cock into me."

Derek did his best to accommodate, his hips beginning to move faster and faster. Ike with no other option gripped the flesh above Derek's hips and started ramming his own prick deeper and harder inside the librarian. Soon the air was alive with groans and puffing, of sweaty flesh slapping against sweaty flesh.

Then Craig cried out.

"I'm gonna fucking shoot, man. I'm gonna spray the fucking floor."

There were three more grunts and then a cry of release as a thick stream of pearly white cock cream came flying out of Craig's piss slit, landing with a splat on the floor, throwing up dust as it landed.

Derek felt his balls tighten. Craig's ass was now tighter than it had been; its muscles spasming. As they clamped down around his cock it felt as though they literally milked his throbbing member.

"Oh fuck," he cried out. "Here I go. I'm gonna shoot. I'm gonna fucking shoot."

He continued to slam into Craig's butt until the first jet of fresh jizz erupted, coating Craig's guts in a thick creamy sauce. He thrust once more, sending another jet spewing out, and another until his cock had given all it had. He shuddered and leaned down on Craig's back. He rested there, trying to get his breath back as Ike continued behind him.

"My turn," Ike announced, his face red and glistening with the sheen of a hard earned sweat.

He had been close ever since his cock had first slid into Derek's ass, but when his fuck buddy blew his load that was the final straw. As Derek's abdominal muscles closed around his stiff pole, he knew he couldn't hold back. He was now going at Derek's hole like a jack hammer, his balls drawing up into his body.

"Here I go."

"Go on, mate," said Craig from somewhere under Derek. "Drench his guts."

Ike didn't need to be told. When the first jet shot out of the head of his cock he thought his balls were going to fly off. His whole body pulsed with energy, his groin was on fire. The second jet came harder and faster than the first. He pushed his hips into Derek, sending both he and Craig forward into the metal shelving. It was only because Craig had been expecting something like that to happen that he held out his hands in time to steady the trio.

When Ike's thrusts slowed to a halt Derek eased himself off the redhead's cock and stood up.

"Well boys that was certainly short but sweet. We'll have to do it again."

Craig turned around, his eyes dropping to Derek's slowly softening cock. A small pearl of cum had strayed to the end of his cock. It was too inviting to resist. He knelt down and took the librarian's cock in his mouth.

"What are you do …?" The surprise on Derek's face was nothing to that on Ike's.

"Ewww Craig. That's been up your butt," he said, immediately feeling like the novice he was.

Craig ignored him and sucked the cock back to its former steel-hard state. Despite his initial repulsion Ike was slowly drawn in by the rhythmic way Craig's lips slid so effortlessly up and down the swollen organ, sucking off the thin coating of jizz it had accumulated when it was deep inside him. Then he stood up and beckoned Ike over.

Together they kissed once more, Craig's lips tasting of cum and smelling of ass, but somehow Ike didn't seem to mind. He even felt his cock stirring again, but any thoughts of another session were brought to a crashing halt by a bang on the door.

Ike nearly had a heart palpitation as he dashed to the small pile of clothes on the box by the door. He dressed in record time and then waited by the door for the other two. His fingernails found their way to his mouth and he bit down on one after the other.

"I'll leave first and get rid of whoever it is," suggested Derek. "Then you guys leave. The door is self locking so don't worry about that."

Derek pushed the door open and peered out. The coast was clear. Perhaps it had just been another student knocking against the door in their pursuit of a hard to find text book.

"Okay boys, out you come. Just let the door shut behind you," he said, his voice hushed and conspiratorial.

Derek walked off and left Craig and Ike brushing themselves down.

"That was hot," said Craig. "I can still feel that dudes cum in my ass."

Ike nervously looked out through the window to give the impression to anyone who might happen upon them that he'd been there all along.

"Hey look," he said, pointing.

Craig tucked his shirt into his cargo pants and followed Ike's finger to a trio of people who had leapt up as the university sprinklers came on. It was Tony Warner and his mates. The sprinklers had caught them by surprise. Tony grabbed his books and in his haste to get away from the water, tripped and went tumbling into the ornamental duck pond a few steps away from where they had been sitting.

Craig burst out laughing and elbowed Ike in the arm. "I told you. Guys like that always get what they deserve."

Tony stood up in the pond, the water only coming up to his knees but he was as drenched as surely as if he had stayed under the sprinklers. He threw his books at his friends laughing hysterically.

Ike soon forgot his nervousness and threw his head back in a raucous laugh that earned him a stern look from the senior librarian who had been slotting books into their Dewey Decimal allotted position on the shelves. He blushed once more and scurried back to his books.

# ROBOT COCK
## Jay Starre

Trey shrieked along with his teammates as their robot pummeled its way past the competitor's machine. The opposing team was eerily quiet as they frantically worked their remote to rally the shattered remains of the robot they'd entered. It looked like a miniature bulldozer that had fallen off a cliff, pieces dangling and dragging as it creaked along after the relatively swifter Robot Junkie's entry.

Trey was proud of their robot. He'd been the one to insist on the swinging pummel arms that had effectively demolished the Machine Mob's losing Dozer. Their robot was tall and ungainly, but light years more maneuverable than the competitor's.

He glanced at the silent team hovering at the other end of the oval competition ring. Not for the first time during the battle, he checked out the slender, dark-skinned dude hanging at the fringe of the group, almost like an outsider.

It was amusing to think of the quiet geek as an outsider, in a group of Robot geeks who were outsiders themselves. But, their eyes met and he blushed, a bad habit of his. Golden orbs returned his gaze with steady directness. The small mouth actually smiled, a silent nod following.

With straight, dark hair that fell to his shoulders, he was obviously Japanese. A broad face with big eyes under pencil-thin brows and a small cleft chin under bowed lips, Trey thought him cute. He was kind of skinny. But most science geeks were skinny, or like Trey, on the chubby side.

His teammates were howling, hopping and slapping him on the shoulders. They'd won! And this was the championship battle! They'd beaten all the competing colleges in Kansas,

Oklahoma and Nebraska! Not that impressive, but to his team it was a victory nonetheless.

Not accustomed to the etiquette of sports competitions, they still managed a modicum of social grace by approaching the vanquished team and filing past to shake hands. Trey pumped one sweaty, limp hand after another until he neared the object of his earlier scrutiny.

Their hands came together as their eyes met again. A slim hand in his plump one, held for longer than necessary, and his cock reared up under his jeans like a rocket about to blast off.

"Good workmanship. You deserved to win. Would you like to see my latest version of Dozer? It's not competition-ready, but perhaps you could assist me in testing it out."

The words were uttered in a rush. No polite name-exchanging or other idle chatter. Trey was used to that in the crowd he usually hung with. Science, and in particular, robots, were their God, and normal human exchange was low on their list of priorities.

The hand didn't relinquish his at an appropriate time either, continuing to pump and squeeze. Trey grinned, flashing white teeth in a freckled complexion.

"Sure. Why the hell not. Now?"

Even though his cock was hard, he wasn't foolish enough to think anything steamy might be on the horizon. This geek was probably keen on showing off his latest robot, and that's what turned him on. But you never knew.

He abandoned his teammates without a word as they headed off for a victory celebration. He managed a quick inspection of the Japanese geek's compact butt, too tightly encased in skinny jeans to be stylish, but hot nonetheless. His cock only got stiffer.

Robot competitions made him horny. It was as simple as that. Still, amongst the other competitors, he rarely found anyone he was attracted to. The exception was today, with this rapidly striding dude he was all hard for.

"I live a few blocks from the college. And I have a cool lab in my grandparents' garage. You'll like it."

The clipped words contained no foreign accent, nor southern, even though they were in Oklahoma City. Trey found his fellow geek more and more intriguing. "I'm Trey, by the way."

"Nikki. Here we are. Come on in. I want you to meet Dozer 2."

They'd reached Nikki's house in minutes. Oaks surrounded a totally normal suburban ranch home. Trey caught a glimpse of an elderly Japanese lady peering out a curtained window before they disappeared into the garage.

He looked around in awe. Robot geek heaven! The garage was entirely given over to Nikki's use, with benches and cupboards lining the wall, and an oval practice station in the middle. It was meticulously organized, with tools hanging in place, and nuts, bolts, metal and plastic parts lined up in precise order.

"Fucking cool," he murmured.

"This is cool, check out Dozer 2."

Nikki snatched up a gleaming silver remote, stepping close to Trey as he aimed it at the practice ring in front of them. He moved so close in fact, his lean thigh and bony knee pressed against the back of Trey's plumper leg and ass.

Trey flushed again at the distracting body contact before he managed to look over at the machine Nikki was apparently so proud of. It was already moving as the dark-haired geek began working the controls in his hand.

Much larger than the robot The Machine Mob had entered that day, it verged on being too big to meet the strict competition regulations. But Trey felt certain this organized dude would have been careful not to disqualify himself or his team.

"He's got some special features. What do you think?"

The clipped words were followed by a sideways glance, golden orbs direct, and a crooked grin making Trey wonder. He looked back at the slowly crawling machine. With tracks instead of wheels pushing it along, it clattered disconcertingly but otherwise clicked and whirred with well-tuned precision. He had to admire the gleaming perfection of gears and sockets of metal and plastic, but it wasn't exactly mind-boggling, at least not until Nikki engaged one of its "special features."

A lengthy pipe of shining black plastic reared up from the front center. Trey imagined it might be an attack tool of some sort, and waited as the tube gracefully descended from its vertical position to 45 degrees, pointing right at him!

Was it about to eject some kind of projectile? He tensed slightly, which only emphasized the thigh and knee pressing into him from behind. Something definitely erupted from the end of that plastic muzzle, but it wasn't a bullet, dart or flying robot.

His mouth dropped open. Glistening with a coating of slick lubricant, a jet-black protuberance emerged slowly but steadily. A tapered knob first, then a thick shank of vein-lined girth following.

It was in fact a big black dildo!

"What do you think of this?" Nikki asked as he worked the controls of his remote with surprisingly cool fingers.

The protruding dildo, already slick with lube, suddenly began to expand around the tapered crown, a realistic piss slit all at once gaping open to ooze a stream of gooey white stuff.

"It's creaming! The fucking dildo is creaming!" Trey blurted out with a gasp.

"There's more it can do. I need a volunteer to test it out though. How about it?"

Trey shuddered. Like most science geeks, he had an active imagination. As he stared open-mouthed at that cock-wielding contraption, he fantasized all kinds of scenarios. A gentle hand on the small of his back urging him forward was all the impetus he needed.

"What the fuck. All in the name of science," he muttered as his face flushed even brighter and he stumbled over to the center of the practice ring.

Dozer 2 performed a little spin on its tracks, impressive enough, if it hadn't also begun to withdraw and extend that glistening black dildo in a lewd manner at the same time.

"You gotta get on your hands and knees. And you have to strip off your jeans and your underwear, too."

He hesitated, but only for a split second. His cock had only gotten stiffer as he'd watched the robot turn nasty, and with it so close and Nikki's bright golden eyes boring into him from behind, he all at once wanted to get naked. He wanted to show the nasty science geek his boner, and his bare butt!

With trembling hands he yanked open his fly and let his baggy jeans drop to the floor. He stepped out of them, fat hard-on tenting his white skivvies. Then, with a determination born of sheer horniness, he hooked his thumbs in the waistband of his underwear and shoved them down to his ankles, bending over at the same time to display the bare cheeks of his hefty can.

Even though he was on the plump side, he was not ashamed of his body. He'd been a swimmer since he was a kid, and still did laps nearly every day at the college pool. He liked his burgers and fries, though, and it showed.

The round moon of his alabaster ass was big and sexy. Freckles, which covered most of his body, disappeared once the curve of those lush mounds swelled out from his waist. Flushing pinker than ever, he wriggled that sweet ass at Nikki briefly before he whirled around and dropped to his hands and knees.

"Let's see what Dozer 2 can do to my big white butt," he challenged.

Now it was a competition, and both geeks were in their element. Nikki grinned, bowed lips glistening with a little drool, golden orbs wide as they drank in the sight of the blond Trey on hands and knees, pants and underwear kicked off and thighs splayed.

"Awesome! We definitely require some training in targeting and insertion. Your asshole will be the prime goal. Your prostate is the location of most desirable manipulation. I'd appreciate a running report, if you don't mind."

The clipped voice grew a little more excited even as the words were controlled and technical. Trey bit his lip and attempted a smile, although he was totally aware of his position, ass in the air and butt-hole exposed. The clanking of the tracks behind him reminded him of the oncoming Dozer 2, with its pumping dildo!

He heard and sensed the robot clattering closer between his spread ankles, his round butt jiggling nervously as the unseen muzzle of the Dozer approached. Nikki's eyes were intent as he manipulated the controls of his remote, a tenting bulge in his tight jeans revealing his own excitement.

Trey jerked as he felt the surprisingly warm tube make contact with his bare ass-cheek. He let out a little gasp before he caught himself and got into the game. "Ten degrees right."

Nikki's grin widened as he nodded and manipulated his controls. The slippery tube swung sideways and all at once slithered up into Trey's deep butt crack. He yelped and heaved his butt up as he dropped down on his elbows in anticipation of imminent impalement.

"Ten degrees lower," he blurted out.

The pumping robotic dildo slid lower along his lower, riding across his quaking butt-hole in a slippery glide. He shuddered and arched his back. The bulbed crown of the black dildo slid up and down in his crack, searching as it pumped in and out. He wriggled slightly upwards as the rubber played across his pink ass-lips, teasing the entrance but then moving away.

"Ten additional degrees lower," he muttered, closing his eyes and focusing on the unseen piston sliding deep in his ass-crack.

"On target yet?" Nikki's voice was definitely shaking now!

"Unnnnhhhh! Fuck! On target! Five centimeters Dozer forward!"

The tapered knob centered on his hole, slowly pumping against the snug sphincter, but not entering until the clattering tracks of the robot scooted ahead five centimeters. All at once, the lubed arm drove into his asshole from behind.

"Insertion achieved!" he yelped.

The rubber cock-head slid into him, plowing past his throbbing ass-lips and stretching the snug muscle beyond. The entire knob pushed inside, followed by an inch of fatter shank. It moved in a steady but shallow pump, rubbing his sensitive butt-lips as it stretched them, but entering only an inch beyond.

"Dozer forward five centimeters ... ohhhh ... increase pump velocity five percent," he bleated out.

"I require a superior view of the insertion process ... in order to maximize the results of our training session," Nikki replied in a strained voice.

The crouching blond glanced up as those lean thighs strode past him. He caught a glimpse of a lengthy brown cock bobbing in front of his fellow geek. Nikki must have fished out his boner while he had his head down and eyes closed! Sweet!

The brief sight of the real thing, long and brown and stiff, waving at him as Nikki disappeared behind him only increased Trey's appreciation of the fake cock beginning to pump deeper into his aching hole. Maybe he'd get fucked by that hard brown boner afterwards!

Or maybe he'd get to fuck his fellow geek's tight round can. He moaned as fantasies swirled around in his head and fat rubber cock continued pumping in and out of his tender asshole. Nikki's strained voice brought him back to the present.

"Sweet! The target area is extremely sumptuous! Two large white globes, smooth and hairless, a deep crevice to invade, and perfectly centered, a deeper cavity to explore. May I insert the device to a greater depth into the cavity?"

Trey felt sweat dripping from his armpits and down his lower back into his spread ass-crack. Lube oozed out of his hole and down over his dangling nut-sack. He shuddered as that pumping probe massaged his ass-lips and stretched his fuck tunnel. More? Absolutely!

"Increase pump velocity 20 percent ... while moving Dozer ahead five centimeters ... ooohhhhhnnn ... yeah that's it," he yelped as Nikki followed his instructions.

The clacking tracks had pushed ahead in perfect time to the deeper pump of the dildo. He was effectively gored twice as deep as before. He felt the tapered crown slithering way into his guts, rubbing places he hardly knew existed. And at the same time, the shaft of the dildo increased in girth, stretching his snug ass-lips wider open.

He groaned and wriggled around the big dildo, his sweaty can flushing bright pink, his husky thighs quivering as he slid them apart in an effort to open up his hole to the deeper penetration. It was awesome!

And his new pal was back there watching it all!

For from being embarrassed, he reveled in the exhibitionist element of their game. He wanted to show off his big sexy ass for the lean robot geek.

"Increase penetration twenty percent ... ugggghhhh ... move Dozer ahead five centimeters ... fuck yeah!"

The clacking tracks moved up against the cheeks of Trey's jiggling butt. The robot was right against him now. And that big dildo was steadily pumping in and out more than six inches deep. He was fucked!

"Is prostate contact acceptable? Should I lower the muzzle ten degrees?"

Nikki's voice rose and cracked. He was definitely enjoying this as much as Trey. Well, not as much maybe, he thought as a strained giggle emerged from his drooling lips.

"Yeah ... go ahead ... go for the prostate....fuck! Like that! Oh goddamn!"

The muzzle lowered, forcing the head and shaft to drive in at the altered angle, this time probing down against his sensitive prostate. It was almost too much! He hadn't been playing with his stiff cock, afraid he'd blow a load if he did. Now, as that probing dildo rubbed against his prostate, his own cock jerked and leaked between his splayed thighs, begging for attention.

No! He couldn't touch it or he'd shoot for sure. And that's not what he wanted. He wanted something more.

"Uhnnnnn ... yeah ... insertion progress excellent. Increase pump depth ... ohhh … and velocity 20 percent ... and how about if we exchange ... ohhhh ... perspectives?"

There it was. Trey made his play. Would Nikki go for it? The whirring robot was planted right between his thighs, metal pressing against his hefty ass, dildo pumping in and out faster and deeper than ever. He groaned and wriggled around the machine invader, his asshole massaged and teased relentlessly as he awaited his fellow geek's response.

"Excellent proposal ... but not before we test out Dozer's Arm Velocity ... how's this?"

And all at once the pumping dildo began to ram in and out at twice the previous speed. The blond grunted loudly, his husky body convulsing around the rapidly impaling robotic arm ramming deep and fast into his ass. The teasing rub against his ass-lips and prostate was wild! He shuddered from head to toe, knees sliding farther apart, hole pummeled and drooling lubricant in a squishing non-stop spurt.

"Report?" Nikki pressed.

"Ohhhh ... unnnnhhh ... yeahhhhh .... excellent ... velocity! Insertion progress ... maximized!"

"Withdrawal initiated. Position exchange upcoming."

He raised his head, shaggy blond hair plastered to his forehead, his bare butt jiggling as the pumping robotic Arm pulled free, and Dozer clanked backwards from between his thighs. His asshole drooled lubricant as it gaped empty then snapped shut. He was all too aware of Nikki's eyes on his spread crack and fucked hole.

But now it was his turn!

"The test subject is required to remove all his clothing in order to achieve true and unbiased reporting status."

Trey blurted that out as he stumbled to his feet and turned to face his competitor. He needn't have mentioned it, because Nikki was already naked! While he was getting butt-fucked by the Dozer's dildo Arm, the Japanese-American geek had managed to strip off! He didn't have a stitch of clothing on, and his lengthy boner reared up to slap against his flat belly like a pulsing brown iron rod.

"Control exchange required. Do you wish instruction on the use of the Control Tool?"

"I'll figure it out," he muttered as he grabbed the remote from Nikki's sweaty hands. He was far too excited to waste another moment. He wanted the geek's hot brown butt!

"Subject on your hands and knees. Ankles as close to ninety degrees as possible," he snapped out now that he had the remote in hand and was suddenly in control.

Nikki flashed a bright grin as he obeyed, his silky dark hair waving against his slim neck as he dropped like a stone to the practice floor. Flat on his belly, the slender Japanese executed a surprisingly limber maneuver, spreading his legs so wide apart, he was effectively doing the splits.

Trey stood behind him, Dozer 2 between them, right now whirling in slow circles in a clanking spin. He wore only his white socks and a tight-fitting green T-shirt. His husky chest and broad back stretched the shirt to the tearing point, emphasizing the breadth and depth of his swimmer-built torso. Below, his thick cock reared up nasty and dribbling. His big butt shuddered, the hole between his sweaty ass-cheeks nicely opened and aching.

"Your turn, pal," he muttered as he experimented on the controls in his sweaty hands. The robot whirled erratically, clanking loudly as tracks attempted to follow the transmitted instructions, while the Arm itself began to extend and withdraw the black dildo at a lewd and menacing pace.

He snorted out a startled laugh, imagining the robot Arm jamming deep into Nikki's poor butthole at that wild speed, before he regained a modicum of composure and focused on the task at hand.

Which was giving Nikki a good butt-fucking!

"Dozer responding to Control. Forward motion initiated. Prepare for approaching insertion!"

Now he was in control. The slender Japanese lay on his belly, legs sprawled impossibly wide apart and round brown butt split in two, as he awaited the same dildo Arm that had just impaled Trey's own tender ass with gut-churning depth and speed.

His pink boner jerked and his fingers trembled as he twisted knobs and punched keys. Dozer 2 jerked forward, spun erratically once or twice, then settled into a direct forward path, right toward the pouting brown hole awaiting it.

"Alignment achieved. Target more than acceptable, sweet brown butt-cheeks split apart, lean brown thighs open, slim belly pressed to the floor, snug pucker ready and waiting ... insertion imminent!"

In his excitement he'd gotten a little ahead of himself as Dozer 2 jerked ahead then halted, then jerked forward again, the Arm rising and falling in confusion. Tearing his eyes from the pouting brown asshole right in front of him, he concentrated on the remote. Yes! Now he had it.

The robot resumed forward motion with clanking steadiness. The Arm slowly lowered, aiming for the spread crack and tight hole. The pumping dildo retreated to leave only the tapered head and two inches of glistening black shank extended.

The Arm was first to make contact, lowered and pointing directly between the spread brown ass-cheeks. To Trey's glee, the lubricated cock-knob slid up against Nikki's puckered butt-hole, directly on target.

"Contact result .... yeah! Insertion commenced! Take that big black dildo up your sweet tight butt!"

Trey's hands shook, and his sweaty fingers slid over the controls as he stared down at the splayed geek in front of him with the robot between his slim legs and that oozing rubber dildo emerging from the robot Arm while pushing against the snug ass-lips it targeted.

He must have over-calculated, because the protruding dildo all at once surged ahead, ramming past tender sphincter, the lubricated knob disappearing in a squishy slurp. He gasped and twirled a knob to slow down the pump speed, but it was too late for Nikki's poor asshole.

The sprawled Japanese yelped and his slim body jerked, but he made no move away from the Arm attacking him.

"Insertion ... fucking ... achieved ... for sure," he grunted out.

The blond geek manipulating the remote tried to get hold of himself, but the sharp memory of his own recent impalement, and the sight of that sweet round butt being fed lubed dildo as the Dozer whirred and buzzed between them was all too exciting. He did manage to steady his fingers, but only so he could command the Arm to probe even deeper into the warm slot it violated.

"Pump depth increased 25 percent, pump velocity raised 50 percent. How's that feel," he asked breathlessly.

The glistening black cock shot out of the Arm, straight into Nikki's tender asshole. It pumped in and out with loud squishes as the brown-skinned geek's compact can reared and jiggled and shoved back for more.

He was loving it!

"Increase ... depth ... fuck! Increase speed ... ohhhhhh ... please ... fuck my poor ass with that dildo!"

The Arm seemed to have a will of its own, pumping in and out ferociously, ramming deep and yanking back out, faster and faster. Wide-eyed, Trey stared down at the wild robotic-fuck almost helplessly. He had to clear his head and realize he was the one in control. His fingers worked the controls, slowing the wild speed but increasing the pump depth. He was rewarded for his efforts as the dildo disappeared far up Nikki's straining asshole and the slim geek reared backwards to cry out his pleasure.

"Fuck yeah! Penetration depth maximizing pleasure ... prostate targeted precisely!"

With his thighs at almost right angles to his body, his asshole was wide open to assault, and it was definitely getting that, the Dozer planted right between his butt-cheeks and the Arm leveled precisely at his targeted slot. The girth of the dildo increased dramatically at its lower end, and he was feeling that as Trey twirled the depth control knob.

"Ohhhhhhh! Sphincter achieving maximum stretch ... fuck yeah! Oral insertion of training subject requested!"

Trey hesitated, wondering exactly what that meant, until Nikki shouted out clearer instructions.

"I want to suck your cock!"

The blond geek let out a snort and a giggle just before he stepped over the pumping Dozer and Nikki's spread brown body. He dropped to his knees in front of him, controls in one hand and cock in the other. His big boner reared up pink and curved in the cute geek's face before he rose on his elbows and gulped it down.

"Yeah! Oral insertion achieved ... fuck! Wrap your sweet lips around that big cock ... subject adequately impaled from both ends!"

Nikki gurgled some kind of response, technical no doubt, mouth full of fat meat, drool dribbling down his dimpled chin, big amber eyes staring up into Trey's blue ones. The warm wetness around his boner had Trey shuddering, while the sight of the Dozer whirring down there between Nikki's thighs while it pumped him full of lubricated black dildo had him rearing forward and driving deeper into the geek's tight gullet.

"Deep throat achieved! Ohhhh ... deep ass-fuck achieved! Orgasm imminent!"

It was too much for him. His chubby body jiggled, his pink cock thrust, he accidentally twisted the velocity knob and suddenly the Arm was pumping dildo into Nikki's puckered asshole at a wild speed.

"Uhhhhnnnnnggg ... uunnnnhhh ... ummmnnn!"

Nikki swallowed cock at both ends, his slender body writhing and flopping naked on the practice floor. The slurping mouth over his cock had Trey jerking, too, flushed pink from head to toe, and then crying out as he shot his load.

He pulled out in time to spray his fellow geek's sweat-soaked face with nut-spew. It was obvious Nikki was coming, too, as he pounded the practice floor with his hips as if he was fucking it. The dildo rammed in and out of his straining hole until Trey fumbled with the switch and managed to withdraw it.

With a slurp it pulled out, as the Dozer backed away obediently then came to a halt. The pair were left thrashing around in orgasmic delight, one on his belly and one on his knees.

Nikki's head cleared first and he finally spoke as he gazed up at Trey from the floor. He winked and grinned as he wiped cum from his chin. "Training well-executed, partner. Fucking well-executed!"

Trey laughed out loud. Yeah, it had been a satisfying experiment, very satisfying. But he more in mind. Much more.

It was a week later when the pair ushered in a prospective initiate for their newly formed club, Dozer Dudes.

"You are required to submit to Dozer Training if you desire membership," Nikki was saying in his clipped manner to the tall geek hovering at the edge of the practice ring and eyeing the whirring, clanking Dozer 2.

Trey grinned from right beside the pair. The tall initiate had a slim waist and high round butt, perfectly suited to a good work-over from Dozer's Arm! "Strip and squat on the practice floor, he means! Dozer 2's vertical targeting needs some tuning up," he said more bluntly.

Timid eyes darting around, hesitant fingers fumbling with the fly of his jeans, the buzzed-cut science geek bit his cute lip and obeyed instructions with a wary eye on Dozer 2, who under Nikki's expert control aimed its Arm directly at the newcomer, and began to pump out its glistening dildo.

They'd replaced the black rubber cock with a fire-engine red one, which looked even nastier as it gleamed with lubricant and pumped up and down lewdly. Their prospective new member gawked open-mouthed as he hastily stripped off his jeans and T-shirt then still biting his lip, turned around and squatted on the practice floor, hands down in front of him, round white ass in the air, asshole pouting and quivering.

"Subject in position! Anal penetration imminent!"

Trey couldn't hold back a giggle at Nikki's somber tech-talk as he made his way behind the squatting newcomer for a better view of the upcoming assault. He stood facing Nikki and their eyes met briefly as they exchanged nods and grins. Their poor victim quivered in place as Dozer clanked its way between his squatting thighs, Arm rearing upwards, pumping red dildo searching for target.

The squeal was loud and satisfying. "Target penetrated! All speed ahead, pump penetration maximum!" Trey called out.

The buzzed-haired initiate's mouth gaped open, eyes wide, and ass totally fucked as Dozer 2 drove its bright red dildo home.

The ensuing targeting test was deemed a total success as the subject squirmed and jerked and finally shot a big juicy load all over the practice floor with that red dildo ramming in and out of his steamy asshole.

Other prospective team members would soon be found, Trey felt certain. Dozer 2 was just too fucking fantastic to waste on mere competitions. Although, the thought of a Dozer fuck competition raised all kinds of lurid notions in his head. He'd have to speak with Nikki about that!

# THE WOOD WIZARD
## J. D Waters.

"She has the biggest tits I've ever seen." This coming from Mark. Big, dumb, two hundred pounds of muscle and empty head Mark. Mark who was currently downing a beer in four big gulps and had sucked up two thirds of a super meat pizza from Maria's.

"Gee, dude. That's great." I tried to smile. Really. But I didn't care about Suzanne Palmers' tits. Not even a little bit. "I'm um ... happy for you?"

He nodded, grinning, chewing with his mouth open. I glanced at the ceiling, the door, my fingernails. Anything to keep from looking into that masticating maw. "You should be because I got to bury my face in 'em right before I turned her over and?"

"Ah, if it isn't the Star Gazer!" There was Perry. Tall and smiling. Hair the color of coffee, skin turning nut brown from working outside in the sun all summer.

"Wood Wizard," I said and got up off the sofa. Something sticky was on the cushion, and I tried not to speculate. The dorm room was impeccable compared to some I had seen.

He nodded and waved me back to his room. "Garrett and Wade had to pass for tonight. Tony will be here shortly." As he walked I tried not to stare. Or fantasize. It wasn't easy. Perry was the stuff wet dreams were made of. Big and wide and handsome. An easy smile, a deep laugh, an ass you could bounce a quarter off of. And besides me being the Star Gazer, I was sure he had no idea I was alive.

I was in the library working on creative writing papers while he was on the football field fending off cheerleaders. And college cheerleaders are full-on sluts, so I've heard, so I was sure he was getting taken care of in the sex department.

Still, it was easy to look at him and slip off into a fantasy. What I wouldn't give to be on my knees doing an oral report on Shakespeare for Perry. To quote *King Lear* while blowing him and?

"… he's not feeling well, so he's not sure how long he'll stay." He turned the full effect of his crooked white grin on me and I blinked.

"What? Sorry. Was woolgathering. Shakespeare and reports that are due and all that." My face felt like I had third degree sunburn. The blush was even heating my ears. If only Perry could see into my head. He'd never speak to me again.

"I said, 'Tony's not feeling well. I don't know how long we'll have him, is all.' And Richie, you really, really need to fucking relax. Not everything is school. Have a little fun, my friend." He motioned me into his room and I dropped my bag by the bed.

"Oh, that's a bummer." Not so much. My brain was already figuring that if Tony bailed, I would be alone with Perry. Or he would just cancel the game and go out and drink and get laid. He was a rarity, our Perry was. A jock who was okay with hanging with the nerds, and he played role playing games. He was the nerd equivalent of the White Buffalo.

"Yeah, it happens. Cold and flu season, wash your hands!" He pointed a finger at me like the old Uncle Sam posters and grinned. I grinned back. It is hard not to grin at Perry. He's too fucking hot to keep a straight face.

"Cool. Got any beer?"

I knew the answer but it gave me something to focus on other than how good his gray sweatpants looked hanging low on his trim hips. And did he have underwear on? Enquiring minds want to know. I shook my head to clear it as he tossed me a Pabst Blue Ribbon. "Tonight we drink in style," he joked.

I laughed. The beer foamed when I opened it, and I slurped the top clean. And for just a second, I caught Perry watching my mouth. Not guarding his expression, just watching.

My heart double clutched. I knew that look. I licked my lips and his eyes narrowed a bit, and he drew in air as if breathless. But then his eyes cleared and he caught my awareness. "Sorry. Zoned out. Just like you did. You must be contagious."

Was it me or were his words a little forced? A little rushed. A tad nervous. No way. Now I was having stalker fantasies. Next thing you knew, I'd be on one of those tabloid shows as the crazed college student who tried to give unwanted blow jobs on campus. I snorted and caught myself. "Dude, I find myself amusing," I said, trying to pass of the faux pas.

Would he ask why I was laughing?

No. He grinned and it shot through me. The want. Fierce and intense, like the sudden thrust of an ice pick through my heart. "Things will be different tonight."

Again my mind went down the wrong path. Supplying me with vivid images of his hands on me, gripping me. How his face would look while he fucked me. What he would sound like when he came. I clenched my hands into fists. I really had to stop letting my brain divert me. At some point I would slip up. He didn't mean different between us, I was sure. He meant the game.

"Oh yeah?" I didn't like how high and reedy my voice sounded. I didn't like the breathless quality, and I didn't like the fact that I was one deep gaze from Perry away from sporting wood. I took a deep breath and held it for a few beats. Willing my heart to slow, willing my cock to behave.

"Yeah. I was talking online to a buddy in Connecticut. He was telling me about some modification to the game. You know, make it a little more real. A little more intense."

"Yeah. Okay. But I'm second level Magii, and I just figured out my powers of mind control," I said. "So, I hope you're not expecting me to, you know, make Tony cluck like a chicken." I was joking. Mostly.

Perry threw his head back and laughed. His abs galloped with the movement, and it was visible even under his white tee. God. Maybe I needed to just stop looking at him. We'd been playing Darkness with Garrett and Tony and Wade for a few weeks now, and every week it got harder. Every week, I wondered if I would slip. Would this be the week where my staggering crush on Perry Evans became crystal clear to all of them? Would this be the week that they all realized I did not give a shit or react when they talked about tits and how much pussy there was to be had in the Women's Studies lectures?

I watched him laugh and studied the pink of his tongue. The rose colored velvet of the inside of his cheeks. I shifted in my chair. I had to think about something else. I started reciting sonnets in my head. It was the only thing I could think to do.

"No. No clucking. You'll see. We'll figure it out. We have all night," he said and my breath solidified in my lungs. When I swallowed I heard my throat click like a dry twig breaking. If only he meant it the way I wanted him to.

A hacking cough preceded Tony. Tony was an Ice Demon. Not really. In the game. His powers tended to stay on the darker side of things, but he could come through in a pinch as a good guy. Not to mention if we were ever to find the relic that would make our quest for the Eternal Light successful, we needed his invincibility. See, in the land of Twilight there lives a demented but talented sorceress. Her name is Ochre and her mission … never mind. It's a nerd thing.

"What the hell. You have the plague?" Perry yelled as Tony dragged his sorry sick ass through the door.

"Yeah, what's it to you?"

More hacking. Coughs too deep and wet they made me shrink back in my seat and cover my beer.

"Dude!" Perry waved his arms. The dice hit the carpet with dull thuds, and I bent to gather them. My head was level with Perry's crotch as he lectured Tony who was still hacking. I paused to wish upon a star, or a cock as it were, and then straightened. "I have a game Sunday. Are you trying to fucking kill me? I can't have the creeping crud. Home!"

"But I'm about to advance," Tony gasped. Another round of coughing hit and his eyes started to water.

"It's a game. Go home."

Tony flipped Perry the bird (which made Perry grin) and then stumbled out the door. Perry turned to me, and I shrugged. "Some people," I laughed. Outside, I was laughing. Inside, I was flipping out. We were going to be alone.

Or he would cancel. I didn't like that option at all.

To shoot myself in the foot, I said, "Hey, I'll bug out and you can plan something else for tonight." I pushed up out of my chair, and he pushed me back. Two tented fingers and he managed to push back into the chair.

"Stay. Come on, I've been waiting all week for this."

He rolled, considered me with big brown eyes shot with gold. I swigged my beer because I was pretty sure I was having some kind of heart attack the way my ears were ringing and my heart was flipping around in my chest. "You need to move through the woods."

"The Captured Woods," he said and winked.

The wink went straight to my dick. Jesus. I was going to make a fool of myself. I could feel it in my bones. Or maybe boner is the more appropriate word. To sum up: I was fucked.

I cleared my throat, and my mind wandered as he did what he needed to do. All I knew was he was pushing the dice into my hands, and I blinked at him as if I'd just woken up. "Right. My turn." I rolled, and my brain tried to call up what I needed to do. Where my character was and what I needed to accomplish.

Perry tskked. I froze. "What?"

"You were captured. Remember, the Rogues are out in force. They caught you. That means you're bound."

"Bound?" God, I needed to clear my head. I was not sure what I could do to save myself if anything. I might need Perry, aka the Wood Wizard, to assist me. When he waved the rope at me. The real rope, my mind stuttered, not processing the information right. "What's that?"

"I said more real. More intense." His face was definitely intense as he stared me down. "Put your wrists out for me, Richie."

"I … yeah, see I um …" I watched, fascinated as my arms straightened toward him all on their own. Seemingly against my will. I watched my pale wrists offered up to him like a sacrifice of white flesh.

"Good boy," he said under his breath, and that did it.

My back shivered and crawled with anxiety and excitement. My cock hardened in an instant, and my mouth was as dry as sand. Surely, I was imagining the tone. The tone of a man about to fuck another man. No way. No way.

The friction of the rope had my cock jerking in my pants. Little tiny spasms directly linked to the harsh pain of the rope on my skin. And the set of his mouth and how dark his eyes had gotten. This wasn't the chug a beer Perry I knew. Or the guy who flirted with cheerleaders or the guy who blew off his term paper research because he only really needed to pull a C. This was an entirely new Perry. A serious and darker Perry who found my gaze and smiled at me. "Don't' worry. It will be okay."

I believed him. I tested my bonds as he rolled. His turn and most of what he said was lost to me as I studied the harsh nip and bite of the rope on my wrists. I shifted in the chair, trying to position my lower body under the table, so he couldn't see. See the hard-on from hell. The hard-on that wouldn't die. Tie me up and I get poker straight. No. That's wrong. Not in general. Perry. If Perry ties me up, I'm done for.

"… turn."

I looked up to see him studying me. He looked concerned and confused. Maybe not confused. Maybe … speculative.

"What?"

"I said, is that too tight and it's your turn."

"No. Intense. More real. More intense," I tried to joke. So guys in Connecticut were tying each other up as they played Darkness? Whatever. I wasn't going to ask. The fact that I was turned on was worth holding onto. Who knew when I'd be alone with Perry again. I could use this as fodder for my fantasies. Late night masturbation sessions dreaming of him tying my wrists while My Chemical Romance blared on the stereo in the dark.

"Your roll. Do you need me to ...?"

I shook my head, grabbed a die and shook. I let it drop and tried to focus on the number and not on the image in my mind of my bound arms looped over his broad neck. Or that fact that in my fantasy realm between my ears he was kissing me.

"Dude, they snagged you again," Perry said.

I glanced at the die. Had that been my roll? I could swear they weren't the same. But I didn't really know, lost in a fog of lust and bondage was I. "What's that mean?" I asked. Because I couldn't remember a damn thing at the moment. My voice was barely a whisper. Clogged up with arousal and want.

"They got you." More rope appeared. "Sorry. I have to." And then he was working my high tops off and my socks and tying scratchy loops around my ankles. He looked up, his head near my lap. My dick poking a very obvious tent in my jeans. "Sorry. You're all tied up. Helpless."

"Helpless," I repeated. I wondered vaguely if I was going to shoot in my pants. Now that would be a bad thing to do. But totally possible, I feared.

"Yeah. Unless I save you."

"Will you?"

He grinned and it was somewhat evil. Playful and open but a twist of something in it. A hint of cruelty. I shifted again and it didn't help. My cock rubbed my jeans and my breath stopped in my lungs. God. What a mess. What a lovely, horny, fantastic, magical mess. Role playing games, wizards and bondage, oh my!

"That depends. Let's see what I roll."

I watched him palm the die. Huge and lopsided. One yellow, one black. They hit the table with a clatter and clack, and his hand settled on my knee. Patting, patting until I thought my dick my actually snap off it was so hard. "Well?"

"If you try to get a head start, I might be able to come up from behind and save you."

My brain registered: come up from behind. And when he smiled, I knew I wasn't fixating. I was reading Perry's secret language. My belly buzzed with anticipation, and my heart did a drunken, little flutter in my chest. God. We were alone. We were finally alone and he was making a move on me. Not as himself. As the Wood Wizard. The name finally hit me for what it was. A brilliant double entendre. A rich easy laughter floated out of me. God, he was hot and a genius!

"How should I?"

"I say you crawl." His big, brown eyes tracked over my jeans and stalled on my zipper. I was still making a tent, and suddenly, I didn't care. I wasn't embarrassed. I was tingling with excitement.

"Crawl. Right." I slid out of the chair without a shred of grace and hit the floor like a fish. The door to the bedroom was shut, but as I flounced around on the carpet, he stepped over me and locked it. The rub of hard floor against hard cock was maddening. I was afraid if I shimmied too far across the floor I'd get myself off.

I stilled, letting my heart steady and my cock regroup. I wouldn't come in my boxer shorts when my walking wet dream had me trussed up like a turkey. I would only come when said wet dream was fucking me. Preferably, had fucked me. I wanted the fucking and the touching and the post coital glow. I didn't want to accidentally go off like a young kid unaccustomed to his own equipment.

The lock sounded like a gun shot. I didn't know I was holding my breath until little spots popped up in my vision. I sucked in a deep breath and looked up. Perry was looking down at me. He walked to the bed and sat. I lay there. Bound wrists under me, bound ankles aching. Cold, white fear speared through me. Maybe I shouldn't have agreed to this. But trust is the better part of bondage, I rationalized. God. Would he ever speak?

I moved to try and get comfortable, and pleasure shot through my pelvis, up in to my lower back, making me groan. I was going to die with a hard-on.

"I'll save you," he said softly, and I stopped. His eyes were moving over me, taking everything in. Perry looked a little glazed, a little drunken and sort of hungry. Like the Big Bad Wolf, but that was a fairy tale, not a game.

"Perry?" I stopped. Perry, what? Help me? Save me? Let me up? Kiss me? Fuck me? Let me go? I changed my mind?

I simply didn't know.

"I'll save you," he said again. A little more sure. A little deeper. His eyes were darker, but the gold stood out like tiny flames in the dark, dark brown. "I've been wanting to save you for a long time."

"Save me," I said, not realizing I was going to say it until it slid out. "Please, Perry."

He was on his knees then, turning me, straddling my chest and leaning the bulk of his broad shoulders and dark shaggy head to kiss me. I realized his lips were almost bubble gum pink right before they touched me. But when they touched me, I fucking forgot what the word pink even meant because his tongue was the hottest and sweetest thing I could remember having in my mouth.

I would have pushed my hands into that thick, dark hair right then, but my hands were bound. I wanted to pinch myself. Surely I was dreaming. But the fact that I couldn't pinch myself in my bondage reassured me. It was real. I wasn't having a wet Darkness dream, Perry was kissing me.

"Save me," I said into his mouth. "Please."

He sat back, his ass on my belly but he held his impressive weight off me, so he wouldn't crush me. Don't crush the skinny nerd who adores you, I thought and snickered. He smiled, looked confused, and then worked his zipper. "Will you? Please?" He was muttering softly. His eyes shy and a little scared.

Was he afraid I would say no? I nodded and opened my mouth for him. Pushed my hips up to make him move, otherwise he looked as if he might stay frozen in place. "Please. Save me," I said.

He slid his cock over my bottom lip. Back and forth, back and forth, until I poked my tongue out and licked the tip of him. Perry let his head fall forward and he groaned. Then he was moving over me, pushing his dick between my lips and down my throat. I struggled against the rope but lost. I settled for pushing my cock against my bound hands. Desperate for some kind of stimulation. I licked up the length of him, inhaling his smell. So much better than I have even fantasized.

Sandalwood and warm laundry and cinnamon. He smelled like the best dessert to me. I treated him like he was, and he shivered over me, his muscles trembling with the effort of holding himself up. "I've been waiting a hundred years for us to be alone."

I swallowed him as he thrust, the tip of him hitting the back of my throat. I wished I could touch him. I would have asked to but my mouth was full. So that was why he'd run Tony out. He saw a chance and took it. He wanted to be alone with me. I lit up on the inside with the thought.

His thrusts grew deeper and greedier and I found him watching me. Whether to simply see his cock gliding over my lips or to see if I could handle him, I don't know. "I'm going to fuck you now? Can I fuck you, Star Gazer?" He grinned when he said it and my prick somewhere between joy and pain seared my heart. I nodded, moving under him. Impatient and greedy writhing on the green carpet.

He flipped me easily. He had a good seventy pounds on me but he was graceful about it. He reached over me, his big arm snaking under the bed. The bottle was purple. That's all I saw. But then his weight was off of me and he said, "Try to get away."

I almost asked why, shook my head, thought better of it. With great effort, I inched, like a worm, over his floor. Until I felt his hand close around my ankles, yanking me back. He pulled me under him, reached under me, wrestled with my fly. Bound further by my own jeans and boxers around my ankles, I stilled at his touch. Warm hands, cool lube, hard breath. "I'll save you."

God. We were both insane. Wood Wizard saves the Magii Star Gazer with fucking. "Yes. I need you to." One arm hiked me up and I was draped over his forearm. Warm fingers slid into me and I let my head hang down. Someone was making a noise. It was me.

Perry was muttering again, and it sounded like prayers or incantations. Another finger slipped into me, and he balanced me on my hands and knees. I splayed my hands and tottered a bit, bound as I was. "Don't let me fall."

"You won't fall." I heard the rip of the rubber packet and the pause where I held my breath and then the head of him pressing to me. Still. Waiting. What was the magic word?

"Now?" I guessed. Here I was bound and on my hands and knees, but he was waiting for permission.'

"Now," he answered, proving me right.

"Wood Wizard," I laughed, sounding a bit drunk.

"Indeed," he laughed, too, and slipped into me. Slowly and easily and perfectly. Just as I imagined.

"Wood is good," I said, laughing in earnest now.

"True. And your ass is magic, Magii." His hand gripped me. A hand I had fixated on, daydreamed about, stared at when I could get away with it. That hand. It wrapped around my cock and started a slow, sure jerk.

"Jesus."

"Nope. Just a lowly wizard."

"Faster," I said, my shyness gone from me.

45

He gripped me with one hands, moving into me, murmuring some more magic in my ear. A shiver skittered down my spine, and he jerked my cock harder. Faster. "Come with me. Is that fast enough?"

I could only nod.

His thrusts inched me across the floor, my knees burning like fire and I didn't care. He worked me and bit the back of my neck, my shoulders, murmuring so that I wanted to demand to know what he was saying. But then the orgasm started to bloom, a hot, white flower, deep in my belly, spreading a leaden pleasure through my lower body. I moaned and he laughed and he said it again, quietly, magically. "Come with me."

He jerked and I jerked. White, warm fluid and soft, wet sounds and lovely sighs. "See, that. You obeyed me."

"You're wish is my command," I teased, letting the rest of my body jump and skitter with the echoes of pleasure still going off in my body.

"Because I'm a wizard," he said with a soft chuckle.

"You're damn magical, that's for sure," I agreed.

# FOUR-EYES AND EIGHT INCHES
## Rob Rosen

The fog had already begun to settle in for the night, turning my sweat-soaked running shorts and T-shirt into a damp, clinging mess. Clearly, I'd lost track of time and distance, finding myself in a usually unexplored section of campus, research buildings on either side of me, lit only from the outside by dim, yellow bulbs.

To top it all off, I had to take a wicked piss, the quart of Gatorade taking no time at all to work its way through me. I sidled up to a wide oak, freeing my cock from my jock, the cool air instantly drying the perspiration that trickled down my balls. A car drove by, then another. Not a good place to relieve myself, I figured. It was then that I spotted the lights on in a corner of the building to my right. I slid my prick back in and jogged over. The door was unlocked. I grinned at my good fortune and walked inside.

A reception desk greeted me, hours empty. Just beyond lay a dark corridor, made visible only by emergency lights; still, I could make out the bathroom at the end of the hall. I tiptoed down, my sneakers squeaking on the polished linoleum, my heart pounding at the thought that I was, if not breaking, then at least entering when I shouldn't have been.

The bathroom door opened. No locks. A bright fluorescent light momentarily blinded me. The piss came fast and furious, my teeth practically floating by that time. The sound of urine striking porcelain reverberated in the otherwise silent room. Then another sound found my ears. Shoes in the distance. Drawing nearer. Fuck.

The door opened. "Oh," came a voice. "I, um, the building was supposed to be locked."

47

I continued peeing. "Sorry. I saw a light on and figured this'd be better than a tree," I explained, still facing the tiled wall.

The door closed behind him as he moved to the urinal to my left. I glanced over for a split second. Short guy. White lab coat. Thick, black glasses. He leaned in, unzipped, and sprayed. "Out jogging?" he asked.

"Yeah," I replied. "In working?"

He chuckled. "Unfortunately. My pager went off. Brief power outage. I had to reset some of the equipment. Check the freezers."

I finished peeing and walked over to wash my hands, checking the guy out in the mirror. Shorter than I thought. 5'7" at most, thin and wiry, tiny ass in baggy slacks that were too short for him, the black of his dress socks peeking out above his loafers. Science geek working late. I dried my hands and turned to leave. "Don't work too hard," I offered, reaching for the door.

He zipped up and turned around. Cute face, all angles, curly black hair, five o'clock shadow that probably started settling in at around 9:00 am. Plus startling blue eyes. Laser intense, shimmering in the harsh overhead lighting. "Almost done. Thanks. Have fun, um, jogging." He hazarded a smile, lopsided, unsure.

I nodded and exited, my shorts, for some reason, slightly bulging. Not my type, after all. Not by a long shot. Then again, alone in a dark building, well, you do the math. Or let him; he seemed the kind to get off on that.

I walked down the hall, slowly, killing some time. He exited the bathroom. "Night," he hollered.

"Night," I yelled back, our voices pinging off the walls. "You, um, okay in here alone?"

He paused, adjusting his glasses, then scratched his head. "I'll be fine; you can lock the door before you leave. Besides, I'll only be another ten minutes."

I nodded and walked the remaining twenty feet. He went the other way, turning a corner, heading for the room I'd seen lit up from the outside. I reached the exit and locked the door. Only I didn't leave. I turned instead, quietly walking back inside, following his route, my breath the only sound, shallow, ragged.

I found the room, a lab. His back was toward me, his hand behind one of the freezer cases. I coughed. He jumped and whirled around. "Oh," he said, his hand to his chest. "Just you."

"Yeah. Just me," I repeated, a sheepish grin wide on my face. "It's later and colder than I thought out there and, um, my clothes are damp. Don't suppose you could offer me a ride?"

His grin mirrored my own. "Sure, no problem. My car is outside. Just let me check the equipment first."

I took a seat on a stool, one leg perched up, the other straight down, offering him a clear view of my crotch. He glanced, briefly, coughed, then moved from machine to machine. Bait taken.

"What is it you do here?" I asked.

"Diagnostic work," he replied, resetting another piece of expensive looking equipment, chock full of levers and read-out dials. "Urinalysis, blood work, clinical biochemistry. Mostly pediatric work. Occasionally some research. The machines run 24/7. If there's a power outage, they stop and need to be restarted. Sometimes the samples misinject, meaning one of the patients could get another one's results. Have to be careful. Hence my pager."

He talked fast, nervous, flitting about as he did so. "Sounds important," I said. "Must've gone to college a good long time."

He stopped, laughed. "Long, yes. Good is a matter of opinion. One science class after the other."

"All work and no play, huh?"

Again he looked up, his eyes returning to my crotch for the briefest of seconds. "No, really, I like the work. Flexing my brain."

"What about the brawn?" I tried.

Again he laughed, walking over to within a few feet of me. He handed me his Coke-bottle-thick glasses. "Um, maybe you need these more than I do. What brawn? I'm a hundred pounds. Wet."

"Speaking of wet, you got a heater in this place? Gonna catch pneumonia. You guys keep it friggin' icy in here."

"Urine and blood and heat don't mix," he informed.

"Outside of the body, maybe," I corrected him. "But not inside."

He nodded and walked past me, returning in a minute with a small space heater that he plugged in and rested on the countertop. "Here you go. Five more minutes and we can leave, anyway." Again he paused, again looking down. "Name's Lenny," he said, his hand reaching up and out in greeting, his small, delicate fingers encased in my mitt of a grip.

"Jake," I replied, with a squeeze and a shake. "Thanks for the heater." I cranked it up, the hot air gratefully blasting across my goose bumped flesh. "Better."

He didn't move. His glasses went back atop his bumpy nose, resting on ears that jutted slightly out. "No problem," he said, his hands in his pockets, the smile returning, crooked, impish. Fucking adorable.

I upped the ante, reaching for the bottom edge of my T-shirt before yanking it up and over my head. I set it down in front of the heater. "Better let it dry a bit before we head outside," I told him. "Do you mind a few extra minutes?"

He looked away, an anxious tic evident on his angular face as he moved again to one of the machines, flicking it on and off, then on again. Busy work. Seemingly unnecessary now. Poor guy. I was making him nervous. Still, he replied. "Take your time. Got nowhere I need to be."

I sat back on the stool and kicked off my sneakers, the rubber soles landing in a dull thud. I rolled off my socks and sat them next to my shirt. "No?" I asked. "No place better than this?"

50

No reply; just a shake of his head, the curly mop bouncing from side to side. More machines flicked off and on, going dead silent than whirring back to life, syringes automatically raising and lowering, injecting their precious fluids. I grinned and watched him work, noticing his hands jut out from his lab coat, small and hairy, the fingernails bitten down, a coating of white powder along the knuckles, evidence of recently worn latex gloves.

The ante now up, I upped it some more. I jumped off the stool and slid down my trunks. His mouth dropped open, his body momentarily frozen in place. The shorts joined their mates drying on the tabletop, next to beakers and flasks and test tubes. "Oh, um," he barely managed.

"Sorry," I said. "Am I making you uncomfortable?"

His face reddened, a flush rising up his neck and spreading across his cheeks. "No, it's just, well, the shades, they're open." He walked over and closed the blinds. "In case anyone sees inside. Looks, um, kind of strange."

I laughed. "What, my being undressed and your not?"

The red deepened. "No. I mean, yes. I mean, well, you know." He pointed at my near naked self, his slender index finger aiming at my jockstrap.

"I see your point," I told him. "That would look odd."

"Yes," he agreed, still pointing, still staring. "Odd."

"Unless," I said, "you got undressed, as well."

He didn't reply, fiddling with his glasses instead. "How, exactly, would two undressed men in a lab not look odd?" he eventually asked.

"Less odd," I reasoned, "than just one."

Again no response. Instead, he nodded and slowly removed his lab coat, hanging it neatly on a hook behind the door. He walked back over and stood a foot in front of me, his eyes locking on to mine, two sapphires glinting beneath the bright light. He kicked off his shoes. 5'6" now. His hands reached up, the slightest of trembles barely discernable. The buttons of his shirt unbuttoned, from top to bottom. He yanked the material out of his slacks and removed the shirt completely, quickly joining it with the coat. A white undershirt still remained, covering a noticeably narrow torso. Again I stared at his hands, the trail of hair flowing up his forearms; thick and wiry black, they came to an abrupt halt at his elbows, only to reappear again within the v-necked collar, dense and matted.

He pulled the undershirt up and off, revealing a lean, tight body, the hairs running rampant across his belly and slender chest, circling around two pink nipples, now erect in the cold air of the lab. The belt came off next, the slacks sliding down, off, until he stood before me in nothing but his black socks, pulled tight up his shins, almost to his knees, and his paisley boxers, which hung down loose around his hairy thighs, but tight in the middle as they rapidly tented.

"See," I said. "Now we don't look so strange. Out of place, maybe; but no longer at odds."

"Huh," he sighed. "Even undressed we look completely different; definitely at odds. You've got half a foot and a good sixty pounds on me. Plus, look how smooth you are and look how hairy I am. Like two different species."

"Same species," I made note, pointing at his growing stiffy and my already rock-solid one. "Both men."

Finally, he laughed, exhaling sharply as he did so. "You know what I meant," he said. "The jock and the nerd. Quintessential opposites."

"Don't opposites attract, Lenny?" I practically purred, standing up and sliding over, my hand running down his slender frame, causing his eyelids to flutter behind his glasses.

"In the lab, maybe. In real life, not so much," he replied, his own hand rising up, his fingers tracing the lines around my stomach muscles, playing with the small patch of fine hairs situated between my pecs.

I bent down, my lips just slightly brushing his, soft and warm and inviting. "You sure about that?" My mouth pressed flush against his, my tongue snaking its way inside. He groaned and melded into me, his short, slight body nestling into mine. A perfect fit.

He inched away, replying with a mischievous grin, "Well, the hypothesis bears investigation, at any rate."

"Sweet talker," I chided, reaching my arms around him in an enveloping embrace, his chest hairs tickling my belly as his prick poked my leg. "And speaking of hypotheses, how about the one about big things in little packages?"

He moved away, his hands atop the edge of his boxers. Taking my hint, he quickly released the beast, his long, fat cock springing up and out, the wide mushroom head already slick with precum. "That one I believe is true," he rightfully proclaimed, giving it a tug that sent his lemon sized balls to bouncing.

I reached down to pat at the underside of the multi-veined shaft. "No wonder you're so pale," I quipped. "All the blood is rushing to this."

I motioned with my finger for him to turn around, so I could check out the backside. He spun in place: bony shoulders, impossibly thin waist, a tuft of hair springing up along his lower back, the smallest ass this side of the Mississippi, covered in a fuzzy down, spindly legs just as hairy. His sum, however, was greater than the individual parts; meaning he was strangely sexy as hell.

I slid out of my jockstrap, my own hefty cock jumping to life, arcing out and just slightly to the left. I gave it a stroke, feeling it pulse in my grip, a million volts of adrenalin shooting out in all directions. "Think there's room for you up here?" I asked, pointing to the ultra-wide countertop.

"You plan on doing some experimenting?" he said, answering my question with one of his own.

"Good place for it," I replied, helping him up.

He got on all fours, resting his small frame on his elbows, his knees wide apart, his perfect, little ass now at face level with me. I leaned in for a whiff, taking in his heady aroma. Musk and sweat. Intoxicating as fuck. I ran my hand across both cheeks, the hairs dense, soft like velvet; then my index finger traveled vertical, following his crack to dead center, landing on his pink, puckered hole, haloed in hair, winking out at me. I took a lick, a suck, a slurp, my tongue gliding in.

"Fuck," he groaned, long and low and deep, mashing his ass into my face as he pushed his prick between his legs, offering up the whole menu for me to enjoy.

My mouth moved from his ass to his balls, tickling his densely hairy nuts with my tongue before taking each one in my mouth for a suck, then yanking down on them with my lips. His back arched as his groans filled the lab. Pleasure mixed with pain. He seemed to dig both. I slapped his ass as I worked his balls. The groan grew deeper. I spanked harder, the flesh turning from white to hot pink.

"Fuck yeah," he moaned, the geek in him turning masochist on me.

I grabbed for his cock, thick and throbbing, a fifth limb for such a slight man. I held it at the base, dangling it straight down, giving it a slap, then another. He moaned, appreciatively, his fat dick-head now drenched in precum. I bent down for a taste, salt mixed with sweat, before engulfing him whole, a happy gagging tear streaming down my face.

I jacked him with my mouth, sending his meaty rod down my throat as I pushed his cheeks apart with my hands, staring hungrily at his hole, which I quickly filled with a spit-slick index finger.

"Yeah," he exhaled, the breath drawn out.

A second finger joined the first as he pushed his cock further between his legs, fucking my face as I worked his mega-tight ass. In and out, in and out; then a miraculous third digit joined the party. He pushed his ass backwards, grinding fist into flesh.

"Yeah, fuck me," he rasped. "Fuck me hard."

With no rubbers in sight, I looked around for the next best thing, something phallic, rigid, firm. "Think the test tubes by your head would be safe?"

He handed me one with a laugh. "Pyrex. Thermal shock resistant borosilicate glass. Tough as nails. Now fuck me."

I stood back up, spanking his ass, his hole, and his cock, his skin turning red, yet again, each swat eliciting a moan, a groan, and a "yeah."

"Hop down, little dude," I told him. He hopped, his head again even with my chest, his glasses reflecting the light as he waited for my next command. "Too fucking cute," I whispered, leaning down for a deep, perfect, soul kiss, gently slapping at his cock as I did so. "Back on all fours," I soon added.

He crouched down on the floor and resumed the position, his fuzzy, little ass beckoning me. I sat cross-legged in front of it, praying at the altar, my reverent tongue offering its wet tithing. Fully slick, I spread him open and placed the rounded end of the test tube up against his chute. He stroked his fat prick as I gently teased it in, tensing for a brief moment before fully allowing the intrusion. The glass held, the cylinder entrenched half way, poking out of his upturned rump.

I jumped back up and walked around him, then plopped my ass on the cool floor, once more face to adorable face. My legs splayed apart, resting on either side of his frame. I slid up, my cock pointing up at his chin. He stared at me, eyes locked, watching, waiting.

"Now fuck that tight ass," I rasped, the breath thick in my throat. He reached behind and slid the tube in and out, slowly, evenly, matching the rhythm with his free hand along his beautiful, porn-sized prick. "Now suck my cock."

His eyes glanced up, the thick lenses magnifying the spectacular blue orbs as his mouth came down around my swollen prick, gliding to the base and setting every nerve-ending in my body on fire. I reached out and down, taking his nipples in between my thumbs and index fingers, giving a twist and a tug and a tweak on each. His muffled groans made my crotch quake. I pulled harder; he sped up the sucking and fucking and jacking.

He popped my prick out of his mouth. "Close. So fucking close," he said to me.

I grabbed my cock and piston-jacked the shaft, aiming my slit toward his face. He stared down, eager for the spectacle. "Come," I told him.

He shoved the tube into the hilt and gave a final tug on his dick. His legs trembled, his back arched, and he shot, a thick, luminous stream of come spewing from his massive prick. I came with him, my own tool quivering and shooting, over and over and over again, the piping hot come launching up and out, drenching his mouth, his chin, and neck, while we both howled in ecstasy, our moans and groans and sighs filling my ears like a veritable symphony.

I wiped the come off his face and leaned down for a soft kiss and a gentle spank on his cheek. He sat back up on his knees and leaned himself into me, his hairy body dripping in well-earned sweat. My arms wrapped around his and his around mine as his lips pressed up tight against my mouth, our tongues doing a slow dance inside.

He reached around and slid the tube out of his ass. "I'll never look at these the same way again," he said, with a laugh, looking back up at me, his glasses brushing my nose. "By the way," he added, "where will I be dropping you off? You live near campus?"

I nodded. "Across campus, actually. Faculty housing."

His head tilted to the side. "You're a teacher?" he asked.

Again I nodded. "Professor. English Lit. Guess that looks can be deceiving hypotheses got tested tonight, too, huh? I'm more geek than jock, little dude. Not so opposite after all."

He frowned, just a bit. "Not so attracted then?" he asked.

My mouth again found his, and I replied, "Oh fuck no. More so. Beautiful brain, beautiful dick, beautiful man. And you're going for a ride on teacher's lap when we get home."

His grin returned, wide and intoxicating. "You certainly have a way with words, Jake."

"I know, Lenny," I replied, my prick already growing stiff. "And I have the degrees to prove it."

# EXPOSED
# Bryl R. Tyne

## *Chapter 1 – Waste of Time*

"I'm not going to have this discussion, Becca. How do you know he's not a poser?" Index fingers registering the keyboard tits, Clay's brain reengaged in his current project before he finished speaking. Working to impress Mr. Minsho by six o'clock, a once in a lifetime shot, he hurried to rerun the simulations for Minsho's newest adult game.

"You can stop acting like a vulture anytime now," Clay said, as he removed his glasses and cleaned the lenses with his shirttail. That's Becca for you, awesome at Game play, but no sense of responsibility. When her normal brand of chatter bored him, he ignored it. Today, all he'd heard from her annoying mouth … Minsho's new hire … some guy she'd never met. Shuddering, he shoved on his glasses.

"Whatever. Everyone's going."

Jesus, shut the hell up!

"Don't you ever chill? It'd do you good to get out, act normal once in while," she mumbled, taking her seat.

Ignoring her, Clay added the final touches to his masterpiece. Mr. Minsho's gonna dig this … Clayton James McCarthy, Lead Engineer. He envisioned the layout of his new business cards, his name plastered across the company Web site and brochures. Clay knew the odds of it happening were slim to none. No one bypassed Animation and jumped from AI to Lead, but who'd they always call on in a crunch? Yeah, he'd proved his skills in animating more than enough. He didn't need a degree to prove his intellect or abilities.

Clay saved his work and logged out. "Watch my station, Becca. I'm gettin' a soda." He stiff-armed the door into the hall.

Meeting new employees means wasting time. Clay considered his features, tucking the shirttails inside his dress pants, before admiring his black Converse high-tops. Two months it'd taken him to save for his shoes, a small feat, but forward progress. Adjusting the brim of his baseball cap against the back of his neck, he righted his glasses and crammed four quarters into the soda machine.

Clay explained the game's environment as he hovered near the monitor. Mr. Minsho's gaze traveled from Clay's shoes to the top of his head. "This is impressive work, McCarthy," he said, clicking another trigger point. His eyebrows twitched more than a few times, Clay noticed. "You never cease to amaze me with your realism."

"Thank you, sir."

Mr. Minsho swiveled around, lacing his fingers together atop his desk. "You are coming to the dinner tonight, right?"

Clay's eyes widened, and he cleared his throat. "I've quite a bit of work ..."

"Nonsense! See you at eight sharp."

Shit! Hoping to circumvent further obligation, Clay shuffled toward the office door, but Minsho's final comment sealed his fate. "Don't be late, McCarthy."

Nobody understood. Never had, never will, and he wasn't about to explain. Clay wanted to crawl into a hole, hide out the rest of the night, the remainder of the week if he could. What's this sudden interest, 'Help Socialize Clay Week'? He found it unnerving to say the least. My life is mine to live, my secrets, mine to keep. Opening up to others meant sharing both. The mere thought of trusting again sent minute pieces of jagged glass scraping down his spine.

"Well, are you coming or not?" Becca asked as she wheeled her chair under the desk and picked up her bag. Clay hoped to avoid the inevitable by pretending ignorance. However, Minsho would never buy that excuse, especially after their earlier conversation. Besides, if it meant finding favor ... he hated caving in – being soft. "I'm not biking 3 miles to Raymond's. I don't think so. Have a nice ...!"

Becca demanded attention as she whipped his chair around. "You're riding with me. So, quit being ridiculous." She yanked him to his feet.

"Let me shut down first for Christ's sake." Clay secured his station, hoisted his backpack, and reluctantly followed her. She seriously needs to get laid ... I'm getting sick of this shit. Becca's twenty years old and single. Briefly, Clay wondered; then struggled to erase the revolting mental images. As she turned on to the street, Clay stared at his clunky twelve-speed chained near the door, calculating how many months he'd have to save for an upgrade.

This many bodies crammed into 4000 square foot must certainly be against fire code. Clay fascinated on the ceiling's beam structure as he shoved his way through the crowd, not willing to fall behind. How does she do it? He fumed. Restaurant patrons eloquently parted for Becca, yet they seemed hell bent on blocking his passage. As she disappeared into the sea of people, panic swept through him. His fear of crowds kicked in ... Enochlophobia, the shrink told me. Yeah, whatever, I just need to stop, recompose ... breathe. Inhaling slowly and adjusting his cap, he wiped the perspiration dotting his temples.

What the hell? He jerked his head toward the owner of the hand that rested on the small of his back. He met hazel eyes ... devilish grin. Exactly the reason Clay hated public places. His tongue wet his bottom lip, as menace transformed into opportunity. The man's smiling face inches from his, Clay toyed with the sudden urge to kiss those full lips.

"Excuse me, are you lost?" the man asked. Even touching a total stranger, the man stood confident. Clay shifted to his right, and the comforting palm retreated.

"J-Just lost track of my friend for a minute," Clay managed to blurt out, tearing his gaze away and scanning the crowd.

The stranger smiled and held out his hand. "Dave Hansen," he said.

Clay pushed his glasses up before accepting the handshake. "Clay McCarthy."

"I'm lost myself," Dave said, "looking for a table of folks from Minsho Software."

"Oh, so ..." Clay's eyes moved to Dave's hand, the one still holding his. Pulling it away, he wiped the sweat from his brow, "You must be the new guy. What's your specialty?" Not a threat, Clay assured himself as his eyes roamed the man's expanse ... Another poser ... noting the scuffed biker boots and faded jeans of his too-casual attire ... Definitely not one of us.

"Oh, so you're with Minsho's?" Dave asked, with his smile widening into what Clay garnered something between sly and sinister. "I'm an animator. One of the best ... So, I'm told."

"Artificial intelligence," Clay said, resolving it'd be a cold day in hell before he'd give Dave any recognition.

"Nice ... I'll enjoy working with you."

"Clay! There you are ... Come on!" Becca snagged his arm and hauled him toward the group. Dave smirked and followed. "I found him, Mr. Minsho." She plopped down in her seat, jerking it under the table. Clay settled at the corner beside her, scanning the vicinity ... perfect, no seats on either side.

"Oh, there you are," Mr. Minsho said standing, and pulling him into a quick handshake. Squeezing between Mr. Minsho and Clay, Dave slammed a stool down and straddled it. After the third brush of thighs, Clay elbowed Becca.

"What the hell's your problem?" she mumbled, sliding her stool to the left.

"Hi, everyone," Dave said, making eye contact around the table. "My name's Dave, Dave Hansen; I'm an animator. I'm excited about working with you all," he glanced at Clay, "and getting to know you."

Clay sensed Minsho analyzing the interaction. Despite his head feeling as if someone just salivated on Pop Rocks, he managed a polite nod.

Lost in musing why Becca's napkin came folded the opposite direction as his; Clay jumped when a hand descended his forearm, and landed cockeyed on the edge of his seat with a yelp. "Chill dude," Dave said, righting him on the stool. Once again, Dave's hand acted like a lonely childhood friend, the kind that refuses to go home. "You gonna finish those chicken strips?"

Clay snatched his arm free and shoved the plate in front of Dave. "Thanks," he said already stuffing his mouth, "I'm starving."

"Sure." Clay pulled out his cell phone checking the time. "Becca, I need to get home."

"Clay ..." she whined.

"Don't give me a hard time. It's already dark," he whispered, "and ... I got a new project to plan." Becca finished her soda, stood, and apologized for leaving. Hopping off his stool, relief washed over Clay as he grunted goodbyes around the table. Fixing his glasses, he snuck a peek at Dave, who sat chin on knuckles, staring at him ... intimidating ... or flirting? Clay figured the latter as he spun around and jogged to catch Becca, anxious for solitude.

## Chapter 2 – Second Thoughts

"Comin' Clay?" Dave hollered, as he opened the door, but kept on walking.

"You're skipping lunch again?" Becca asked. Clay motioned for her to go without him. "What's going on? You've been avoiding all of us for over a week!" Again, she stood directly behind his chair. His fingers flit over the keys, and five seconds later, the screen faded to black.

Screaming came to mind, but he chose civility. She cared about his well-being ... the motherly type ... no biggy. "Listen Bec, I've got a million things to finish on this project."

"What project? I finished my work two days ago. You should've been done already."

"Don't worry; I've been snacking, see?" Clay held up the half-eaten bag of candy.

"Jesus Clay, candy's not lunch."

"You mean dinner, Bec. It's seven o'clock at night ... called, dinner."

"Whatever ... I'm going."

Heat rose from Clay's neck to his temples as he batted his eyelashes. "Gees, I didn't know you cared." She threw him a half-hearted wave stomping away. He waited for the door to click before rebooting his screen. If his estimations were correct, he had exactly fifty-two minutes of paranoia-free time, and his fingers moved into action.

At fifty-one minutes, forty-six seconds, Dave, Becca, and the rest of the crew moseyed into the room. Becca slammed onto her chair with a sigh. Clay shrugged, his monitor reflected the company's latest work, special project saved and closed. All of a sudden, his senses flared to high alert as foreign pressure lifted the brim of his cap. "Missed ya, Clay," Dave said.

Clay clasped his cap against his head as he shot up, whirled around, and poked Dave's chest. "Don't ... ever ... touch ... the hat!"

"Whoa ... God man, so temperamental." Dave stepped back, grinning. Clay glowered at him. No one touched his hat, ever. "Okay. Gees ... a joke man, it's a joke." Dave retreated to his station after Clay settled in his seat.

With frazzled nerves, Clay struggled to make sense of the remaining evening's assignment. Ten minutes before his shift ended, he lost it. A half-empty soda whizzed through the air, smacking two feet above an empty station, bouncing off the desk, and rolling to a lopsided stop. Amber syrupy liquid patterned the white wall. All sets of eyes on him, Clay twisted around and buried his head in his hands regretting his asininity.

He heard the door open and click shut several times. Good, they're gone. At least his coworkers realized when a guy needed space. "God Damn it!" he yelled, slamming his fists on the desk … only to hear a clearing throat behind him. Oh, Fuck!

"I'm sorry," Dave repeated for the third time. Clay spun around wondering why he kept yapping. His gaze narrowed on the upturned view of Dave's perfect ass outlined in tight jeans as he sopped up the splattered drink with paper towels. "Listen," Dave started, as he discarded the towels, "I'm sorry I got you so riled up. Those weren't my intentions."

"Screw you, Hansen." Clay redirected his attention to his computer feigning occupation. "You're certainly full of yourself tonight, no?"

So close, Clay swore he could date his cologne, Dave leaned over his shoulder. "Show me where you're having trouble." Dave's breath ghosted across his cheek, goose bumps prickling every limb. Temporarily immobilized, Clay managed a curt nod. His rationale pleaded reprieve, but his body held an opposing viewpoint. Dave's chest now, pressed against his upper back. "I am sorry," Dave whispered, standing upright, manipulating Clay's tense muscles with a firm grip. Electricity surged along Clay's spine, to his tailbone, and accumulated just under his balls. Every nerve ending inside snapped at once.

He secured his computer, shrugging off Dave's hands as he stood, and picked up his backpack. "I'll work on it first thing tomorrow afternoon." He marched for the door.

Dave's arm blocked his path like a railroad guard. "Wait."

Clay remained paralyzed as logic fought body, one seeking the exit, the other longing for Dave's touch. "Here," Dave said, handing him a paper towel. Clay snatched it from his hand and removed his glasses.

"Thanks," he stammered, cleaning his lenses then drying the sweat running down the sides of his face. Not the first time Dave had shown kindness, he'd offered assistance since day one, copping feels wherever possible. Clay knew what Dave wanted.

He wasn't sure he'd anything left to give, not now … not yet, maybe … not ever. He slid his glasses on and reached for the door.

"Clay."

Holding his breath, he paused.

"You ever think of wearing contacts?"

"Save it, Dave. See you tomorrow."

Five miles in ten minutes, not bad … Clay clocked his time then pulled off his shirt without unfastening the buttons, threw it in the washer, and slid in three quarters … One more day this week. He bound up the steps and into his apartment. After resting his bike against the wall by the TV, he stalked to the bathroom.

Large, blue eyes the bane of his existence. Clay cut a hole in the steam searching his reflection. Every new person commented on how beautiful his eyes were, or worse yet, "such lovely eyelashes". He shuddered. Exacerbating his woe by adorning contacts not his idea of a good time. Hell, he'd worn glasses his entire life. He'd be hell pressed to spend money on something so frivolous. Three months and he'd be on top, at least out of the hole his ex left him … bastard. Clay wrapped the towel around his narrow hips. Two years it'd taken him to right the mountain of debt his ex compiled. Rental centers and pawnshops, not to mention the freaking mail orders charged to his credit card. He vowed, never again. Then he met Dave Hansen.

Pulling up his sweatpants, he plodded downstairs and returned from the laundry room, with his damp shirt in hand. Dave seemed different, but they always do. He's two years older, twenty-two, Becca told him. Clay wrapped his shirt around a hanger, hooking it on the shower rod; should dry overnight. He pushed his pile of comics off the bed and lay down. He welcomed the ceiling fan's hypnotic trance. If he let Dave in, Clay vowed not to forget the keyboard of life this time. His finger would remain poised over that escape button, and he'd make sure Dave knew it.

## Chapter 3 - That's Life

ALGORITHM TO DAVE'S – Shit! Clay's five-second program shutdown, now took less than two. He caught his breath as Becca took her seat. He'd titled his project, and finished timing the marquee when his coworkers shuffled in the door. A month and a half ago, completing before Christmas seemed a lofty goal. The next step, presenting it ... he refused to get cold feet now, damned if he'd wasted two months of his life. He wiped his sweaty palms on his pants. By the holidays, he'd have saved enough for his dream bike. If Minsho promoted him, he'd don a newer wardrobe, too. Same style though, hell if he'd wear a T-shirt. Dave's idiosyncrasies still irked him, but Clay conceded, a poser, he was not.

Clay found himself anticipating Dave's casual touches, his baritone voice. An intricate game of cat and mouse, Clay skipped breaks, not trusting the atmosphere ... not trusting himself. He'd joined them at the movies twice, but only as a group. His financial situation an issue, he feared losing ground. Along with his ex's number, he'd no help from family either. They'd disowned him five years ago.

"Hey Clay, how's it going?" Dave's arm brushed his back as he strolled toward his station.

Clay concealed a smile. "So far, so good." He kept Dave at arm's length, despite how close he wanted him ... Close enough to suck my cock. He resolved Dave suffered long enough. He'd fix it, and soon.

"Come on, I wanna show you something." Clay followed Dave outside during the break. "Whadaya think?" Dave introduced him to his new wheels, opening the driver's door and motioning for him to slide behind the wheel.

"What happened to your motorcycle?" Clay ran his hand over the dash, registering the many gauges ... two tachometers. Dave informed him he'd traded it for the down. "It's nice, but can you afford it?" Clay asked.

"Hell yeah! Minsho's promoting me to Lead Engineer. Can you believe it?"

Of all things, he'd expected to experience outside with Dave, hearing this wasn't on the list. Death by suffocation sounded better. He staggered out of the car, upended Dave, and bolted into the building.

Backpack on; he fumbled with the chain looped around his bike as Dave jogged toward him. "What the hell's wrong?" Dave grabbed his arm, but Clay straddled his bike, and shoved Dave backward. Launching off the bench and out of the parking lot, he flew into oncoming traffic.

"What's going on?" Becca asked, rushing out the door.

"I don't know ... I showed him my car a-and, he flipped."

"He'll be back."

Dave didn't move. He stood staring at the cars passing on the road. He looked ... Confused ... Hurt? Becca didn't know, but Clay taking off obviously bothered him. "How bout we ask for the rest of the night and go look for him?"

Dave's face lit up. He whipped the door open and raced to shut down his station.

After receiving permission, Becca and Dave piled into his car. As Dave barreled down the streets, she directed him to Clay's apartment. One intersection after another, they searched for any sign of Clay or his bike along the way. No lights shown through the windows, and Clay never answered the door or his cell phone.

Becca called work, but they hadn't heard from him either. After three hours of searching every place she knew he frequented, they began to worry. "Call the cops," Dave said.

"Huh? Isn't that a little dramatic?"

Dave slammed on the brakes and swerved to a stop alongside a curb. Fingers tightening on the steering wheel, his jaw clenched. "Where is he, then? You've got a better idea?" Becca stared at him wide-eyed. "Do you?" he screamed, a single tear streaking down his cheek.

Becca dialed information for the number to the police station.

"He's in ICU, sir." That was the last thing Dave remembered before seeing his apartment door. He stepped inside not bothering with the lights and trudged for the shower. Water should regain his senses.

Every part of his body felt numb. He leaned against the tiles as the water cascaded over his tensed muscles. No washing, he allowed the spray to rivet his skin until his legs began to weaken. Running the towel over his head, he glanced at his reflection. His skin glowed cherry red. He went through the motions, of shaving, brushing his teeth, and combing his hair. Nothing helped. He'd instructed the nurses to call him if Clay's condition changed. Would they though, he wasn't related.

Dave flopped onto his bed and tried rationalizing the situation. He ended up settling for closing his eyes, hoping to still the tears … no luck. "Why'd Clay get so angry? Why do I care?"

His cell phone rang less than once before he grabbed it off the nightstand. "Hello?"

"Mr. Hansen, please."

"Speaking … Is this the hospital … Is Clay okay?"

"Calm down, sir. Mr. McCarthy's in stable condition. I'm only calling you because he claims there's no family."

"Nobody? Can I talk to him?"

"He's awake, but they're medicating soon … It might be better if you ..."

"Just give me his room number."

"Room eight seventeen, Mr. Hansen … please try ..."

Dave disconnected the call and dialed the hospital. "Room eight seventeen, please."

After handing Clay the receiver, the nurse promised to return in fifteen minutes. "H-He-llo," his voice groveled over the line.

"Clay, it's Dave. God, are you all right?" Expecting a reply, he heard muffled voices, and received the distinct click of

69

disconnection. Phone still in his hand, he dropped his arm to the bed. He'd never been so attracted, so patient in the hunt, or agonized like this over anyone. God, I practically jumped him the moment I met him in the restaurant. He took on a corpse-like pose. He'd always liked computer nerds, fucking animals in the sack. Clay's different. Not that he envisioned anything less than a tiger in bed, but he actually liked the guy … a lot.

He'd blown that all to hell. As a squall of remorse trickled into his ears, Dave wished he'd never applied at Minsho Adult Software Developers.

## *Chapter 4 – Just Cause*

Thursday, the doctor told him. Five weeks had passed quickly. Last week Clay's left arm evolved from traction to a partial cast. His cracked ribs although still tender, had healed, and the Doctor allowed him to return home. "Doc told me I can work Christmas Eve … yeah, tomorrow … B-But, not even just half a day …?" Clay paused; his spirits had been high, until Mr. Minsho's unbearable response. "Yes sir, Monday."

"Damn it!" He chucked his cell phone and it slid across the coffee table. Not much of a Christmas present, if it's late … He and Dave had made amends. Dave called the hospital every day before and after work until he'd given in. Now, his Christmas ruined, he shoved off the couch, catching his left side … Damn, be more careful. The hall mirror called attention to his disheveled cap. Fiddling with escaping strands of hair, it dawned on him; Dave said he'd stop by around dinnertime.

Clay glanced at the alarm clock by his bed … six-thirty. He brushed out his hair, gathered it into one fist, and wrapped it into a ponytail, before tucking it under his cap. Right on time, he chuckled, as he heard the knock. He secured the shambles of his cave, straightened his T-shirt as well as possible one-handed, and adjusting his cap, opened the door. "Hey."

"Clay." Hands in pockets, Dave shifted his boot clad feet, taking in the sight of bare toes protruding form-fitting jeans ... and a T-shirt? "You didn't get new glasses yet?"

"Trying contacts ... Come in." Clay motioned to the sofa as he padded to the refrigerator. "Want a beer?" More of a rhetorical question as he handed a bottle to Dave. Clay cracked his open and took a swig before strutting across the carpet mocking a runway model's turn. "So, your curiosity satisfied? Told you I was fine."

Dave glanced at his cast then met his gaze. He smirked and toasted to recovery as Clay settled beside him. Dave picked at the label on the bottle. "So," he said, taking a sip, his eyes fixated on his lap, "you really aren't mad at me for Minsho's call?" He scratched the back of his head, twisting just enough to see Clay's response. Clay's assurance included leaning on his shoulder.

"Good ... God," Dave choked out, as his heart beat faster. Blood raced through his veins, damming behind his zippered jeans. He killed his beer, but its icy chill evaporated as it met the fiery heat below.

Clay stood, set his beer on the coffee table, and grabbed Dave's empty bottle. "You want another?" Dave declined. He tossed it into the trash and scurried back, hurling himself onto the sofa. Dave chuckled, imagining what lie ... or stood ... behind ... those damned jeans. He locked eyes with Clay and draped an arm over his shoulders.

Pulling him flush, he stroked his face from temple to chin. "I am sorry."

"In the past ... drop it, will ya?"

"Yeah ... drop it," Dave whispered, capturing the lips he'd longed to taste for months.

Clay's good hand gripped the back of his neck, and held him close as Dave's tongue explored, searching for an opportunity. Clay needed little coaxing and eagerly parted his lips. Dave smirked.

71

"What's so funny?"

"I didn't realize you were so hungry."

"I'm starving."

"Really? Well then ..." He reclaimed Clay's mouth, cupped his face, and delved deeper, exploring, and parting for air. "Lose the hat."

Clay sat upright. Reaching behind his head, he flicked the brim and the cap toppled onto the carpet. Astonished, Dave watched as three feet of banded hair, spilled down Clay's back. His fingers laced through well-kempt, coffee brown strands. "My God, Clay ..." He carried a handful over Clay's shoulder and pressed it to his nose, inhaling. "Let it loose."

As Clay unwound the band, hair furled down the length of his arms. Too silky, too much, Dave couldn't touch it enough. He attacked Clay's mouth and lowered him onto the cushions.

"Humph," Dave groaned, as Clay's cast gouged into his stomach. He fumbled for a minute, dislodging it from between their bodies, and leaned it against the sofa's back. Hovering above, he pressed his aching bulge against the excitement in Clay's jeans. "God Clay, why hide your beauty?"

Damn it ... Enough talk ... Clay bucked upward. One set of fingers fumbling to rid Dave of his pants. Dave's body heat disappeared as he crawled off him and pushed to his feet. Dave cut off his protest by shedding his boots, pants, and shirt in less than ten seconds. "Jesus," he gasped, and Dave helped him wriggle his own jeans past his knees. Clay scooted against the sofa's arm until seated, and kicked them past his feet.

He yanked Dave onto the cushions, and scrambled on top of him, reversing their situation. "Can you breathe," he teased as his hair smothered their kisses.

"God ... yes ..." Dave's hands squeezed Clay's underwear clad buttocks, rocking him against his length. "No, God. Don't stop." Dave sighed, as Clay's lips abandoned his mouth, but as he attacked his throat, licked over a collarbone, and started teasing a nipple with his teeth, his protests turned into pleas for more.

Clay obliged. Months of pent up fantasies, mixed with the aroma of Dave's woodsy cologne drove him wild. He needed release. His mouth roved down Dave's packed torso, tongue dipping in and out of his navel, and snagged the waistband of Dave's boxers with his teeth. One hand and a strong jaw pulled the material over his erection, down his thighs, and off his ankles. Clay hesitated, stilling his own burgeoning cock. He straddled Dave at the thighs; tracing the rigid vein along the bottom of Dave's shaft ... perfect. Dave stretched toward his discarded clothes. "What?"

He snagged his pants, digging into a front pocket, retrieving a condom. "Here." He tossed it to Clay, who immediately tore it open and covered Dave's cock.

Dave's exhales came short and fast as Clay's tongue flicked over the latex sheathed head then moved to the skin between his cock's naked base and his scrotum. He enjoyed his exploration ... until Dave pulled his hair. He scowled, snarling, and knocked his hands away.

"Sorry ..." Dave blurted as Clay slapped his cast over him, pinning his lower abdomen to the sofa.

"Now, calmly," swirling his tongue around the head of his coated cock, Clay whispered, "lie there," and fingered his sac, rolling the balls gently, first one, then the other, "and take it." Dave groaned as Clay wrapped his fingers low around the base and he disappeared inside Clay's mouth.

Clay swallowed Dave's cock inch by inch then removing his mouth to the head, raked his teeth lightly over the swollen ridge. Dave's hips strained against the weight of Clay's cast and his back arched. "Please ... Dear God ... You're killing me," he panted.

Clay's lips applied pressure as he engulfed him again, this time his chin and nose brushing coarse blond curls. Dave's hands grasped the back of Clay's head as he continued sucking, long to the head then hard to the base. He let out a growl as Dave tensed and erupted, thick and hot, swelling the end of the condom in the back of his throat. He sucked and pulled as his fingers ghosted the bottom left of Dave's scrotum until he'd drained his cock.

Amid crushing lips and battling tongues, Dave slid his hands inside Clay's boxers and stroked his neglected erection while the other hand fondled his ass. So many showers he'd fascinated over the flesh he held in his arms.

"Jesus," Clay gasped, "I can't last. I wanna fuck you."

Dave tugged on his boxers. "Left front pocket."

He chuckled as Clay crawled from the sofa, discarded his shorts in haste, and retrieved another condom and … lube? He lifted a brow. "Call me hopeful," Dave teased, as he watched Clay waste no time tearing the package open and rolling the condom over his leaking cock.

"Knees on the carpet," Clay ordered.

Dave rolled onto the floor and assumed the position while Clay downed his warm beer, shoving the coffee table over with his leg. Closing his eyes, he enjoyed the feel of the hands mapping his back as Clay knelt behind him, his slick hardness rubbing along the seam of his ass. Clay wedged his legs further apart. Anticipation raced through Dave, his cock stiff again from the fingers plunged into his tight hole.

"God …" He lowered his head, tensed for a moment, and then relaxed. Clay's fingers backed out then eased inside with a twist, increasing in depth and speed as Dave pressed for more. He heard Clay mumble something about being ready and the fingers disappeared.

Feeling Clay at his entrance, he shoved his ass toward him, but Clay's hands stilled his eager hips. "Damn it! I'm more than ready." Dave threw a defiant glare over his shoulder.

"Grab your ass and open it wide." He never pictured Clay as demanding, but found the more barked orders the more tension built behind his balls. He leaned forward; face buried in the cushions, he gripped his ass, and spread his cheeks as instructed.

Clay entered just past the tight ring of muscle and held his position. His cast-covered arm wriggled under him and pulled him upright. He leaned his head to the side, taking Clay's lips, thankful for the distraction as he sheathed all of Clay's eight inches with a gasp. Clay seemed anxious, but held him, caressing his face and throat.

His insides quaked and he bucked against Clay's belly. Clay pulled out to the head and entered to the hilt, balls slapping Dave's ass. They set a steady pace. Dave's cock, hard and swollen, begged for release, every nerve ending heightened. Oh yeah … more than ready. He leaned forward, arms bracing the sofa. Clay followed. His mane falling over his shoulders, and brushing back and forth over Dave's sweat glistened shoulders.

Clay palmed at Dave's chest as his tempo increased, and Dave arched, driving himself into his thrusts, matching his rhythm. Dave's balls ached and drew upward preparing to expel, and his fingers curled around his cock, fisting its length. Clay bit into his shoulder, pounding, frantic, and erratic, into Dave's ass. "Yes-yes … yeah …" he exhaled, as thick white essence creamed over his knuckles. Body rocking, hips jerking, Clay grunted incomprehensible words as liquid heat rushed into the condom.

He trembled as Clay eased out of him. "God, that was great," Dave panted, sprawling across the carpet. Clay reclined and pulled him into yet, another heated kiss as Dave tried in vain to distract himself from the tug on his heart.

He knew. Nuzzled into the crook of Clay's neck, he opened his mouth to speak, but snoring said they'd discuss motives later. He lowered his eyelids in satisfied exhaustion.

Dave awoke well past midnight. Not wanting to disturb Clay, he took a quick shower, dressed, and found a blanket in a hall closet to drape over him. He knelt, gently threading his fingers through Clay's hair. "I think I'm in love," he whispered, and kissed his forehead before quietly leaving.

## *Chapter 5 – Exposed*

Disoriented, Clay rubbed his eyes, hardly recognizing his cell phone's muffled ring. Shit … where's my fucking … He found it entangled in discarded clothing. "Hello?"

"How are you this fine morning?"

He turned one way then the other. "You left?"

"I'll drop by tonight if you'll have me. I had some things to take care of before work. Besides, you were out like a rock," Dave chuckled.

Clay snorted. "Yeah … come over tonight. I'd like to have your ass again."

"I bet. Listen, I gotta run."

"What time is it?" Eyes dry, Clay tried to read his display.

"It's noon, Clay. Gees, one round and you're wiped out?"

"Well that was one hell of a round, smartass."

"Talk to ya later, gotta go. Love ya."

Clay stared at the phone's darkened display … He loves me?

Dave called again after he arrived at work. Minsho needed an old file saved on Clay's desktop. "Just give me your password. I can move it to the server. No problem." Leery at first, Clay offered the funky eight-character combination, only in exchange for Dave's password. They trusted each other now, but he never gave anything free ... not anymore.

Clay expected Dave that night, Christmas Eve. Aware his shift ended at ten o'clock, by the time midnight rolled around, he didn't know whether panic, worry, or a broken heart owned the pain in his chest. He phoned twice, and twice Dave rejected his calls … twice. He wouldn't push.

Ass on the carpet, Clay slouched against his sofa, elbows on his knees, every now and then, twisting, and inhaling Dave's lingering scent from the cushions. What transpired between their night of mind-blowing sex and last night? What a way to spend Christmas Day … longing, wondering what went wrong, where, or when. His gaze traveled from his second-hand furnishings to his fisted hands. *Maybe he balked over my financial situation?*

Clay made it through the weekend, determined to confront Dave at work today. *An explanation's all he'd request.* One last ten-point check, hard to believe the mirror reflected the same person. Concealing his mop, Clay pounced downstairs to Becca's car. "Thanks for the ride," he said, sliding onto the seat and buckling his safety belt.

"Nice touch, Clay ... special occasion?"

"You like the new me, huh?" Elbow on the door rest, Clay stared out the window, "Good." He tuned to the passing buildings and trees during the ride.

Posture stiff, Dave's eyes stayed on his monitor as they entered. "Afternoon Dave," Becca said. He gestured a curt wave.

Clay noticed Dave no longer sported jeans and a T-shirt, but formal attire; navy dress slacks and a pressed shirt ... *Must come with the new title.* He shrugged and settled into his work. He'd missed his routine; there'd be plenty of chances to corner the bastard later.

Despite his recent concerns, Clay found solace in his creations. When they say absence makes the heart grow fonder ... *Clay figured they must've been referring to one's career,* but dinner break arrived much too soon. "Come on, Clay. You gotta eat," Becca said.

"Bring me something. I can't stop." *Truth is he didn't want to stop.* They exchanged opposing philosophies smoother than normal. *A good thing,* he reckoned.

So busy, he'd forgotten his project, but with an hour of solitude, he opened the program. Stunned, staring at the marquee, Clay sat speechless ... YOU MANIPULATIVE FUCKWAD flaunting his vision. Handing his nerves over to nausea, it took him all of two minutes to realize the meaning. *Passwords are like underwear ... Change them often, and never lend them out to strangers.* "That son of a bitch." He shoved his chair away from the desk.

With forty minutes remaining, he engaged his greatest asset, his mind. Ecstatic that his paranoia come in handy, he weaseled into Dave's desktop ... Thinks I'd hand over my password free. Proud, he'd bargained the exchange. Idiot, should've changed it, his eyes narrowed, and he grinned, strumming the keys with intensity and purpose.

Serves him right, Clay smirked reclaiming his own station seconds before the door opened. He heard Dave snort as he passed, but reminded himself the real fight had yet begun.

"What the fuck!" Dave's cursor blinked on a darkened screen, a single line of text displayed: ALERT, USER ERROR. REPLACE USER AND PRESS ANY KEY TO CONTINUE. Within seconds, uncontrolled cursing infiltrated the heavy door and pervaded the halls, bringing a fuming Mr. Minsho barging into the room. Clay nudged Dave's shoulder to still his fit. He whipped around, meeting a snarl on Minsho's face. Recomposing himself, he offered his apology for the outburst.

"Not the best way to start out the week," Mr. Minsho said. "I expect you have an explanation, Hansen."

"Sir, Clay ... he ... Never mind." Dave stood and stalked toward the door. "I quit!" Minsho grabbed his arm.

"Not so fast, Hansen. It appears McCarthy and you have unfinished business." Minsho's gaze traveled between the two men before scanning the room. "All of you are excused for the evening, nothing that won't hold until tomorrow." Becca rolled her eyes at Clay and joined her coworkers filing out the door.

"I'm going home myself ... Mr. Hansen," Minsho waited for Dave's attention, "you're in charge of locking up ... after, you and McCarthy sort this out. We barely made it through his accident. I can't afford to lose either of you right now." He released Dave's arm. "Get your act together, men. We'll talk later." Mr. Minsho closed the door behind him, leaving the two alone.

His back to Clay, Dave seethed. He'd nothing to say to the lowlife.

"Sorry," Clay offered, although, almost too quiet to hear.

"Heh! It's not everyday my sex life is depicted in graphic detail on a video game … and, process? What the fuck is process to Dave's love? What are you, a fucking control …?"

"It's not like that!"

Dave spun around, lunged for Clay, grip tightening on his upper arms. "Fuck you, McCarthy! Did you rack in a pretty penny for such detailed smut in the underground, scumbag?" Dave shook him. "You … you, freak! I trusted you ..."

"Damn it! It's not what you think!"

Dave's arms flailed. "Yeah … How do you classify it then?" His fingers dug into Clay's flesh. "A joke? Therapy?"

"A present ..." Clay lowered his defiant glare. *I knew I shouldn't have opened up to anyone.* "… for Christmas," he whispered, fighting a hopeless battle with the moisture welling up in his eyes.

"A … what?"

Clay shoved Dave backward. "A fucking Christmas present!" he screamed. "Fuck you, Hansen. You ungrateful bastard." Clay shut down his station, slung his backpack over a shoulder, and headed for the door.

"Clay … don't." Dave embraced him from behind.

He turned in Dave's arms, but refused to look him in the eye. "Let me go. I'll be fine."

Dave pulled him against his chest. "No, I didn't know. Please don't leave." Clay closed his eyes. *Jesus, why am I so weak? Why'd Dave have to smell so good? Too good.* "I'm sorry," Dave said, swaying the two of them as if lost in a slow dance.

Clay reached up to wipe his face, but Dave finished the task as he brought Clay's mouth to his. "I'm sorry," he breathed against Clay's lips. He defiantly knocked the cap off Clay's head and untied the dark mane. "God …" he whispered, entwining his fingers in the loose strands.

79

Clay maneuvered them toward a vacant desk, reversing their order. The edge of the desk pressing into the back of his legs, his good arm tugged Dave closer ... I love him ... "I love you." Dave chuckled, breaking their kiss. "Shit, I said that out loud, didn't I," Clay whispered, staring at his feet.

"It's okay, baby." Dave brought his face upward and reclaimed his mouth. His fingers worked to rid Clay's pants. "I love you ... in jeans," he spoke, varying kisses down Clay's neck, "but better without." His hands found their way inside Clay's boxers. On his knees, he wriggled the works down his legs in a rush of excitement.

Clay gasped as he watched Dave dress his cock before taking it deep into his throat. "Jesus, Dave ..." he panted, and threw his head back as Dave's tongue massaged along the bottom of his shaft, to the base and back, teasing just under the head. "Don't ... stop." His voice traveled on short exhales.

Dave agreed with a low hum as he sucked long and hard, working Clay's hips into motion. Clay's thrusting grew uncontrollable, and Dave allowed him to hold his head steady and fuck his mouth. Clay's cock rammed into his throat and Dave welcomed the warm load streaming into the condom.

He kissed Clay's pelvis then licked his way upward, shoving Clay's shirt over his head, and attacking his mouth as he ground his own erection into Clay's thigh. Catching his breath, Clay cradled Dave's face, his thumb ghosting over Dave's full bottom lip. "Guess we're done fighting."

Dave illustrated his reply by kissing Clay's chest, paying his nipples extra attention with his teeth, and nibbling a path to his neck. "The animations were awesome by the way ... I watched the bedroom scene twice ... It's ... amazing."

"Really now," Clay smirked, fingers struggling to get past Dave's waistband. "Did you realize it's interactive? Two players can perform all sorts of acrobatics, including purposely tea-bagging your counterpart."

"Jesus, Clay … I think I'm in love." Dave relieved him from his single-handed fumbling.

Skin to skin, Clay bathed Dave's lips in a heated kiss. "Now, that we've established your respect for my genius …" He turned and leaned over the desk, eying Dave over his shoulder. Exposed, spread legged; flowing hair framing his dimpled ass, he ordered, "Take me."

# HAZARD PAY-OFF
## Landon Dixon

I tipped the paving stone-loaded dolly back, walked it ahead a few feet. Then I hit a rock on the half-completed driveway and the bricks shifted, pulling me and the dolly forward. I struggled to keep the stack upright, running now. And I clipped the dolly with a steel-toed boot and sent the whole thing flying over, pavers spilling everywhere. Right in back of my foreman where he was kneeling on the driveway.

Once the dust had settled, Blake pushed a couple of pavers away from his backside and got to his feet. I sheepishly grinned at him. He shook his head. "Hazard, try not to live up to your name, huh? For the good of the health of me and the crew."

I nodded, amazed and gratified that the guy hadn't fired me on the spot. I'd only been on the job an hour, and this was already my second dolly wreck.

Actually, not a bad hour for a guy with my safety record. That's why they call me Hazard. I'd lost my previous three summer jobs when I'd: (1) accidentally pulled the ladder out from under a residential window-washing colleague, (2) smacked three guys in the head with a sheet of drywall at a house construction site, and (3) spilled boiling grease all over the brand-new shoes of my boss at a fast-food fry job. My placement counselor at the student employment office even called me Hazard.

But I kept applying because I needed tuition money for my first year of college in the fall. And I kept getting hired, because the skyrocketing price of base metals had turned the northern mining town into a boomtown.

Blake crouched back down, started once again picking up and placing the pavers into their interlocking pattern, building a driveway to last a lifetime, while I started restacking another load onto the dolly from the pallets at the end of the driveway. That was my job: delivering the stones to Blake who then fit them together in the sandy jigsaw puzzle. Ideally, delivering them smoothly right next to the guy, rather than catapulting them onto his back.

It was hard, hot, muscle-straining and forearm-scraping work. But the job had its good parts: all on Blake.

He was in his mid-twenties, with short black hair and warm brown eyes, muscular all over from lifting and planting and stamping pavers for a living. He filled his faded jeans tight and taut, round in all the right places, his cheeks looking hard as the stones he was setting down. And since it was so hot, the work so heavy, he had his shirt off, his chiseled torso gleaming smooth and pumped in the sunshine. The guy was actually a good half-foot shorter than I was, but then I'm a carrot-topped beanpole.

I ogled my boss's rock-hard, glistening body constantly, my mouth hanging open and eating dust, craving to lick the salty sweat from his muscle-humped chest and rigid nipples. I strangled the handles on the dolly, yearning to finger the soft, perspiration-slick crack of his apple ass. And what with all my sweating and drooling, I was soon parched with thirst.

"Uh, is there anywhere I can get a drink of water?" I croaked, towering over Blake's broad, muscle-bunched back like a loving shade tree. The rest of the crew had gone on their dinner break, so it was just me and the boss.

He turned his head and squinted up at me. Making sure I wasn't holding anything that could fall on him, no doubt. "Yeah, sure. The people who own the house are gone for the weekend, so it's locked up, but there's a hose in the backyard they said we could use." He grinned, adding, "Don't flood the basement or anything, okay?"

I grinned back, said, "Okay." Then tripped over the heel of his boot and went sprawling onto the front lawn, as I tried to move around him.

I managed to make it through the wooden gate that led into the backyard with only a slight tear to my T-shirt from a snagging nail, and spotted the hose hooked up to a faucet at the rear of the house. And as I was cranking the handle, getting the water to flow (after lifting my big feet off the hose), I heard some yelling and splashing coming from the house next door. So I walked farther into the yard, past the garage that blocked my view, playing out the hose and sucking sweet, cool water from the spout.

A six-foot-high plank fence surrounded the entire backyard, but that was no eyeball obstacle for a galoot like me. And when I peeked past the garage and over the fence, I choked on the water and just about swallowed the hose.

There was a swimming pool next door, two guys waist-deep in the middle of it, in each other's arms, in the midst of a hard, hot, passionate kiss!

I gaped at the men blatantly sucking face. They were really feeding on one another, lips chewing, tongues flailing, arms octopusing all over each other's backs, locked together so tight not even a sliver of light showed between their suntanned and water-washed bodies.

One guy had blonde hair, the other a shaved head. And Blondie pulled back from Baldy's ravenous mouth and sealed his lips around the guy's tongue, sucked on it, the bald dude groaning his encouragement. I openly watched them go at it in that neighboring dunk tank, dropping the water hose and wrapping my fingers around my own hose, which had filled with something other than water in my jeans. I squeezed and rubbed my cock, eating up the erotic aquatic action next door, the two water sports too wrapped up in each other to notice my jug head floating over the fence.

Baldy reeled his sucked-dry tongue back in and dropped his head down to Blondie's chest, started licking the guy's protruding nipples. He swirled his chunky pink tongue all around the slick, tan buds, Blondie tilting his head back and moaning, gripping his lover's cinderblock shoulders.

The dude with the high-polish chrome dome vigorously sucked on Blondie's nipples, bit into them, tugged on them with his shiny white teeth. Like I was tugging on my pulsing prick through my jeans, my body burning with a heat more than sun and work-related. This was the kind of manual labor I could really get into.

And after working over his tub-buddy's boyish chest for a good, long while, Baldy steamed the guy through the water and up against the side of the pool. He lifted the sleek little blonde out of the water with the greatest of ease and plunked him down on the pool's edge. Which is when I gleefully noticed that the guy was totally naked, his hard, all-man cock bobbing like an inflatable beach toy as he splashed down on the rim of the water bin.

Baldy quickly swam in between Blondie's legs, latching onto the guy's lean thighs and capturing and swallowing glistening cockhead. Blondie groaned, sprawling his hands back to hold himself up under the muscle-stud's onslaught, Baldy's head diving down between his quivering legs. My hand froze on my bulging cock, as I witnessed the dick-defying sword-swallowing. Baldy consumed his buddy's entire prick like it was nothing, and everything.

I held my breath, along with my writhing neighbor. Until finally, Baldy pulled his head back and gleaming meat oozed out from between his thick lips, like a greased snake. When he got to the cap, he bit into it, then inhaled the whole shaft again, his tongue shooting out to lick at Blondie's blonde balls.

I started squeezing, rubbing again, singing the bald man's deep-throating praises with the palm of my hand. As the shaven muscleman gripped his buddy's legs and bobbed his head up and down, earnestly sucking cock. Blondie rode his lover's cranium with one of his hands, his lithe body quivering with the wicked vacuum power of the awesome blowjob.

"You workin' or jerkin'?" a voice exploded in my ear.

I twisted my head around, and saw Blake lounging in the open fence gate. He was looking at me, at where my sweaty paw clutched my thread-straining cock. "Uuuhh ..." I stammered, my face going even redder than my sunburn.

He walked over to me, then went up onto his top-toes and peered over the fence, taking in the erotic sights. "Not bad technique. You might actually learn something," he casually commented. "Wanna give it a try, Hazard?"

I stared at the stud, hardly believing my burning ears. He just smiled and placed his warm hand over mine on my throbbing cock. And I just about jumped out of my work boots.

Blake unfastened his belt and unzipped his jeans, as I sank to my knees in the grass, ready and willing and eager to worship. He pushed his pants and briefs down, and his cock flopped out into the sunlight, big and getting bigger. I trembled with delight, inhaling the musky, ball-sweated scent of the man, watching his beautiful vein-ribboned tool rise up and up and expand and point at my face. Here was finally something I could truly handle on-the-job, the best job in the world.

"Suck it, Hazard," Blake rasped. And I went to work.

I seized his thick dong with just my forefinger and thumb, forming a ring that I rode up and down his pink, pulsating length. Quick and light and teasing. He grunted, urging me to grab on and fist him. But I O-ringed his cut cock from balls to cap, sailing up and down his bumpy shaft with my circle jerk, neat and clean and tantalizing. I might be all thumbs in the workplace, but in the sexplace I consider myself a bit of a master craftsman.

Blake groaned and grabbed at my hair, as I pumped him fast, then slow, then fast again, tickling his tight, shaven nut sack with my other hand. Moans and groans from across the fence mingled and merged with Blake's gasps of lust in the superheated air. Until the guy just couldn't take my sexual taunting anymore. He yanked my head into his groin, begging me to suck him.

But I didn't suck him, at first. Instead, I noosed his hood, pressed it into his grated abs, and licked at his meat, up from his tightened balls and along his pulsing shaft in one smooth, wet, tongue-beaded motion. He clawed at my hair, his legs shaking, as I sensuously painted his pipe – delicate and bold tongue-strokes that left him drenched in saliva and sweat, my fingers sticky with precum.

Then I dropped his cock. It strained in the still, electrified air, sniffing at my lips. I breathed all over it, steaming it raw, driving the man wild. Before clipping the jumping cap with my teeth, causing Blake to cry out his sweet torture.

I sank my teeth into his meaty cockhead and slowly chewed it into my mouth, until I tasted shaft. At which point I shot my head forward and swallowed the guy right down to the balls. Then bounced back up again.

"Fuck!" he gasped, stunned. He stared down at me, unsure if what'd just happened had actually happened.

I proved that it had, sealing his cap between my lips and dive-bombing his shaft again, hands-free and balls-deep, over and over. Blake dug his fingernails into my scalp and hung on, growling, his cock filling my mouth, bouncing off the back of my throat and beyond.

Then I took a page out of Baldy's X-rated book, quick-downing my man's cock and holding it. And holding it. Nose pressing into his abdomen, chin pushing into his balls, I locked him down tight and wet and let the superheated, vise-like pressure build to outrageous proportions. Fortunately for the both of us, my gag reflex is like the rest of my reflexes – virtually non-existent.

"Holy shit!" Blake cried, pulling on my ears, banging on my head. His watery brown eyes were frantic, his pressure-packed cock gone from his sight for an excruciating minute and counting.

The tension tightened like a wrench on a bolt, sweat pattering down off Blake's agonized face and onto mine. Humid breath steamed out of my flared nostrils and bathed his stomach, my cheeks and throat bulging with meat.

Until at last he grunted and shoved me back, before his balls boiled over. His dong burst out of my mouth in a gush of saliva, a slickened spear still tied to my lips by strings of spit.

"Want me to fuck you, Blake?" I asked, breathing hard hardly at all.

The guy nodded in amazement, and respect.

He ended up on his back on the picnic table, stark, stunningly naked, legs up and spread. Very receptive to learning a further thing or two from his work-inept apprentice.

I shoved my jeans and shorts down around my ankles and shuffled in between his legs, letting him get a good look at the fat, squat tool that was going to pound him like the compactor he used to pound the paving stones together in the sand. Then I gripped his ankles and slapped my cock against his cock. He moaned.

His legs were as gorgeously muscled as the rest of him, just as smooth, and I slid my hands down and around his clenched calves, squeezing them. Then I shouldered his legs and ran my hands along his thighs, inner and outer, digging my fingers into his big, bunched quads. His muscles twitched and his cock bounced up and down on his flat belly all on its own, as I felt him up.

"Fuck me!" he implored, playing with his golden nipples and staring up into the sun.

I could see the perverted neighbors over the fence again. Blondie was on all-fours on the diving board, like a tawny animal, Baldy at the top of the steps gripping the steel railings and hammering the guy's upraised ass. The board quivered like the pair of them, hanging out like Blondie's tongue as his chute got reamed. I nodded my approval at the workmanship and then teased Blake's asshole with the tip of my prick.

"Yeah, fuck me!" he responded, rolling his nipples, rolling his head back and forth on the smooth-sealed slats in sexual agony.

I squatted down, his legs riding my shoulders, and dug around in my grass-level pants pocket, came up with a one-session portable packet of lube. A good worker always comes prepared, with his own tools. I greased up my dick, nice and slow for Blake's benefit, and mine. Then I oiled his crack, wriggling a couple of fingers two knuckles deep inside the hunk just to hear him squeal, see him squirm. Finally, I steered my shiny cockhead up against his smooth-as-silk asshole again.

But if he'd thought I was going to take it slow and gentle, ease my way into his tight crevice, then my cocksucking hadn't taught him anything about the way I work the body. I punched through his starfish and plunged bowels-deep inside him, buried to the hilt in an instant. He jumped on the table like he'd been electrocuted, shouting obscenities to match our neighbors.

I gripped the pale soles of his feet and thrust sure and deep, full-cock fucking the stud, out to the cap and all the way in again, over and over. He was super-tight and burning hot, smooth-riding, the sight of his prone, cock-rocked body sizzling. The firm smack of my thighs against his shuddering ass filled my ears, the sensual feel of his gripping chute milking my churning cock stoking my body with heat.

He frantically tugged on his own prick as I crammed his ass strong and steady. I tickled his feet, licked at his puckered soles, sucked on a tender toe or three, all the while pumping my hips, fucking his sweet anus with authority.

A scream sailed over the fence. Followed by another. I jerked my head up and saw Blondie shaking out-of-control on the end of Baldy's ramming cock, jacking ropes of sperm out of his own cock and onto the diving board. As Baldy tilted his head back and let out a roar, emptying his balls in the blonde bottom's rippling ass.

"You're going to come all over yourself!" I instructed my boss, pumping faster. "Right after I do!"

He groaned and flung his head from side-to-side, his sun and cock-blasted body shaking.

I grasped his armored thighs and dug in, force-fucking the gorgeous man, brutally slamming his ass. We smashed together, my cock pistoning his chute, the wet-hot friction unbelievable. I surged with an incendiary heat, balls flapping and boiling, Blake's hand flying up and down his shaft, in rhythm to my savage fucking.

I caught fire, and my cock exploded in the stud's sucking hole. I ripped out of Blake's ass and fisted wildly, spraying white-hot semen onto his jacked-up cock, torquing his action even more. He cried, "Fuck!", and sperm jetted out of his jizz-slick cock, splashing down onto his heaving chest and stomach in great, sticky gobs.

# # # # #

I still have plenty of goof-ups on the job. But it's great finally having a boss who's so forgiving. Among other things.

# GAN HAATZMAUT YERUSHALAYIM
## David Muller

There are many differences between Jerusalem and Tel Aviv, but this park wasn't one of them; both cities had a *Gan Haatzmaut*, Independence Park, where all the gay men go to meet other men. In Tel Aviv, *Gan Haatzmaut* is more secluded and located right next to the beach and it's also much bigger with more places to go for quickie outdoor sex. I'd probably walked at least a mile wandering around that park. In Jerusalem, *Gan Haatzmaut* is right in the center of things; the Israeli flags flying atop the internationally renowned King David Hotel can be seen from *Gan Haatzmaut*, and the American consulate is just across the street in plain sight.

My experience with the park in Jerusalem also stood in contrast with my experience with the plot of land bearing the same name in Tel Aviv. For starters, I only went to *Gan Haatzmaut* in Tel Aviv during the day en route to and from the beach. In Jerusalem, I only went to the park at night and, on more than one occasion, I went to the park simply for the sake of going to the park to get my dick sucked; I'd even taken a taxi to nearby Rehov Hillel only to wander into the park seconds after paying the driver more times that I care to remember. Of course, there were also times I would take a one-day, overnight trip to Jerusalem just to visit the park.

Men were men no matter where you are and, like any park for such activities anywhere else in the world, men made no bones about what they wanted and; once they found a guy to do it with; they went off and did it. In Tel Aviv, however, you had to do a little dance before you went off to fuck. There they liked to flirt and beat around the proverbial bush, talking about the weather or stupid shit like that before getting down to business.

Everything in *Gan Haatzmaut* in Tel Aviv was done behind trees and bushes in pseudo-privacy.

Things were slightly different in the park in Jerusalem. One time, I went there and went to sit on the grass at the top of the park, not too far from that little wall I sometimes liked to sit at, and watched men, (and, in Jerusalem's case, women, tourists and, for lack of a better term, the entire town), come in and out. Once, as I sat and watched a guy wearing a tight red shirt with Japanese letters, some guy sat down next to me and told me his name was Amir. In the middle of this wide open, albeit dark space, he pulled his pants down and showed me his dick, (it was pretty big and I was certainly tempted). He asked if I wanted to go with him into the bushes and "do something."

I told him, *"Lo rotzeh, todah lecha,"* which means, "Thanks but no thanks" not because I really didn't want to but because I wanted to see what else there was in the park that night. He was nice about it as he smiled and got up and left me sitting there alone.

Less than two minutes later ... another guy came up and sat down next to me in the very same spot that'd been occupied by Amir, the first guy. The thought that ran through my head at that moment was "And here's our next contestant." This second guy never told me his name, but he did tell me he wanted to show me his "big penis." It turned out he was more shy than the first guy; we walked over to nearby rock under a tree and took his dick out, (his was also pretty big and two toned; his head was a lighter shade of pigment than his brown shaft). Just like the first guy, he asked if I wanted to go with him into the bushes and "do something."

I told him, *"Lo rotzeh, todah lecha,"* just as I'd told that first guy, not because I really didn't want to but because I wanted to see what else there was in the park that night.

I went and stood motionless in the darkness in the center of the park, near a gaggle of trees, and waited for someone to appear. I was kind of surprised when an Orthodox Jew with the whole Orthodox garb; black hat, black pants, tallit and a beard; he appeared out of nowhere.

In Hebrew he asked me, "*Tafsiki?*" or something that sounded like that and I shook my head. He asked me if I spoke Hebrew.

I shook my head and said, "*Anglit*," even though I could navigate my way though a sexual liaison in Hebrew. I had absolutely no interest in hooking up with this guy; aside from being Orthodox, he was way too old for me, probably in his forties, and he looked as if he probably had a wife and kids somewhere beyond the boundaries of this gay meeting place.

In English he asked me, "Do you suck?"

I shook my head, "No," and he quickly walked away looking for the love that dare not speak his name.

A half hour later I found myself sitting on a bench at the other end of the park. I was looking down at the American consulate and admiring all the black Chevy Suburbans parallel parked on the street when; lo and behold, I was approached by two young yeshiva boys.

How young were they? I found out: one was nineteen, the other eighteen.

What did they want?

What do you think?

Were they cute?

Cute enough … the younger of the two, I don't think, had even started shaving as both of them had the sprinklings of a soft beard under their chins. The older of the two was named Yosef, the Hebraic equivalent of Joseph, and the other was named Ezra. In Hebrew I asked them what they were doing here and why they were talking to me. They told me they didn't know what they were doing here, but they saw me first. Then again, we all knew why we were here, I certainly did, at least, so I started walking toward a dark spot in the trees at the foot of the nearby Sheraton hotel and they of course followed me.

We talked as we walked; I asked them if they had ever had sex before; both of them nodded yes. I asked them if they had sex with a man and their answer, (I was hardly surprised), was no; they'd never had sex with a man but only, as it were, with each other. They were awkward, gawky, shy, nervous, nerdy and horny and eager for a screw all at the same time. I admired their boldness, they'd come crawling out of a Jerusalem seminary in the middle of the night to bust a nut with a secular heathen. Although not religious myself, I knew I wanted them out of those black and white clothes and I wanted them naked and sucking on something right quick.

We came to the dark place in the trees, and I asked them, "Do you guys want to do something with me?"

Yosef and Ezra turned to each other and laughed slightly. I could tell they were nervous, so I endeavored to make this transaction, for lack of a better term, as easy as possible for them.

I asked them, "Where do you guys live, in a seminary?"

They nodded their heads.

"Do you have a place we can go to?"

They shook their heads.

"That's okay," I said, "I have a place we can go to."

"Where?"

"Katamon."

"Do you live here?"

"I live in Tel Aviv; I'm staying at a friend's place."

Yosef asked me, "We can go there?"

"He's not there. No one is there."

Ezra asked, "What can we do there?"

I said, "Duh, we can fuck there."

Ezra and Yosef smiled and giggled. In the darkness I rolled my eyes.

"Can I see your dicks?" I asked them.

"What?" Ezra asked, "Here, now?"

"Yeah, take them out and show them to me."

Yosef shrugged and nodded at Ezra but Ezra exhibited signs of inhibition.

I said, "Oh come on, no one is here. Take it out; let me see your dick. Is it really small?"

Ezra shrugged and Yosef nudged; the older of the two was already unzipping the fly of his black trousers getting ready to expose himself to me. Ezra mumbled something to Yosef that I couldn't understand and they started talking quietly in a language that sounded like Yiddish or what I imagined Yiddish to sound like.

"Listen," I told them, "If you show me yours, I'll show you mine, okay?"

Ezra and Yosef bantered for a moment longer. Yosef unbuckled his belt and pulled his pants down slightly, letting his cock and balls come out for all to see. I started to unbutton my pants just the same when Ezra unzipped his fly, pulled his underwear out of the way and showed me his incredibly tiny penis. His dick was like a small little head poking out of the darkness of his black trousers; his penis was smaller than a pigeon's egg.

I said, "Wow, Ezra; that is tiny." I reached down and touched his penis, all its length, with the tips of my fingers. When I touched him, I could tell he was not hard at all, I tried to toy with his little penis and coax him into erection, but Ezra got nervous suddenly when we heard the sounds of a car alarm beeping in the distance beyond the park.

I turned to Yosef, his dick was much bigger in comparison to Ezra's. His was long and thick; his dick hung nicely and was also yet erect. I unbuttoned my jeans and let my pants fall to my ankles. At the first sight of my rod, Ezra and Yosef gasped.

Yosef said, "Yours is the biggest one here."

I looked at their dicks and down at mine, "You got that right. So," I looked at the two of them, "you guys want to go back to my place? It's not far, we'll take a cab." I stuffed my dick back in my pants.

Ezra and Yosef zipped themselves up and turned to each other. Yosef smiled and winked and Ezra shrugged.

Yosef said, "Sure, how long does it take to get there?"

"Ten minutes." I asked him, "Are y'all really horny?"

Yosef nodded, "I am very horny."

"What about you, Ezra?"

Ezra wore eye glasses; he pushed the glasses up on his nose and only shrugged. We walked out of the darkened spot beneath the trees and crossed the vast expanse of the park heading toward the American consulate. I'm sure the sight of two religious teenagers leaving the park with an American raised some eyebrows among the security team at the diplomatic facility on Gershon Agron street, but I didn't give a shit, and I don't think Yosef did, but I bet Ezra was feeling more than a little nervous by the whole experience.

We hopped a taxi and took off toward the German Colony, driving down Emek Refaim, arriving at a building in the Katamon section along Rehov Ben Zakkai. This building functioned as a hostel, or something like a hostel; groups and travelers and backpackers from all over the planet came to stay at this place and, occasionally, I was told, weddings took place in the large main room off the entry salon. For whatever reason, I had a key to this building and so, this was where we were headed, me and these two yeshiva seminary boys, Yosef and Ezra. I'd checked the place out earlier, before I headed out to the park. True to word, the building was empty, except for a few straggling volunteers, one of whom was an Asian-American girl named Rosemarie. Lucky for us, Rosemarie was fast asleep in her bed when the three of us arrived very late at night, around two or three in the morning.

I think they were quite surprised by the décor of the first room; the place was gaudy, like a Jerusalem version of Las Vegas; portraits of Orthodox religious leaders, rabbis and right wing politicians past and present adorned the wall surrounded by flashy velvet print frames with feathers, flowers and lights. There was a thick Arabesque rug on the floor with a hypnotic pattern of design that almost induced a hallucinatory trance. I looked back at the boys as they looked around the room and stole a quick glance with each other; I don't think this was what they expected when they arrived; the stark, drab building, built with Jerusalem stone, looked like every other apartment building in the neighborhood; which, like many neighborhoods in Jerusalem, was home to a large majority of religious Orthodox Jews.

I led Ezra and Yosef upstairs and into a maze of hallways painted with murals of memorable scenes from the *Tanakh*, the Hebrew acronym for the *Five Books of Moses*. Again, I could tell my two religious companions were surprised by these frescoes; I took them into one of the bedrooms and pushed one of the beds in front of the door to prevent anyone from coming in. The décor of this room, unlike the rest of the building, was practically naked; the walls were bare and the beds nondescript with rusty, socialist-era metal frames and thin mattresses made of foam. On the wall, an El Al Airlines poster of the amphitheater in Caesarea hung dead center as the single piece of art in the entire room. I flipped on a light and the three of us looked at each other.

"Okay," I said after a second, "let's get naked." I started to unbuckle my belt.

Ezra pulled his white shirt out of his black pants while Yosef took off his skullcap.

I told them, "Take everything off; I don't want to see any religious garb, I don't want any *tzit-tzit* or *tallit* or *kippot*." I told them to strip out of every last article of clothing, and I hid their religiously-prescribed clothing in a nearby closet. Yosef, the older of the two boys, had a growing erection; my cock was alright filled with the hot oil of my blood and standing at attention raring to go. Poor Ezra, the younger boy; his little penis barely poked out from his mop of pubic hair; he wasn't hard at all.

Yosef came up behind me and stuck his stick in the crack of my ass, my butt held his prong upright like a rod as he pulled me closer to him, running his hands down my chest and stomach. Yosef reached down and caressed my rock hard organ as he smothered the back of my neck with petite little kisses. Yosef was very skinny; I could tell he didn't work out at all; he was probably too busy studying Torah and Talmud at the yeshiva to get to a gym with any regularity. He was hairy all over and this reality was driven home as I felt the brush of his youthful beard wipe across the back of my neck as he slobbered all over me from behind.

Ezra, on the other hand, had good smooth body definition, despite his youth in years; his butt was soft, plump and round and his hands were warm and manly. Yosef had long bony fingers and longer-than-average finger nails. I reached out to Ezra and pulled him into me. I held my arms around him, letting my hands land on his supple butt. Our two cocks met each other head to head, my throbbing muscle of love and sex pressed up against his pubescent flaccidity.

Ezra had smooth, hairless skin; his nipples were big and pink and his chest was soft and his abs flat; as I touched the smooth skin at the bottom of his rear ravine, I knew I had to have his tiny little prick in my mouth; I wanted to suck that little cock to life and make him hard with my tongue.

I sat Ezra down on the bed and pulled away from Yosef, who'd been slowly humping my backside with his stick, pushing the two halves of my ass together to create skin friction as he humped up and down on my butt. I left Yosef as I pushed Ezra's legs apart and kneeled before him. I leaned in and first started to cuddle his nuts; I nibbled on his nads and licked at them lightly with my lips. I quickly moved up to his tiny penis; Ezra had grown with the first initial springs of arousal; his tiny chorizo swelled to the size of an egg but he still had far to grow before he was hard all the way. I suckled on his knob and almost swallowed his genitalia entirely. I swirled his little member around on my tongue like a candy before I felt him spring to life with the beginnings of a boner. His penis came up suddenly as I felt him rise with the delights of my oral pleasure; I jerked my jaw and head around on my neck as I toyed with the little wiener, coaxing him closer and closer to hardness. One inch became two and two became three; Ezra's baton filled steadily with the heat of his horniness as his little pisser grew into a stiff pickle.

Once I knew Ezra was on his way, I stood up and shoved my trunk of flesh into his face. "Now you suck on my dick." I grabbed Ezra's head and steered his lips to the purple head of my love wand. In the dim lighting of the room, I could see the reflection of my tool in his eye glasses level with my prick.

"No," Ezra shook his head, "I don't want to."

I ignored him as I jammed my cock into his face; I packed my pecker up against his nose and moved my dagger of my kosher pork around his mouth and eyes.

"You suck that cock, little boy," I told him, "you're going to like sucking on my bone." I pushed my head onto his lips and pried his mouth open with my drill. My shaft entered through his lips, impaling his jaw as I forced the young religious lad to kiss and suck on my phallus. I held his head in my hands as I face fucked him; I could tell Ezra was getting into it, he started to groan with happiness; he grabbed onto my legs and held on as I thrust my member into his mouth.

Yosef, who I presume had been watching all of this, started to finger my hole; I moved my legs apart, giving Yosef more room to prod into my rectum. Yosef's long bony finger quickly caned my can. I looked over my shoulder and saw Yosef drop to his knees and I felt him push apart my two buttocks. His long, slender wet tongue licked my rim; he tongued my sphincter and kissed the lips of my hole with his own; I was surprised; Yosef was very good at it and my cock got hot and wildly hard as he gnawed on my rear entry. I looked down and around me, here I had two nerdy yeshiva boys; one eating out my hole, the other sucking on my dick and still, I wanted more from them.

I lifted Ezra off my pipe and off the bed; he stood before me as I French kissed him. I squeezed the soft muffins of his ass as our tongues met and caressed each other and then I pushed him out of my way. I stepped away from Yosef, gnawing on my cavity, and lied down on the bed.

"One of you," I said, "you!" I pointed at Yosef, "Go down on my dick."

Yosef bent down at the side of the bed and took my spear of his mouth. He pushed my throbbing meat all the way down his throat. He wetted my horn with his saliva and kneeled beside the bed. I felt his jaw and his lips on my shaft; I watched him go up and down on my penis and felt his *peyes*; the twin sidelocks of hair worn by the religious that dangled ahead of his ears; rise and fall on my pelvis as Yosef bobbed up and down on my lengthy, meaty truncheon. I looked up, Ezra was standing next to the bed watching Yosef; his little soldier was growing still; his slit willie grew into a little general, as he polished his purple helmet.

"Turn around, bend over," I said to Ezra, "I want to play with your anus."

Ezra turned around and bent over; he held his butt open for me as I pointed my index finger straight out and plugged into his dark and tight little hole. Inside, Ezra was tight and warm; his o-ring was soft but firm, fresh with virginity and still yet to be popped.

"Oh Ezra," I said, "you have such a sweet little ass." I sat up and my dick fell out of Yosef's mouth. "Yosef, get on the bed, lie down." I pulled my finger out of Ezra's asshole and got up off the bed. Yosef came to lie down on the mattress; I said, "Ezra, you get on top of him, you know how to *shishim v'taysha*? Do you like to sixty nine?"

Ezra nodded and climbed on top of Yosef; nervously he held up Yosef's erect cock and started to drop his jaw over his head. Ezra's cock, still rising incrementally with each second, swelled into Yosef's mouth; I heard Yosef gag and cough as he struggled to suck on Ezra's growing horn. I watched them suck on each other simultaneously and marveled at the heretical nature of the entire liaison.

I leaned over to my backpack and brought out a condom, slipping the protective prophylactic over the hood and shaft of my penis. I came around to Ezra's bent over rump and kneeled at his behind, poking the rubber reservoir of the condom into his dark chasm. I slapped my hands on his hips, my fingers curling into the soft plump melons of his butt and pulled him down onto my shaft. I jammed my rod into his hole in one fell swoop, slipping his colon around my cock like a glove. Ezra groaned and shrieked, but then his bone hole eased up and he easily took in all of my inches. I began to horn into and pump away at his dirty little secret.

Ezra's magically inflating wand of sex continued to strengthen and expand. At first, Ezra was hung like a prepubescent child but now, over time, his phallic attribute had multiplied five to ten times; his member had grown larger and harder than Yosef's and was quickly approaching a bracket on the scale far surpassing my own numbers. I knew, once I witnessed this fascinating prodigy that grew and grew, that Ezra was a total bottom, probably praying to God every morning with *tefillin* to be fucked like this every day and twice on the Sabbath. Ezra grew to be huge.

Ezra moaned and cried and inhaled Yosef's cock as I sodomized him through the rear in an unorthodox manner. I butt fucked the *hechshure*, (the certificate of "kosherness"), right out of this young yeshiva boy and what I didn't fuck out of there I'm sure Yosef sucked out. I hammered into Ezra's soft dark pocket; I pounded into his ass with the force of a rhinoceros. I felt my pudding leap up the inside shaft of my cock; I yanked my dick out of Ezra and sat back on the bed. I pulled off the condom and stroked my own shaft as I watched the two yeshiva boys go down on each other off. I could clearly see Ezra's bloated genital, forcing Yosef's mouth wider as he grew. Ezra was hot and bothered; he munched down on Yosef's religious rod and painted his shaft with his tongue and lips. The next thing I saw, Ezra's waterfall of thick white protein stream into and around Yosef's jaw, raining down Yosef's neck and into the slight hairs of his beard, hot lava overflowing out of his mouth, tumbling onto his chest and onto the bed below him.

Yosef shot his load then; his entire body stiffened up like stone and his cock exploded with the treasure of his manly seed; gushing like a geyser into Ezra's face like a sprocket spewing boiling oil. Both necks rose and bobbed on their dicks as they choked their cut bishops with their religious lips. I stroked my dick and twisted my wrist until I, too, dropped a load and shot out semen like bullets of wet dripping sex all over the two yeshiva boys. I punched out globs and globs of man paste and aimed my equipment with precision, firing at them with wet glowing darts of my burning human seed.

Ezra's stallion drained like a pipe; he was so overcome with sexual fulfillment he started to recite one of the most sacred and revered of prayers in all of Judaism, *"Baruch atah adonai, eloheinu melech haolam ... "* Ezra pulled Yosef's cock out of his mouth and cried out the hallowed words of the *Shehecheyanu* as he continued to ejaculate more and more pails of protein from his loins.

I came until I could cum no more, and I clutched my rod once I was spent and shook globs of sperm around the bare room. Eventually Ezra crawled off Yosef and walked to his pants in the middle of the floor; he had to move slowly, I'd so powerfully reamed into his ass he had to take his time bending over again to retrieve a pack of Marlboro reds from a pants pocket.

Yosef sat up on the bed and wiped Ezra's cream off his lips with the back of his hand. He asked Ezra to take a cigarette for him and Ezra, the sweet young yeshiva boy that he was, offered one to me.

This, more than anything else that transpired in the park that night or in the events that followed, was the real moment of truth. I stared at the single cigarette that Ezra held out to me. I was stoked and spent and I certainly wanted to smoke that cigarette, but I declined his offer in the end. It wasn't that I didn't want to smoke, I just didn't want to smoke a Marlboro red; those cigarettes are very harsh and too strong for me. If Ezra had offered me any other cigarette, I would have probably lit one up that night, but in any case I didn't light up. Instead, while they smoked, I had Ezra lie face down on the bed while I sat between his spread-apart legs and fingered his nubile young hole with my two fingers. I made his hole ooze with sweat and perspiration as I dug around in there, toying with his rectum and playing with his o-cavity for no apparent reason. After they finished their cigarettes, Yosef and Ezra left the building, and I took a shower.

In the shower I got hard again and I stroked my cock of erotic hearsay. I declared proudly:

"The only thing better than a yeshiva boy is ... two yeshiva boys at the same time."

# A NIGHT IN MIDGAR
## Augusta Li

Brandon's costume, on which he'd spent hundreds of dollars along with his entire summer break, provided an advantage that he never would have predicted. The man perched on the stool by the door to the hotel bar barely glanced at Brandon's cousin Mike's driver's license before deciding the person behind the goggles and gravity-defying fronds of blond hair and the one pictured on the card matched closely enough. He stamped the back of Brandon's hand and motioned Brandon inside with a tilt of his head.

Brandon made it only three steps into the dark and smoky space before a young woman blocked his path. She had cobalt hair teased up like an eighties metal star, almost high enough to hide her cat ears. Her tiny blue pleated skirt matched her tie.

"Oh my god," she said, touching the high collar of Brandon's shirt, "You're the best Cloud I've ever seen."

"Thanks," he said.

She motioned frantically with her hand until her friends joined her. "Isn't he the best Cloud?"

The three young women nodded their hot pink, violet, and banana yellow heads respectively. Their fingers traced the rounded piece of armor over Brandon's shoulder, the hem of his single, flowing sleeve, the metal wolf's head ornament with the ring in its mouth, the embossing on his thick belt and the buckles on the straps that stretched vertically over his chest.

"Oh, you're perfect," said Violet. "Just perfect. Where did you get your costume?"

"I made it myself," Brandon said, enjoying more attention than he'd received in the last year combined.

"Wow," said Banana Yellow. "Is that your real hair?" She touched one of the locks flat-ironed and sprayed into a ninety-degree spike. "The color and everything?"

"Yep, it's mine."

"You just have to take your goggles off," pleaded Pink. "Let us see your eyes."

He slid them up, letting them rest in his hair like a headband. All of the girls leaned in, their faces pressed together in anticipation. Then they squealed in unison, "They're blue!"

"And they're so big!"

"You are just so beautiful," said the girl with the cobalt wig. "You look just like him. It's amazing. I mean your bone structure and everything. Even your lips."

"Thanks," Brandon repeated. He'd begun to feel a little awkward. The four girls just stared at him, as if they expected something. Girls didn't normally stare at or speak to him, and he wasn't sure what to do. He considered asking them if they wanted to see his sword, but, thankfully, he realized how bad that phrase would sound before it escaped his lips. Though normally a loner who spent most of his time in his room drawing, watching anime and playing video games, Brandon had wanted to attend the costume party after the Con and show off his efforts. The praise felt good, but he sensed something more behind it, something he neither fully understood nor desired. In truth, he wanted to escape.

"I, um..." he began.

"Well we have to go," said Pink. "We're Convention volunteers, and we have to help organize the costume contest. Maybe we'll see you later?"

"Maybe," he said, relieved.

"Bye then," they said, spinning and prancing away, watching him and waving over their shoulders. "Bye, Cloud!"

Exhaling, Brandon headed toward the bar. While he wanted to order a drink, at nineteen he wasn't legally permitted. But he had Mike's ID in his pocket, and he never bent the rules.

All through school he'd never so much as blown off a class. He felt as if he deserved, needed, a little bit of misbehavior, even if it made him nervous. He needed to live a little, take a risk.

"What are you supposed to be?" the bartender asked when Brandon sat down.

"Cloud Strife," Brandon answered enthusiastically. The bartender was attractive: thirty-ish with short dark hair and a nice build beneath his black T-shirt.

"And what the hell does that mean?" the older man asked as he poured away the contents of an ashtray.

"He's a character from *Final Fantasy Seven*," Brandon said.

"Is that like one of those Japanese comic books?" the bartender asked.

"Well, Cloud has been in some manga," Brandon explained. "But he started off in a video game. Then they made a movie based on the game."

"What's he do?"

"The plot is really complex," Brandon said, too inexperienced to recognize the feigned interest as just part of this man's job. "He's a mercenary. He thought he was a soldier, working for Shinra corporation, but his memories had been tampered with. A scientist named Hojo experimented on him with Mako energy and Genova cells. Genova was an alien being that fell to earth and ..."

But the bartender raised his hand, smiled and shook his head. "You lost me a long time ago, kid. What can I get you to drink?"

Brandon froze. He hadn't planned what to order. He didn't even know the names of any drinks. Whenever he went with Mike to watch football and eat wings, Brandon would hear his cousin say "Whatever you got on tap, buddy."

"Um, what have you got on tap?"

"Bud, Coors Light, Miller, Harp, Guiness, Lowenbrau, Magic Hat, and Woodchuck."

Brandon chose Magic Hat because he liked the name. The bartender set a tall glass of amber liquid on a little napkin printed with the name of the hotel. He asked for three dollars and Brandon gave him a five. Then he left to serve the other patrons.

Pivoting on his stool, Brandon rested his elbow on the bar. More and more people filed into the space, most in groups of four or more. They talked excitedly to one another. Brandon had come to the Convention alone, and no one paused to converse with him, but that was okay. Just sitting, sipping his drink and watching satisfied the young man because all of his favorite characters paraded past. He smiled every time he noticed someone he loved from a manga or a game. He really did love them, though he'd learned not to share his feelings with most people. These characters had been his friends. He was able to relate to them, understand their motivations and support their struggles in a way that he'd never been able to with the people he met. More times than he could count, he'd closed a book or turned off his television filled with longing to join the world inhabited by those characters, a world that he not only desired but was certainly meant for. Being surrounded by them gave him a sense of belonging that had eluded him all of his life.

A row of lights turned on at the end of the bar, illuminating the stage area. Brandon swiveled his stool to face it. The blue-haired girl, standing behind a microphone off to the left, announced that the costume contest was about to begin. The top prize would be five hundred dollars. A basket including some rare manga, videos and action figures awaited the participant winning second place, and an autographed poster could be claimed by the third place contestant. There was still time, she said, to sign up. Brandon watched as groups of costumed attendees crowded around the little table to fill out the form.

"Hey, Cloud," said a voice, elegant, soft and yet masculine, like a leather-bound book.

Brandon turned. Behind him stood a man dressed in a black trench with straps criss-crossing over his bare chest.

Distressed metal guards rode on his shoulders, and shimmery silver hair spilled past his hips. He had fair skin and electric-lime irises with vertical pupils. Sephiroth. He was greatest of the soldiers, and Cloud's enemy in the game. He'd gone insane after discovering the experiments that created him, and tried to destroy the world. Looking at him, Brandon knew how the girls must've felt. He was perfect: his height and carriage, the angle of his jaw, the little smug smile tugging at the corners of his mouth. His every aspect almost convinced Brandon that the real Sephiroth stood before him; no mere mortal could nail every detail with such precision.

Aware suddenly that he'd been gawking, his own lips parted, while this man waited for a response, Brandon croaked, "Hey. That's a really sweet costume."

"I could say the same to you."

He even spoke like Sephiroth, in both his inflection and his choice of words. "Thanks," Brandon said.

"We'd go quite well together, don't you think?"

"I ..." Heat spread across Brandon's face from one ear to the other.

With a knowing grin, Sephiroth said, "In the contest. Most often the winners are groups of people. We'll stand a better chance together. Will you sign up?"

"Oh, I don't know," Brandon said.

"Come on, Cloud. It's five hundred dollars. Besides, why not show off your hard work?"

Emboldened by the beer, Brandon finally nodded, and the two of them wrote their characters' names on a piece of paper. Then they went to wait in line by the steps leading onto the stage.

"I think we should say something from the game," Brandon suggested to the taller man standing stoically beside him. "And then we should draw our swords and attack each other."

"That will be beautiful," Sephiroth said. "Just perfect."

As they watched the other contestants, the two of them continued to discuss their performance. They compared their favorites moments and lines from both the game and the movie. Brandon felt glad that this man understood how Sephiroth was tormented and tragic, not just a hack and slash cliché villain.

Finally the blue-tressed emcee said, "And next we have Cloud Strife and Sephiroth from *Final Fantasy Seven*, property of Square Enix. Give it up for Cloud and Sephy!"

Amidst hollering and applause, Brandon followed Sephiroth up the steps and into the blinding white light, sweating and feeling as if he might be sick. Their booted feet thudded against the wood beneath them until they reached the center of the platform. They stopped and faced one another, and the crowd went quiet. Some sort of vent sent Sephiroth's hair off to the side in silver streamers. He stood with his face slightly lowered, looking up at Brandon with just his eyes. He looked so cold and deadly and gorgeous, like a gemstone with his hard-edged, precise beauty, that Brandon's pulse raced. He stood staring at a corporeal dream, a fantasy made flesh.

Then Sephiroth said, "It's been a long time, Cloud."

Several voices, mostly feminine, shouted out in approval and recognition. Brandon couldn't respond; his throat felt swollen shut. The whole world seemed to be waiting for him to do something. Sephiroth took a step toward him, his expression unreadable.

"Tell me what you cherish most Cloud," he said. This time Brandon felt like Sephiroth spoke to him, for him, and not for the people watching. As he watched Sephiroth's lips moving, his hair waving in the air current, and his chest rising and falling beneath the leather straps of his armor, Brandon nearly forgot that he was on a stage.

"Tell me what you cherish most," Sephiroth said again. "Give me the pleasure of taking it away."

Swearing to himself he wouldn't disappoint Sephiroth, maybe even a little afraid to do so, Brandon stepped forward and drew his thick-bladed sword from its scabbard on his back. As he arced it down slowly, giving the other man time to parry, he said confidently, "There's not a thing I don't cherish."

Brandon's sword met Sephiroth's famous katana, Masamune. For a second Brandon panicked, realizing from the sound of the impact that Sephiroth carried a real metal weapon. Brandon's replica of Cloud's Buster Sword was wooden. He'd signed up for a shop class and suffered the ridicule of the other boys just to construct it. An entire semester spent sweating over a belt-sander after school had earned him an elaborate and detailed weapon that he didn't want to lose. He held tight to the hilt, his fist over his forehead as Sephiroth bore down. Not wanting to embarrass himself, reveal himself as a scrawny nerd unfit to represent Cloud, Brandon pushed back until sweat glazed his limbs and he panted at the exertion. They stood locked in their struggle for a long time, blades crossed and bodies straining. Many people snapped pictures.

Just when Brandon's muscles threatened to give out, Sephiroth gracefully swung his sword upward. It scraped along the side of Brandon's blade and bounced off of the tip. Sephiroth lifted it above his head and sheathed it behind him. Brandon stumbled forward and almost collided with the other man. Before Brandon knew what was happening, Sephiroth's fingers had closed around his collar and yanked him even closer.

Leaning in, Sephiroth whispered in Brandon's ear, "How about something for the yaoi fans?"

Then, lightning-quick, Sephiroth kissed him. He wrenched Brandon's chest hard against his own and drew Brandon's lower lip between both of his. Cheering erupted from the audience, though Brandon only perceived the first few seconds of it. After that nothing existed but this man, the texture of his teeth and lips, the fragrance of his artificial hair, the firm grip of his hand, and the solidity of his chest. The rush of blood inside Brandon's skull drowned all other noise. His grip slackened on his sword and it clattered against the stage. If he hadn't felt himself getting hard and remembered that probably a hundred people watched him, he might have remained entranced, paralyzed. Luckily he managed to break away before he got a full-fledged erection that his snug pants would do little to hide. He hurried to retrieve his weapon and escape the merciless glare of the stage. The audience applauded and shouted for more as he staggered down the steps.

A metal-winged woman, her avian armor reflecting light, shouted after him, "That was so hot! You guys should totally win!"

Unlike Brandon, Sephiroth stopped to talk to the line of people that met him at the foot of the stairs. For a while Brandon waited, thinking that Sephiroth would join him, that they could discuss more about the game and the characters. Soon it became achingly clear that the other man didn't share Brandon's desire for companionship. Sephiroth basked in the attention that the other Convention attendees, particularly the women, lavished upon him. Brandon returned to his place at the bar and watched Sephiroth moving through the crowd, enjoying himself and displaying about as much genuine amiability as a case of hypothermia.

After ordering another Magic Hat, Brandon asked himself what he'd expected to happen. Conflicting answers warred within his mind. Sephiroth kissed him. He'd instigated the whole thing. A person didn't just kiss another person if he wasn't attracted to that person, did he? Or had it just been a stunt, a means to the prize money? Brandon, along with most of the people here, had read dozens of fan comics and doujins centered around a romantic, or at least a physical, relationship between Sephiroth and Cloud. And besides, the kiss had lasted only half a minute and their tongues had never made contact. Though Brandon had felt as if he stood in a shaft of heavenly light where all time was suspended, to everyone else it had just been a peck: cute but meaningless. Likely Sephiroth was straight. Brandon looked across the room to where the silver-haired man sat at a table. If

Sephiroth wasn't hetero, he put on a good façade for the three girls in the sailor suits.

The night passed. Now and then someone approached Brandon and complimented his costume or his sword. A Japanese pop band played, and Brandon declined when a woman in a white kimono asked him to dance. He kept watching Sephiroth as previews for new anime flashed across a screen on the stage. A few times the strangest thing happened: Brandon's eyes sought out Sephiroth, only to find that the other man had been watching him. When Brandon made contact with Sephiroth's cat-green eyes, the other man quickly looked away. Confused, Brandon wished real people were as easy to understand as characters. If he were really Cloud and the other man really Sephiroth, they would be mortal enemies. They would try to kill each other, cut each other to ribbons with their swords, and it would probably hurt a lot less than this.

Brandon ordered another drink. He wandered over to the vendor tables to inspect some explicit manga that wasn't allowed to be sold during the main Convention. He looked at Sephiroth. Their eyes locked and then Sephiroth looked away. The scheduled events had concluded for the evening, and the people mingled, socializing, getting tipsy and flirting. Some of them danced to the techno background music. The alcohol he'd consumed made Brandon much less insecure than he normally felt around strangers, but he didn't attempt to talk to anyone. If he spoke with these people, got to know them, it would shatter his vision like thin glass against concrete. He'd discover that they were dentists and plumbers, not half-demon warriors and space pirates.

Sephiroth looked at him and looked away. After the winners were announced, Brandon decided, he'd go back to his room and leaf through the prints he'd purchased earlier that day. He vowed not to lie across his rented bed and remember that kiss, nor fantasize about where it could have led.

Several of the convention volunteers took the stage, and the music faded and died. The pink-haired woman lifted the microphone from its cradle and said, "It's been a difficult decision this year, but the judges are ready to announce the winners of the costume contest. A big round of applause for everybody who participated! Great job everybody!"

When the crowd settled down, she called the winners to the stage: a group of eight people, four of whom had constructed giant, robotic suits of armor while the rest donned the tight unitards of their pilots. Brandon clapped. They deserved the prize. Maybe he'd even ask them how the costumes had been made.

"And second place goes to Cloud and Sephiroth," the woman said. "How about that kiss?" She fanned herself with her hand while everyone clapped. Brandon went to stand beside Sephiroth on the stage, surprised at how much resentment he felt toward the other man. He managed a half-hearted bow before hurrying away, certain that what he felt showed as brightly as an electrical fire.

This time Sephiroth followed him, carrying the basket of prizes that they'd won. When Brandon sat down at the bar, Sephiroth took the stool beside him. The bartender sat a beer in front of Brandon even though he didn't order one. His throat like sandpaper, Brandon downed half of it in one swallow and muffled a belch.

"What are you drinking?" Sephiroth asked.

As much as he wanted to, Brandon could find no logical reason to be rude. "Magic Hat," he said.

"Is it good?" Sephiroth asked.

"Not really."

"I'll get you something," Sephiroth said, motioning for the bartender, who presented Brandon with a blueberry martini.

"Matches your eyes," Sephiroth said.

"What are you trying to do?" Brandon asked.

Sephiroth scrutinized him, staring at Brandon's face while his own remained an icy mask. Eventually, though, he turned to the prize basket and peeled away the sparkle-coated cellophane. "Let's see what kind of treasures our presentation earned us," he said, lifting a pack of trading cards.

"Some of this stuff seems pretty cool," Brandon said as he dug through the pins, key chains, and DVD's. "We'll have to divide it up."

"You can have it," Sephiroth said.

"You don't want any of it? Why did you compete?"

It was the second of Brandon's questions that went unanswered. He drank what Sephiroth had offered him. The remainder of his beer tasted even more bitter after the richness and sweet.

"Another," Sephiroth told the bartender. "Gin and tonic for me." He turned to Brandon and asked, "Why Cloud?"

Brandon considered giving Sephiroth a taste of his own medicine, but felt sure that if he remained silent he'd seem inept and slow-witted rather than enigmatic. "I don't know. He's cool and I kind of look like him."

"And that's all?"

"What else would there be?" Brandon asked. "Why do you want to be Sephiroth?"

"Sephiroth represents the pinnacle of achievement. I respect him for his abilities and his unwavering pursuit of his goal."

"His goal is to kill everyone," Brandon reminded the other man.

"I just can't help but to admire a person who will let nothing stand in his way. What is it about Cloud that you relate to?"

"His friends," Brandon said quietly, without looking at the neon eyes that drilled into him. "Cloud has Zack and Tifa and the ninja Yuffie, and Vincent Valentine and Cid. All of those people who care about him and will do anything to help him.

They see something in Cloud that inspires them, something noble and good that they can get behind. That's the kind of person I want to be. A person that other people care about. A person worth caring about."

"You don't see anything in yourself that others would find valuable, is that it?"

"I guess," Brandon said, unsure why he'd divulged so much.

Sephiroth's fingers curled around Brandon's chin and gently inclined and turned his head. The pad of his thumb stroked the center of Brandon's lower lip. His smile, while not deranged or cruel, sizzled with wickedness. "I'm going back to my room now Cloud," he said. "And I assume you'll be joining me. But bear in mind that none of your friends will be there to protect you this time. It will just be you and me."

Sephiroth's tongue battered its way into Brandon's mouth, forcing its way past his teeth and toward his throat as his hands wriggled down the back of Brandon's tight pants. Grasping his hips, Sephiroth spun Brandon around so that his back smacked against the hotel room door. Crazy desire moved in currents through Brandon's body, making him squirm in his partner's embrace even though flight was the last thing he wanted. Picking at Sephiroth's buckles, groaning with frustration when he couldn't undo the straps, Brandon's hands moved frantically from one elaborate article of clothing to the next, desperate to peel something away and find the flesh beneath: the genetically-perfected skin of Sephiroth.

Brandon's hand clutched Sephiroth's fly, his fingertips disappearing inside the fabric, finding a soft trail of hair that grazed his knuckles. He pulled with all of his might, popping the button open and driving their cocks together. Holding tight, Brandon ground his erection against the other's as they kissed violently, biting and suckling each other's lips and tongues until they throbbed and swelled.

Then Sephiroth caught both of Brandon's wrists and pinned Brandon's hands against the door, beside his ears. Silver hair hung disheveled in his face, a strand in front of his mouth fluttering with his heavy breath. His eyes, traffic-light-green, glowing with passion, found Brandon's, and this time he didn't look away, or even blink. Brandon stretched his neck, trying for Sephiroth's lips, but the other man held them a maddening inch out of Brandon's reach.

"Cloud," he huffed, licking up the side of Brandon's face but pulling back before Brandon could catch his lips or tongue with his own mouth. "It's not like you Cloud, just to take it. Not to fight."

Through the heavy haze of his arousal Brandon finally comprehended what the other man wanted. By standing up from his stool and following this man back to his room, Brandon had agreed to play out a fantasy. He'd agreed to be Cloud and only Cloud, and in exchange he got to have Sephiroth. He'd do this part as well. He actually found he wanted to, that the idea turned him on, and he tried to free his wrists, only to have his hands pounded hard against the door.

"Let go of me, Sephiroth," Brandon said through gritted teeth.

"No, I don't think so," the other responded. He wrapped both of Brandon's hands in one of his and squeezed hard, making the bones crackle. Holding him immobile, Sephiroth used his freed hand to undo the zipper that ran down the center of Brandon's shirt. The shirt fell open, exposing the smaller man's slender, freckled chest and torso. The shoulder armor Brandon had made from a hub cap landed beside him with a hollow, resonant ring. Chartreuse eyes devoured Brandon's flesh unapologetically as Sephiroth's tongue traced the sharp edges of his teeth. "I've always wanted to do this to you, Cloud."

As Sephiroth's head dropped and his lips met Brandon's neck, Brandon wanted to tell him that he'd always wanted it done, but said instead, "No, I'll kill you, Sephiroth. I'll defeat you just like I did before."

"You won't win this time Cloud," he said, his hot breath moistening the side of Brandon's neck. "You're all alone. You're mine for the taking." He bit into the muscle that stretched from Brandon's neck to his shoulder, forcefully enough to make Brandon grunt in earnest. Slowly, tauntingly, he sunk further down, his mouth traveling along the cords of muscle between Brandon's rib and hipbone. Even though Sephiroth's nail scraped down his forearm, Brandon kept his hands against the door, just where his lover wanted them. He did, however, rest his shoulder blades against the wood, curve his pelvis forward and spread his legs a little farther apart. He couldn't help it. He'd never wanted anyone so badly. This was his impossible dream coming true before his eyes. Sephiroth's silver head waited beside Brandon's lower belly, his tongue lapping wide paths up the center and his teeth denting the flesh.

Sephiroth tugged at the hem of the one long sleeve Brandon wore. It wasn't attached to the shirt, but held on his upper arm with elastic, and it slipped away easily and floated down. His unzipped shirt followed, and then Sephiroth started on his belt and straps, effortlessly undoing the buckles. Only the thick piece of leather separated his hands from Brandon's aching cock, and Brandon wanted to feel them on it, see them there, more than he'd ever wanted anything. But he'd have to pretend he didn't want it, pretend to fight. It seemed impossible, but he'd try.

"No, what are you doing?" Brandon stepped to the side, but Sephiroth seized him by the hips.

"Now, Cloud. You may have grown up in that little mountain village, but I know you're not that naïve."

"Get away from me you monster!" Brandon lifted his foot and kicked Sephiroth in the shoulder, sending him sprawling on his back. Scared at first that he'd gone too far, he saw the other man's smile and smiled back. Both of them knew the same thing:

this was what would happen. It was hot and exciting because this was how it would really be.

Springing back to his feet, Sephiroth tore away his black trench coat and tossed it on the bed. Nothing covered his sculpted body but the two leather straps that crossed over his heart. Brandon hoped he wouldn't remove them. Beneath his black pants waited an unmistakable erection. Long, shining hair, battle-mussed, brushed against his ribs.

"Just stay away from me," Brandon said. "I'm warning you."

"Just try to stop me, Cloud."

Lunging forward, Sephiroth tackled Brandon to the bed and trapped him beneath his body, kissing him hard, brutally. As their teeth knocked and scraped together, Brandon toed off his boots and let them fall to the floor. Sephiroth's hand sliced between their tightly-pressed groins and unbuttoned Brandon's military-style trousers. He seized Brandon's cock and squeezed the shaft hard, using his thumb to swirl Brandon's pre-cum over the head.

"No," Brandon whimpered without conviction, as his pelvis bucked involuntarily, driving his dick against the other man's palm.

"You can do better than that, Cloud," Brandon's partner panted beside his ear. He raised himself up on his elbow and looked down at Brandon as he continued to churn Brandon's cock in his fist.

Brandon lifted his hand to strike. When he hesitated, the other man nodded and whispered, "Go ahead."

The heel of Brandon's hand struck Sephiroth's shoulder forcefully, making him recoil but not topple off.

"Not good enough," he said with a maniacal, perfect-Sephiroth smile. He sat up and straddled Brandon's thighs, leaving the slighter young man caught beneath his weight. Slowly he unzipped his pants and freed his erection. A few pearls of semen escaped the slit when he grasped it, making the head darken and pulse. It left a slick trail as he rubbed it back and forth over Brandon's stomach, poking the head against Brandon's belly button suggestively.

No longer able to act, robbed of the ability to even think clearly by his desire and the throb in his balls, Brandon lifted his ass from the bed and pushed his own pants to his thighs. With one hand he grasped his own penis, not to make himself come but to alleviate some of the tension, and with the other he touched his partner's silver hair.

"Sephiroth," he panted. "I always wanted you. Dreamed about doing this. You doing this to me." His hand moved to the back of the other man's neck, and he pulled him downward and kissed him, loving the way his long hair covered both of their bodies like a silken sheet.

Deftly Sephiroth straightened his legs, so that his thighs lay flush with Brandon's. As he had done with Brandon's wrists before, he took both of their cocks in his hand and pressed them together. For many minutes he just held them there, as he kissed and nibbled along Brandon's jaw line and ear with real, not pretended, passion. Slowly his hand began to move over their erections, summoning more fluids. Both of them moaned and twisted with growing need, need that rapidly became unbearable.

"T-take me, Seph. Please."

The silver-haired man rose from the bed and removed his shoes and pants. He stood a minute for Brandon to admire, in nothing but his bit of black leather, with his balls huddled close to his body and his cock glistening and bouncing. Brandon continued to touch himself as he drank in the beautiful, surreal sight, tickling the sensitive groove on his head with his finger.

"Stand up," he finally told Brandon. "Take off the rest of your clothes."

Hurrying to comply, Brandon stripped clumsily and left his pants, shorts and socks balled at the foot of the bed. As his partner had done, he waited, let himself be looked up and down. After Sephiroth had satisfied his eyes, he stepped forward and stroked Brandon's blond hair with heart-wrenching gentleness. Sadness shadowed his brilliant eyes. Brandon wondered if he was thinking about how they would be enemies, how one would destroy the other, how fate had made it inevitable.

"Seph," he whispered, draping his hands over the other's knuckles.

"Shh," he responded, lifting Brandon into his arms, holding him beneath his knees and under his back, kissing him softly as he carried him into the bathroom and turned the light on. He set Brandon on the counter, beside the sink. The mirror was cold against his back. Sephiroth guided Brandon's heels to the edge of the tile slab. Across the tiny room, Brandon could see the two of them in the mirrored door of the shower stall. He saw Sephiroth's amazing hair spilling over his back, stopping just at the crack of his muscular ass. His own calves looked thin and frail on either side of his partner. The side of his face that was visible over Sephiroth's shoulder bloomed pink with lust. When Sephiroth closed the door, Brandon got a view of them from the side, courtesy of a third, long glass.

"Ready, Cloud?" Sephiroth asked, urging Brandon's legs further apart.

"Don't hurt me," Brandon said. "Not for real."

"No, I wouldn't," the other man responded, kissing Brandon's forehead and brows as he took lube and a condom from a plastic travel case. He positioned Brandon's ass just where he needed it before he twisted the cap off of the small bottle and drizzled the clear gel over his fingers. He let it warm before smearing it between Brandon's legs, working some of it inside his hole with first his fingertip, then his finger. Brandon relaxed back, let his burning cheek rest against the coolness of the mirror, let his eyes flicker closed. He moaned as Sephiroth's fingers infiltrated his body, delving deeper until they hit Brandon's gland and drove a sprinkle of semen from him. He bit his lip at the twinge when Sephiroth scissored his fingers, spreading him open, preparing him. Then the fingers withdrew, and he heard the tear of the condom wrapper.

"Look at me. Open your eyes."

He did, turning to face his lover, his fantasy, his Sephiroth. The other man reached down and stroked Brandon's penis, twisted the head in his hand.

"God, Cloud your eyes. Fucking beautiful," he murmured as he guided himself into Brandon's anus. Despite the foreplay, it was a tight fit and Brandon's eyes clamped shut and his spine stiffened at the stretching sensation.

"No, look at me," Sephiroth said as he thrust in, making Brandon groan. "Hold on to me." He steered Brandon's hands from the edge of the counter to his shoulders, where the nails bit in as he drove his entire length into Brandon.

"God, Seph," Brandon moaned, his head thrashing from side to side, trying to focus on his lover's face amidst the torrent of his ecstasy, Seph's emerald eyes guiding his gaze like a beacon in a storm. The other man stabbed into him, deep and hard, his cock slamming into Brandon's prostate.

"Is it okay?" he asked, waiting for Brandon to nod before doing it again, and again, and again, harder and faster. Brandon circled his groin to meet Sephiroth thrust for thrust. He grasped his shoulders franticly, feeling the skin break but unable to stop, unable to let go, lest he be swept away by rapture. Seph inhaled sharply but didn't complain as they fucked like it was the first and last time. Brandon's head lolled to the side as he took his cock into his hand and stroked it to the rhythm of Sephiroth's thrusts. His eyes blinked open, and he saw them again in the mirror: himself blushing from head to toe, practically flat on his back on the countertop, pleasuring himself, with his perfect Cloud hair and perfect Cloud eyes, even a sandy-blond happy trail. Sephiroth's hair swayed back and forth as he labored above Brandon. This was just the way Brandon had always pictured it. He'd seen it depicted in manga and even flash animation, but nothing as good as this. This was the real thing: not a drawing of Sephiroth fucking Cloud, not a story about it, but real.

"Seph, Seph look," he breathed. "Look at us."

Both of them faced the mirror, and the scene gained even more startling beauty with their eyes reflected back: his, Cloud's, wide and ocean-blue and Sephiroth's chemical jade. As they watched, Brandon's hand left a quartet of red furrows down Sephiroth's arm as he jerked himself to completion and shot his seed over his stomach. He whimpered and thrashed, mouthing words whose sound never left his lungs. The spout of semen that poured from him felt endless; it pooled on his belly and dripped from the sides of his waist as he writhed, practically sobbing at the intensity and pleasure. On top the other man moved with growing urgency. Sweat sparkled over his ivory skin. He lifted Brandon's foot to his shoulder and kissed Brandon's ankle.

"Oh fuck. Oh Cloud," he seethed as his body shook with the tremors of orgasm. "Always wanted. You." Then his head drooped, his hair blanketing the both of them, veiling the once-in-a-lifetime-scene.

Brandon's whole body, his every cell, tingled and glowed. It had been better than anything he could ever imagine, especially since he'd never thought it could happen. Some people dreamt of rock stars or movie stars as their lovers, but movie stars actually existed, and, a possibility, no matter how remote, existed alongside them. But the things and people Brandon loved inhabited only the realm of imagination, at least until tonight. They'd made it happen, made it genuine, willed it into existence.

"We were really them," Brandon said sleepily, unconsciousness threatening to claim him even before he made it out of the bathroom. Just then he remembered a line from the movie, a line that seemed to have importance beyond his exhausted comprehension. "Seph, stay where you belong. In my memories."

The last awareness Brandon enjoyed that night involved a warm cloth wiping his stomach, strong arms depositing him on the bed, and a steel and satin voice saying, "Sleep, my Cloud. And thank you."

Seph still slept when Brandon woke the next morning, so he replaced his black pants and tried to tame his hair a little bit. Then he borrowed a faded T-shirt that said "Got Mako?" from Seph's suitcase. He didn't think the other man would mind; they were lovers now. Then Brandon went to the hotel lobby and filled two cups with coffee and a Styrofoam plate with assorted donuts.

When he returned to the room, Brandon found Seph, or the man who'd been Seph last night, sitting on the edge of the bed, tying a pair of charcoal canvas sneakers. He wore dark jeans and a lavender and white striped button down shirt. He had short brown hair and light brown eyes that slanted ever so slightly, like he maybe had an Asian grandparent. Surprisingly, Brandon found him just as attractive as he had beneath the leather and silver wig. He smiled, but the other man kept looking at Brandon like he was some sort of ticking bomb, or a poisonous snake ready to strike.

"What's up?" Brandon asked.

"Just, please god, tell me you're legal."

"Yeah," Brandon said. "I'm nineteen. I got us some breakfast."

The older man sighed with relief, but wouldn't meet Brandon's eyes. Long moments of silence stretched on, before he finally said, "Could you leave my T-shirt?"

"Leave it where?" Brandon asked.

"Here. When you go."

"Go?"

Seph (Brandon didn't know how else to label him) sighed again, this time with exasperation. "Yes go. I'd hoped you'd have done it before I woke up."

"But why?" Brandon asked.

"In order to avoid this extremely uncomfortable moment."

"What's your name?" Brandon asked.

"Why?"

"Because I want to know."

126

"Why?"

"Because I like you."

"I guess you don't understand how this is supposed to happen. It's a one nighter. A game. Now it's over, and you go."

"That's not what I want," Brandon said. "I want to get to know you. At least be friends."

"You wanted to fuck Sephiroth, a character from a game that no living person can live up to. I helped you out. You reciprocated, of course. We both got to live out a fantasy, for one night. It only works for one night, Cloud."

"My name's Brandon."

The man on the bed shook his head, as if he could rattle Brandon's name loose from his memory. "It only works for one night because you can't build a relationship on this. This is game. Fantasy. Do you think we could live as Cloud and Sephiroth all the time?"

"No."

"Exactly."

"Why can't we get to know each other? Why is that so wrong?"

"You don't want me for me. You don't want a real person, Cloud."

"Stop it."

"You hide from real people. You can't relate to them. I saw you at that bar last night."

"Maybe that's true. But give me a chance to try. I don't want to hide. For once. Tell me your goddamn name at least."

"It's Travis."

"Travis," Brandon said. "I think you're afraid."

"Of what?"

"A real friendship," Brandon said. "Of caring about someone. Of how that can make you vulnerable."

"Please. You discerned all that in one night of drunken sex? You don't know me at all."

"No," Brandon admitted. "But I understand all about Sephiroth. You're too good of a Sephiroth, and not just aesthetically. You're too detached as him. Not all of it can be an act."

"And you're too damn needy, just like your hero."

"Careful, Travis. We're getting to know each other."

"Shit."

Brandon sat down and proffered the donuts, and this time Travis chose one. He held it and just looked at Brandon, looked at him with more amazement than he had when he'd been Cloud.

"Your eyes really are beautiful," Travis said.

"Does this mean..."

"It means we can talk," Travis said. "Email. Maybe be friends. Meet once in a while."

"You mean as them," Brandon said.

Travis nodded. "I've been looking for a Cloud for a long time. I've been to Cons, seen hundreds of people try. You, you're flawless. You're him inside and out."

Standing, Brandon walked to where he'd leaned his Buster Sword against the wall. He picked it up and inspected the blade with his hands, his fingers stopping over a deep notch in the wood. "You damaged it," he said to Travis. "You can't keep doing that. Your Masamune is too sharp."

"I'll try to be more careful," Travis said.

"It's more fragile than your sword. It could break apart."

"I know, Brandon. You'll have to decide if you want to risk it. But if you just want to keep this in your memories, keep your, your sword from getting hurt, I'll understand."

"No," Brandon said. "It's stronger than it looks. I think it will hold up, prove its worth."

"Yeah," Travis said, tracing the edge of Brandon's ear with his pinky. "I have no doubt that it will."

# TREE HUGGER
## Jay Starre

Sam and Davy hauled their heavy chainsaws up the wooded slope, huffing for breath from the climb. They were surprised when they spotted a young dude seated in front of an enormous fir tree in their path.

"What's going on, bud? We're fucking working here," Sam warned the stranger as he checked him out.

He looked like a college kid, short and lean, with shaggy gold-blond hair, a sparse beard, square-framed glasses too big for his narrow face, and jeans and T-shirt that had seen better days.

"I'm with the Tree Protectors of North America. You aren't cutting down this tree," the environmentalist proclaimed as he stood up and spread his arms defiantly before the huge bole of the ancient tree he'd chosen to defend.

The loggers glanced quickly at each other before bursting out in laughter. "A tree-hugger for fuck's sake!" Davy snorted.

"There's a million fucking trees all around you. How the hell are you gonna protect 'em all?" Sam asked, shaking his head as he set down his saw.

"If I save one tree today, it'll be worth it!" the conservationist nerd declared loudly, as if he was in front of a score of TV cameras, rather than in the bush in the middle of nowhere.

Davy chuckled, looking at his pal and winking. "For an airhead, he's actually pretty cute."

The pair just happened to be gay, and fuck buddies, too. They didn't put up with any shit from their fellow loggers who were mostly straight. They weren't about to allow this skinny punk to get in their way.

Carter stood his ground, although he was actually scared out of his wits. When he'd taken the dare offered by his buddies in the Science and Nature Book Club, he hadn't really anticipated meeting a pair of rough-and-tumble loggers who had muscles bulging from every conceivable crack and crevice of their redneck bodies.

He also hadn't expected to be so turned on by their threatening size – or their hooting derision!

His cock stiffened under his torn jeans, his asshole twitched, and he even felt drool pooling inside his mouth. What the hell? He was supposed to be saving the environment, not turning into a quivering pussy-boy for a pair of brainless loggers!

It was the more brazen of the two loggers, Sam, who saw past the bravado and recognized the tree-hugger's hidden fear. Tall and built, with buzzed dark hair, he was also the more menacing of the pair. He decided to really put a scare into the nerd tree-hugger. His weapon of choice was his big hard cock. To the shocked surprise of both the young blond and his own pal, Sam tore open the snaps of his fly and whipped out his fat fuckstick.

"Here's a tree worth saving! Why don't you snuggle up to this wooden pole? You might find it more friendly than a goddamned fucking tree trunk."

Sam's cock was quick on the trigger. It only took a few pulls and the fat thing rose in a dangerous-looking curve, the purple shaft lengthening and thickening almost instantly.

Davy was quick to follow his buddy's lead, grinning as he glanced around to see if the tree-hugger had any friends lurking about. When he spotted no one else, he whipped out his cock, too.

"How about two big poles? Two big poles for your two hot holes," he chuckled, winking lewdly.

The defiant environmentalist had his arms out wide and his back to the big tree he'd chosen to champion. But his eyes were on the two cocks rising up only a yard in front of him. Bright blue orbs locked onto those fat cocks while the college student's jeans tented up at his crotch, betraying his tight-lipped silence as surely as those hungry, darting eyes.

A grunting moan escaped Carter's clenched lips. A pair of stiff cocks like these at any other time would have been a welcome sight. But right now, they only meant he'd have to be stronger and more defiant if he was to save this majestic Red Cedar.

Most of all, he was afraid of what he'd have to say about himself when he reported back to his pals in the Book Club! They'd be just as derisive as these pair of red-neck loggers, only much more capable of lashing out with witty and biting comments about his lack of commitment to the Conservation Cause!

The husky loggers glanced at one another and shared a nod. They were far from any of their crew, and the tree-hugger appeared to be alone. Evidenced by the tell-tale tent in his scruffy jeans, he was definitely horny. They moved toward him with cocks in hand. He leaned back against the tree, still shielding it, but his entire body was quaking by then.

"Not gonna run away like a fucking little scared rabbit?" Davy laughed coarsely. Short and powerful, wavy brown hair outlined a wide, handsome face. His lips smacked lewdly as he blew a kiss to the defiant nerd and moved in to stand directly in front of him.

"Down on your knees and suck this fat cock. I promise I won't cut down your fucking tree if you swallow my cum."

Face to face, barely a foot of space separated them. Sam hovered on the right, almost as close, grinning and pumping his cock as he checked out the nerd's tight ass from the side. He realized his pal was merely baiting the blond, but he also knew how irresistible his masculine appeal could be. They'd often fucked guys who claimed they were straight, and that was primarily due to Davy's sexual charms.

This college boy with the big glasses looked as if he was wavering, and about to fall prey to that vulgar magnetism. His whole body quaked while his crotch bulged with an unmistakable boner that actually jerked as it leaked a spot of precum to stain the worn denim.

Sam couldn't help hooting with laughter. "He's jizzing his jeans! The nerd ain't even wearing any underwear I bet! Let's see if that's true. Come on punk, show us you got no undies on!"

No one moved as that jeer echoed in the forest silence.

Finally, Carter let out an explosive whoosh of air as he let go of his held breath.

"Ok. If you guys promise not to cut down this one tree, I'll suck your cocks. But you've got to promise me!"

It came out kind of whiny, and Carter bit his lip and groaned. Was he really going to suck the rude loggers off? And would they even keep their promise not to cut down the cedar?

All of the sudden, he didn't give a fuck anymore! Hovering in the air between them, the brawny pair's lust was palpable. They wouldn't be waving those thick boners around at him if they weren't randy and ready. He'd show them what a real suck-job was!

With a determined grunt, he dropped to his knees. His hands dropped down, then reached out and grasp Davy's broad hips. His mouth opened, and with his eyes on the prize, he swooped down to swallow up half the logger's plump poker in one gulp.

The two loggers exchanged looks of surprised mirth. This was an unexpected bonus, an afternoon sex romp instead of the usual, sweaty, dirty, manual labor they had to look forward to!

And the cock-sucking activist was actually kind of cute. His scraggly blond hair hung around his ears framing elfin features. Bowed lips smacked loudly around the head of Davy's big cock. A tight T-shirt clung to slim but well-proportioned shoulders and torso.

He was hot! Sam had checked out his butt, which swelled outwards in a sexy curve from his narrow waist, and decided it was extremely fuckable.

"Nice job, tree-hugger. Wrap your lips around that big meat!" Davy was ordering between grunts of his own.

He shoved up with his hips into the wet mouth slobbering over his boner, then pushed one thigh up between the kneeling college boy's thighs and pressed it against his crotch. His heavy work jeans and thick boots looked rough and sexy against the lean body of the kneeling nerd.

"I think he needs his ass fucked, too. Maybe if he opens up his butthole for me, I'll cut down one or two less trees today. Just to be nice," Sam sneered as he moved in.

There was no way he could just stand by and watch the hot cock-sucking scene without joining in. The small mouth, surrounded by the short stubble of the nerd's sparse beard, dribbled drool over a quivering chin as thick shank pumped in and out. Davy's plump nads swung back and forth in the air banging against that slobber-coated chin. The nerd's bright blue eyes gazed fixedly through the lens of his big glasses at the meat he swallowed.

From the looks of that excellent suck-job, Sam had a good hunch the tree-hugger would take cock up the ass like a champ. He sure gulped up Davy's juicy meat with plenty of enthusiasm! The logger moved in behind Carter and roughly booted his legs apart. He knelt in the pine needles behind him and reached forward to tear at the blond's jeans. There was a mewling grunt from his cock-filled mouth but no other protest as he shoved his pants down to his knees.

No underwear! Just like he'd guessed. The naked butt quivered as he gave it a few playful slaps. Two globes of pale muscle jiggled as he took hold of them with his calloused hands and pulled them apart. The deep crack was hairless and sweaty.

Hot butt! Very hot! The tall, confident logger, was actually shaking as much as the cock-sucking environmental as he scooted forward and crammed his stiff cock between those sexy mounds.

133

A loud moan escaped the blond's bellowing cheeks as that fat boner rammed up against his tight sphincter. Sam pushed against the convulsing butt rim as he leaned down and spit into the juncture of cockhead and asshole. He spit again, the gooey drool landing directly on target. His plump cock-head glistened with saliva as he rubbed it into the snug, yet pliant butthole. Two or three good shoves, and the flared bulb drove past snapping, flushed butt-lips and sank home.

"Oh fuck yeah!" he muttered as the clamping walls of the nerd's butthole wrapped around his knob. It was like a pulsing vice had taken hold of him. He shoved deeper, amazed at how that snug orifice opened up for him so easily. Another good shove, and he was balls-deep in hot nerd asshole.

"We're plugging him from both ends! The little fucker really is working hard for all this tree-saving bullshit!" Davy chortled as he pumped his cock between the activist's stretched lips.

The blond stared up at the stocky logger with wide blue eyes. There seemed to be no question he was enjoying the double-fuck. He'd taken Sam's cock without a whimper, and he was now wiggling his butt back over that fat poker with enthusiastic humping motions. His head bobbed up and down over one cock while his plump ass rode up and down over the other. The pair of loggers couldn't help but assume they'd stripped away the tree-hugger's defiance with their plowing cocks. He was all theirs for the using!

Carter knew what they were thinking, and he encouraged it by wagging his fucked ass all around the giant cock drilling it, while slurping noisily up and down the juicy shank the stocky one was pumping so lustily between his drooling lips. He might have told himself he was doing it to save a tree, but that was probably a lie. He was doing it to get cock up the ass and down his throat! He was determined to make the burly loggers shoot their loads!

Maybe they'd be too exhausted from a good fuck and a nasty orgasm to cut down any more trees for the rest of the day! Or the entire week!

Davy had his thigh pressed up into the student's naked crotch, his rough jeans rubbing against his stiff cock. Carter humped that thigh as he sucked cock and opened up his legs to take another cock up the ass. All three grunted and moaned lewdly in the forest stillness, intent on the sexy three-way.

"We've got a ... uggg ... live one here, Sammy! He loves cock as much ... uhhnn ... as he loves trees! Shove your fat dick way up ... uhhhmmm ... inside his guts and I'll ram mine down his throat. Maybe they'll meet inside him!" Davy grunted rudely from above.

Meanwhile Sam was in butt-hole heaven. The tight slot massaging the length of his drilling boner constantly pulsed with waves of heated convulsions around his sensitive meat. The student's lush white butt squirmed continually as he sought to get as much cock up his tight ass as possible. The tree-hugger rubbed his crotch over the Davy's thick thigh like a horny slut as he sucked the stocky logger's fat boner with loud smacks. Davy thrust in and out of his slurping mouth steadily as he grinned down at his pal fucking him from behind.

The usual sounds of the forest, woodpeckers' staccato drilling, ravens cawing, squirrels quarrelling, and the wind in the bows above, were punctuated by the nasty trio's grunts, the smacks of Carter's lips around cock in his mouth, the squishes of Sam's pole as it rode in and out of clinging sphincter, and the slap of rough logger jeans against naked nerd ass-cheeks.

Then, in the distance, the buzz of chainsaws felling forest giants returned to remind them of what all that hot fucking was about. The rest of the logging crew were back at work after their lunch break.

The rude reminder only seemed to incense the kneeling activist. He gurgled and snorted as he burrowed into the stocky logger's crotch with determination, managing for the first time to swallow up the logger's entire fat shank, right to the balls. His big glasses banged against Davy's flat belly.

"Oh man ... oh yeah ... oh fuck ... he's deep-throating my pecker," Davy yelped. Reaching down, he grasped the sides of Carter's face with both calloused hands as he squirmed around the wet mouth and tight throat encasing his cock.

At the same time, the kneeling nerd reared backwards to swallow all of Sam's lengthy shank with his heated asshole. Furry logger balls nestled up in his smooth ass-crack as he began to writhe and hump at twice the previous speed.

"He's jerking off my cock with his butthole ... fuck! Oh yeah ... he's gonna make me blow if he keeps that up," Sam gasped out as he clung to the nerd's humping ass while slamming back with savage pumps of his own.

Carter gurgled over cock down the throat and thrashed around over cock up the ass, writhing uncontrollably between the two loggers. His entire body drove forward against Davy's thigh while his pale moon ass slammed back over Sam's big boner.

Suddenly Davy felt something wet and gooey soaking the material of his jeans.

"The little tree-hugger ... ohhhhh ... is coming! He's shooting jizz ... ummmmnnn ... with two big logger dicks fucking him from either end!" he chortled between gasps.

The blond nerd shuddered from head to toe as he unloaded all over the stocky logger's rough jeans. He snorted around the cock in his mouth as his lean body convulsed in the throes of orgasm. He writhed over the thick thigh pressing into his crotch while his asshole convulsed around the huge cock drilling his slick, heated asshole.

But it was not over for the hapless activist. The two loggers were incensed by the sight of the blond squirming around their cocks and shooting jizz at the same time. They'd fucked the jizz right out of him! Now they'd fuck him until they blew a nut too!

"You still gotta suck a load outa my fat pork-slab," Davy growled as he cupped the blond's chin and lifted his face to gaze down into his blue eyes. His face was flushed and sweaty, his hair hung in damp ringlets around his ears. His slim body was wracked with convulsions, exhausted and sated.

But strangely enough, he made no attempt to tear away from the two brutes who fucked his ass and throat. Instead he renewed his sluttish behavior with all the wild fervor of before.

As the tree-hugger resumed his rearing slam over Sam's cock, and bobbed his head rapidly over Davy's hard rod, the two loggers exchanged looks of awe. They had a real wild one on their hands!

That thought spurred them on. Sam's big paws gripped their victim's ass fiercely and pounded into his tight ass. He stared down at that gaping slot as it clung possessively to his driving cock like an elastic piston, pushing out when he pulled out and caving in when he shoved in. There seemed to be no bottom to the hot hole. He rammed his cock to the balls and pulled all the way out, then slammed right back in. The kneeling nerd took it without a single complaint.

Davy watched his pal fuck that white, lush ass. It was very hot. The tall logger was still dressed in thick coveralls and tight, dirty T-shirt. His fly was open and his fat cock stuck out like a purple battering ram. It glistened with sweat and spit as it rammed in and out of the student's willing, pouting asshole. Carter had his thighs wide open, taking all that cock effortlessly. It was a sight that drove Davy over the edge.

The wet mouth slurping over his cock was suddenly too hot and moist and sexy to withstand. He was coming!

"Take my hot spunk down your throat! Save a tree today," he howled as his load rocketed out of his cock-head and down the blond's gullet.

Sam had driven himself into a frenzy of his own. The quivering butt he roughly impaled was a pit of wet lava. The fluttering anal walls and ass-lips rubbed over his pistoning pud without respite. When Davy shot his load down the activist's throat, Sam could no longer hold back. He began to come, too.

"I'm filling his ass with logger nut-cream! That's two trees he's saved today!"

The pair held the activist between them as they filled him with their steamy jizz. He gulped down Davy's spunk and sucked in Sam's with his tight sphincter muscles. He drained them dry.

They pulled away, stumbling toward the nearby path and collapsing beside each other breathlessly. "What an awesome fuck!" they chimed in together.

Carter was on his feet, smirking with self-satisfied smugness. His cock dripped jizz, cum glistened on his lips and some was smeared over his cute white butt-cheeks. He lazily pulled up his torn jeans while as he laughed out loud.

The loggers stared at him like he'd gone nuts. He waved to them jauntily as he began to trot down the path away from them.

"I couldn't give a fuck about a bunch of trees! Cock is what I care about. Especially a pair of brainless logger's big juicy cocks! Thanks for the creamy loads! See you later," he jeered as he disappeared from sight.

Sam and Davy looked at each other in astonishment. Then they burst out laughing. That was one tree-hugging nerd they wouldn't mind running into again!

It was only two days later when Carter offered his report to the Science and Nature Book Club.

"The two idiot loggers shot their loads and collapsed on the forest floor. I saved more than one tree from their rapacious actions that day," he claimed dramatically to the four members of his Club, all of whom had listened in open-mouthed disbelief to his blow-by-blow rendition of the hot fuck he'd experienced

"Yeah, right! Have you got any proof? Sounds like a bunch of crap to me. I bet you never even went out to the forest to protest," one of his buddies sneered, a plump and snotty senior who usually tried to run the Club through sheer nasty will.

"Or if you did, you just jerked off against a tree trunk and pretended it was a logger's big boner," another Club nerd chimed in, a red-head with a lanky frame and a big toothy grin.

The other two book club nerds laughed derisively while Carter stood his ground and merely laughed back. This aplomb surprised his Club pals, but not as much as what happened next.

"I do have proof," he shouted above the laughter.

A door at the rear of the small basement meeting room swung open with a loud bang. The activists jerked in their chairs and spun around to see Sam and Davy strolling in from the broom closet they'd been hidden in.

"Here's Sam and Davy, two reformed loggers about to offer you guys a chance to save some more trees, just like I did!"

The pair wore logger's helmets, big logger's boots – and nothing else!

"Save a tree today! Ride a logger's pole," Davy called out, his big hand gripping the base of his towering fuck-tool, his hefty, naked thighs striding forward into the group of seated, open-mouthed activists.

The snotty senior recovered first. "Did you hire a pair of actors to wave their cocks at us and pretend they're really loggers?"

"Hey chubby, I've seen more trees up close than you ever will! How about a closer look at logger dick?" Sam, tall and intimidating, booted chairs out of the way as he stomped over to the startled senior and shoved his massive meat right in his face.

Surprised and definitely intimidated, the senior jerked backwards, upending his chair and sprawling on the floor between Sam's big boots. With a sneer, Sam dropped to his knees, straddling the felled activist. He gripped the student's face in both calloused palms and thrust into the gaping mouth.

"Now that we've taken care of the loud-mouth, who else is gonna call our pal Carter a liar? Any takers?" Davy waved his fat poker around at the group as they gawked in shock at their snotty friend gurgling over cock buried between his slurping lips.

The red-head's hand shot up in the air. "Me! I won't believe a word until I get some proof. Are you real loggers?"

Davy and Carter exchanged smirks as the blond activist intervened. "Drop your drawers and bend over, Red. You can see for yourself how logger cock feels up the butt!"

Red, one eye on Davy's big cock, the other on Sam's hefty pumping ass as he drilled the senior's gurgling throat, didn't waste any time as he reared up out of his chair and turned around to yank down his jeans and bare his lean white butt.

"Prove you're a real logger then! Fuck an activist," the tall nerd dared with a nasty giggle

The handsome logger shoved his way past the other two seated Club members, who eyed the fat boner and big hairy ass with unadulterated interest, then seized Red's compact can in his big paws and rammed his cock between the quaking cheeks with a rude laugh.

"I'll fuck every one of you tree-huggers, just like my logger pal and I fucked Carter the other day out in the woods. He saved a bunch of trees that day, and now it's your turn to do the same. Got the balls to save some trees? Then give up your holes for logger poles!"

Davy's sexy grin and nasty wink sent shivers through the quivering spines of the watching Club members. Red, feeling the blunt crown of logger cock knocking at his puckered sphincter, yelled out his own ratification of the nasty proposal.

"I concur! Yeah! Give me some logger cock up the butt and save a tree today!"

A yelp followed as the rough but sexy logger kicked Red's long thighs apart and pushed his head down over the back of his chair, thrusting beyond palpitating sphincter into nerd asshole with a thrust of his naked hips.

The senior on the floor blubbered something incoherent as he swallowed logger cock eagerly, his chubby hands fluttering all over Sam's hefty, hairy butt as he pulled that ass down toward his fucked mouth. Whatever he had to say, it didn't seem to be a complaint!

"I move that this chapter of the Tree Protectors of North America strip down and line up for logger dick! Let's do our part to save the forest! Anyone second?" Carter shouted out, tearing off his own clothes as he spoke.

The pair of remaining un-fucked Club members made up their minds, raising their hands and chiming in together. "I second the motion! Give me some logger cock! Let's save some trees!"

The remainder of the evening Sam and Davy spent proving their stamina as they manhandled the Club members with their work-calloused paws and pounded their willing holes with their logger poles. No one was left a skeptic, nor was any nerd hole left unsatisfied.

It was definitely the best damn meeting the Science and Nature Book Club ever had! And not only was Carter elected the new Club President, Davy and Sam were admitted as the newest members!

# HARDBOILED
## Landon Dixon

He fanned the pictures across my desk.

It was all there in black and white – me sucking 'Big Deal' Rigoletti's cock, licking his balls, getting fucked deep in the ass, the expression on my rugged pan one of inescapable ecstasy. I had to hand it to the mug; he could really handle a Speed Graphic camera and a flash gun – hiding behind a two-way mirror.

But this was face-to-face. And I wasn't passing out any kudos.

"It's gonna cost you plenty, Mr. D.A.," Convey sneered, gathering up the smut pics, stuffing them back into a manila envelope. "The big, tough, manly crime crusader for the people gettin' all swishy with the state's number one gang boss. You'll be ruined."

I sat back, crossed my legs, smile tugging up the corners of my Valentino-like kisser.

Time dragged, sweat spreading in trickles across Convey's clock. He tried a grin, but it didn't take. He pushed a shaking mitt through his short, blonde-white hair, his blue eyes watering.

"I-I want money – lotsa dough!" he bleated.

Two-bit blackmailer.

I knew something about the guy, could read him like a cheap pulp magazine. "You don't want money," I stated.

His gob dropped open. "W-what? Either you make with the geetus – and plenty – or I cart these sex shots on over to the papers … or maybe the Governor." He shook his envelope at me.

I rubbed the cigar I'd been toying with underneath my nose, repeated, "You don't want money."

His Adam's apple did a jig. "Huh!?"

143

I filed the fifty-cent stogie in the breast pocket of my two hundred-dollar pinstripe, climbed to my feet. Then I strode around the wide expanse of desk toward Convey.

He backed away, eyes bugging, hands thrusting out the thick envelope like a shield. I swatted it aside. Pictures of two big-dicked, hard-bodied he-men fucking up a storm spilled out all over the carpet. I grabbed Convey by his bowtie and shook him like my prick after pissing.

"What're you gonna do!?" he screamed. "I'll scream!"

I jerked his sweaty expression close, knocking his fishy glims down with my blazing headlights. Then I planted one on him – square on the mug's moist, red lips.

His eyes just about popped out of his head.

"You don't want money," I snarled, breathing his hot breath. "You want me." I plugged his pucker again, holding the lip-lock longer and harder this time, really working the guy's soft, wet mouth. Until his body went limp as Sammy Wong's famous egg noodles.

"I saw it in your eyes – and groin. Those pictures turn you on. You got all hard and hot lensing me and Rigoletti. Didn't you, blackmailer!?"

He nodded so hard his neck creaked.

I sent a hand sailing down to his crotch, grabbing onto the pole testing the seams of his checkered five & dime suit. He groaned, eyelids all a-flutter. I kissed him again, shooting my tongue into his open mouth, exploring, hand squeezing, rubbing, his stiff, clothed cock.

"You want to suck my cock?" I growled.

His eyes burst open. He bubbled affirmatives.

"Then do it," I rasped, shoving him down to his knees.

He had me unbelted and unbuttoned in the time it took to spring a dirty crook with a pile of filthy lucre. He pulled my semi-hard out of my drawers and clung to it, like it was the stuff that wet dreams are made of. Then he started fisting my swelling dick with a damp paw, two, really pulling. Getting me hard as the Law's supposed to be on mug's like him.

"It's b-beautiful," Convey marveled. "So ..."

"So, do you have an answer for the class, Mr. Schiller?"

I blinked blur out of my eyes, mouthed, "Huh?"

The class laughed. Professor Convey didn't. "My question was: how did Raymond Chandler reshape and refine what Dashiell Hammett had done earlier in *Hardboiled*, turn it into true literature?"

I blinked again, the fog lifting slowly from my brain. I stared at Professor Convey, the man's tanned, rugged face, his shock of blonde-white hair and piercing blue eyes, full lips, thick body immaculately clothed in a soft, brown turtleneck and tan, gabardine pants. "Hammett?" I stalled.

The class erupted with more laughter. Professor Convey snorted. "If you have any intention of passing Hardboiled American Literature of the 1930s, Mr. Schiller, I suggest you start paying attention in class."

He moved on to another student, one who was actually compos mentis. I crossed my legs, burying my achingly-hard erection between my hot thighs.

\# \# \# \# \#

Class over, I waited for Professor Convey in the hallway. Not to talk to the man, to tail him. I just had to know more about the thirty-something literary hunk – where he lived, and with whom, his hobbies, his turn-offs, and, god yes, his turn-ons. Although I appreciated the hardboiled scribblings of Horace McCoy and Edward Anderson and James M. Cain and Raymond Chandler, I appreciated the hard, boiled body and hot good looks of Professor Convey even more.

He finally exited the classroom, strode down the hall, smooth-leathered folio tucked under his left arm, as always. I loitered over the water fountain, spraying the side of my face, absorbed in the man's taut, round buttocks as they shuddered back and forth in his tight slacks.

"You gonna take a shower, too, bub?"

I jerked my head around, stared at the gum-smacking co-ed waiting for her turn at the tap. Then I fled down the hall after the professor. He was just exiting the Arts Building, striding out into the crisp fall day. I trailed after him.

His house was a couple of blocks off-campus – a modest, blue and white bungalow that smacked of singlehood. I rejoiced, from behind a big, old oak tree in the tiny park across from the man's house. A light went on in the living room, and I settled in alongside the bark.

Three minutes later, my mind was wandering off on its own again. Back to a Depression-era scene playing out in a big-city D.A.'s office. There was a man on the floor, on his knees, the hardboiled D.A.'s huge cock in his trembling hands …

"So big and hard and smooth," Convey breathed, stroking in awe.

The mug was really getting through to me, my cock throbbing, body seeping heat and balls tightening. Shivers of sensual delight prickled my skin, as the guy vigorously two-fisted my prick. But I didn't let on to Convey. I was the one doing him a favor.

"I told you to suck it," I gritted.

He looked up at me with his baby-blues, drool crowding the corners of his mouth. Then he bent my rod down with his humid mitts and gulped my shining hood.

I shook, a little.

The guy's warm, thick mouthflaps stretched over my mushroomed cockhead and he started sucking on my cap, wet, eager tongue swabbing the pulsing underside of my dick. He moved his head forward, taking rigid shaft into his hot, damp maw.

I stripped off my jacket and tie and shirt, draping them carefully over the back of a green leather chair, then letting the

Nerdvana

dirty blackmailer get a good gander at my gleaming-white, muscle-humped torso. He got an eyeful, all right, along with his mouthful, watching me pinch a pair of stiffened pink nipples even stiffer, as he shifted his head to and fro, slid his lips up and down my dong, sucking on my cock.

He grabbed my balls and squeezed. I bucked my hips, fingernails biting into my nipples. Convey's eyes lit up like a Wurlitzer. He excitedly pulled my gleaming rod out of his mouth and slammed it up against my washboard abdomen. He stuck out his tongue and lapped at my pinned prick, painting pipe with hot spit, dragging his beaded, red velvet tongue over the length of my shaft, up from my hairy balls to my bloated cap, over and over.

Until my sacked sperm started heading for higher ground. "You're going to take it in the ass," I informed the ardent cock-lick, pushing him away in the nick of time.

He shucked his pants and drawers like it was bath-time at the flophouse. He spread out on his hands and knees. His ass was small, tight, the mounded half-moons dusted with blonde-white hair. I got in behind and spread his crack, spat into his asshole.

"Fuck me, big man!" he squealed.

And I obliged.

I speared my slimy dickhead into his manhole, popping his rim, barging meat down his chute. He groaned, grabbing up his cock and tugging, hard, urgent strokes, as I sunk shaft inside him to the fur-line.

"You're not going to the papers with those pictures of me and Rigoletti, Convey – if you know what's good for you." I gripped the mug's narrow waist and pumped him, once, slamming the statement home, making my case.

"Yes … I mean, no – I won't go to the papers!" he cried, feeling the full impact of what was good for him.

I started churning his chute, reaming him, setting his body to rocking and his cheeks to gyrating. I surged with the wicked sight, the wanton feel, of my cock plunging that man's ass.

I slammed back and forth in Convey's hungry chute. His face was buried in the broadloom, hand desperately working his own cock. The crisp smack of my powerful thighs against his rippling butt cheeks filled the heated room, making a sweet mockery of my oath, and office.

Convey clutched at a chair leg for support. It knocked against the wall as I cocked him, knocking …

Someone was knocking on Professor Convey's front door.

My eyes came back into focus. I pulled my fingernails out of the oak.

A guy about my age was knuckling the professor's door. The door opened, and my hero appeared. The two men exchanged greetings, then quick glances up and down the quiet, leafy street. Before the door closed on them.

I looked right, left, back at the three kids sitting on the swings staring at me. I raced across the street, in behind Professor Convey's bungalow. His backyard was as small as his house, withered tomato plants filling most of it. A light burned in the partially-open kitchen window, and I ducked down and latched onto the frame, peeking over and in.

"Five hundred dollars, Brady – give it or leave it," Professor Convey stated, holding up a manila envelope.

Brady was a buzzcut blonde, with the cinder-block head, lantern face, and brick house body that spelled 'football' in big, white letters on his university jacket. "That's a lotta green," he groused, rubbing the back of his sun burnt neck. "The test's only worth ten percent of my final mark."

"Ten out of ten's better than zero. And don't complain to me about money, Brady. I happen to know you're receiving more alumni support than the college's endowment fund."

I bit my lip, eyebrows skying. Professor Convey was selling exam answers! The guy was as crooked as Francois Sagat's dick.

I watched, wide-eyed, as the flat-top jock reluctantly forked over the cash, five C-notes. Professor Convey handed him the manila envelope for his efforts.

I studied the situation, the professor's rugged body and Daniel Craigesque face, wondering: what would hardboiled PI Philip Marlowe do in this situation? The Continental Op? Any twenty-minute yegg from the pages of the hardboiled literature the 'good' professor taught?

And as I was pondering, a bird suddenly let loose a caw and took a swoop at my head. There must've been a nest or feeder nearby. Tweety taloned my hair, and I slammed my face up against the kitchen window to get away. Alerting the parties inside.

Brady tucked the answer envelope under his arm like it was made of pigskin. He barreled out of the kitchen, steaming for the front exit. While Professor Convey dashed out the back door and splayed me up against the wall like a cockroach.

"Mr. Schiller," he growled, shaking his head. Before yanking me off the wall and marching me inside his house.

He slammed me down into a kitchen chair, towering and glowering over me. "Just what did you see, Schiller?"

I swallowed hard and looked up at – but no longer 'to' – him. He wasn't a revered sexpot scholar anymore; he was just a man – a greedy, grubbing man like the rest of us, with five bills in his pocket and plenty more where that came from. And I was just a hard-up college kid – like any student outside of the athletic program and the blueblood set – who could really use some extra dough. Tuition and textbooks didn't come cheap, like academic integrity.

I stood up, standing tall, thrusting out what little chin I had to the point where it just about poked Convey in the chest. "I saw you selling test answers to the starting D-line, is what I saw. Grades for *gelt*." I squared my bony shoulders. "And now I want a piece of the action. And a boost in my grades."

Convey rubbed his dimpled chin with a big, brown mitt. Then slapped me across the face, sending my glasses and bravado flying.

"You pay attention here, but not in class, eh?" he mused. "Just why were you watching me, anyway?"

I hung my head like a bum in a breadline.

"I think I know why," Professor Convey continued. He reached out and lifted my chin, staring into my watery eyes. "Maybe we can make some sort of ... arrangement."

I lit up like a Philco radio.

Professor Convey gripped my shoulders and shoved me down to my knees, had his belt and zipper undone before my brain had even stopped spinning. Then, like an astute educator, he observed, "I've noticed the looks you've given me in class ... Melvin. I understand why your attention wanders."

I gulped, staring at the big bulge in the big man's blazingly white briefs. It was moving, growing, uncoiling, taking shape long and hard right in front of me, stretching the fabric and the edges of my endurance. Professor Convey dug his hand in and pulled his cock out, slapping my burning face with it.

"This is what you really want, isn't it, blackmailer?"

I answered by eagerly grabbing onto the man's monster erection, the both of us shuddering with the erotic impact. His huge snake pulsed in my hot little hand, both hands, as I took hold and tugged.

The professor's cock was beautiful – pink and smooth, clean-cut, purple hood thick and shining. I pumped and pumped his pulsating shaft with my sweaty hands, pulling so hard his balls flapped.

He stood firm, hips outthrust, thunder cock filling my worshipping hands and eyes. "You want to suck on my cock, don't you?" he said. "Well, do it."

I pulled his awesome tool down until his bloated hood was level with my mouth, slit staring me in the eyes. Then I opened wide and engulfed his cockhead.

"Yes!" he groaned, clutching my black curls.

His hood was soft and chewable. I pulled on it with my lips, scraped it with my teeth, tongue swabbing shaft. I felt the man's entire body vibrate through his cock.

He yanked my head forward, forcing more of his meat into my mouth. I happily consumed all I could, before gagging, his cap bumping against the back of my throat. He grunted and pumped his hips, fucking my mouth.

I gripped Professor Convey's moving hips and went cross-eyed watching his gleaming pole glide back and forth between my stretched lips, pulsing shaft bulging my cheeks, hood tickling my tonsils. He tasted so very good, filled me up so very well.

He churned my mouth until snot bubbled out of my nose and spit hung down in spaghetti strings from the corners of my overfull kisser. Then I grabbed his hairy balls and squeezed, and he pumped even faster, fucking my face like it was his own personal glory-hole.

I gained strength from the man's strength, from what he was doing to me and what I was doing to him. I jerked my head back, leaving him dangling and dripping. I gulped for air and courageously stated, "I'm going to fuck you."

"Like hell you are!" Professor Convey roared. "That's a man's job."

He shoved me backwards, toppling me onto all-fours. Then he pulled my pants and shorts down, digging in behind me with his now-latexed prick and a bottle of lube. I clawed at the tile, as he greased my crack, brought the hardboiled home by busting my butthole and cramming cock down my chute.

"Fuck me, big man!" I squealed.

And he obliged.

Professor Convey hung onto my hips and pounded his cock into my ass, stretching my chute like never before. I flooded with wicked, tingling heat, sliding back and forth on the linoleum, desperately pulling on my own numb-hard dong whenever I could.

"Now you're getting what you deserve!" the professor bellowed, spanking my cheeks with his heavy balls, blowing me wide open with his sledge of a cock.

I frantically jacked in rhythm to the man's pistoning prick, face mopping the floor, body and ass swollen with sexual electricity, brimming with sensual joy. The sharp, quick smack of the professor's powerful thighs against my rippling buttocks was erotic music to my ears, striking just above our ragged grunting and groaning.

"Here it comes, Melvin! The payoff!"

His rugged body jerked, his cock jumping in my butt. Hot cum spilled into his condom, deep within my ass. Just as my own balls boiled over, and I was jolted by ecstasy, spurting jizz all over the floor in rapid, fiery bursts.

We danced around like we were dodging bullets, coming and coming and coming, connected at the ass and cock. I full-body quivered with the ball-draining strength of my hand-cranked orgasm, the wicked rush of the big man emptying himself inside my raw, fucked-over anus.

My bank account and grades are as low as ever these days. But at least I'm getting all the hot, hardboiled sex and literature I can handle. Professor Convey gives me what I want, if not always what I ask for.

# LUST CONSULTANT
# Dalton

I drove onto the sprawling office campus and parked my Prius in the visitor's section. I stepped out of the car into the cool morning air and smelled fresh cut grass and mulch from the manicured beds that surrounded the buildings. I hadn't been to this particular office park in several years, and they'd both added buildings and made it look a whole lot nicer. I reached back into the car and grabbed my laptop bag and my tool bag and headed for the reception desk. I'd gotten a call from their IT director the day before asking if I could help iron out some issues that were popping up on the network in a new building they were about to staff.

The lobby was all light hardwoods, soft lighting and neutral colors, but my eye was immediately drawn to a very tasty young man behind the main desk. I stood a little straighter and tried to put on my best friendly but sexy smile as I stood before him. "Can I help you?" he asked in a low, very provocative voice that made the hair on my neck stand up.

"I'm here to work on the network problems in the new building. I think I'm supposed to see someone named Todd," I said, pulling a slip of paper out of my shirt pocket and looking at it.

"Oh good, he's been expecting you. Just let me call Todd and could I have your name?" He looked up at me expectantly, a certain gleam in his eye. Was I seeing things? He did look vaguely familiar as if I'd seen him in a club or bar in the past.

"Sure, I'm Terry."

"Nice name. I'm Stu by the way," he said, extending a hand and picking up the phone with the other. His hand was soft, dry and his grip firm. He smiled at me meaningfully as he spoke into the phone then he stood up and came around the desk. "Todd

153

wants me to bring you over to the new building," he said, motioning me to follow as we turned and headed out the front door. As we walked along the paved paths to a building about 200 yards away, I caught him checking me out, and when we got to the new building, I felt his crotch brush against me as we went through the door after he had swiped his card through the lock. It was a very nice, firm crotch.

We stood in another lobby much like the one in the main building, but it was all deathly silent. We walked through a door down a long corridor with cube farms every so often and glassed in offices in between. This was obviously one huge operation. The company, a well-known Internet firm, was obviously doing well. I saw gleaming desks and fresh computers all over the place. It was like they were just waiting to bring in the people but everything right down to paperclips was in place.

I saw a light at the end of the hall coming from an open door on the right when Stu stopped and put a soft hand on my arm. We turned to face one another in the dim hallway, and he smiled, his brown eyes twinkling beneath his unruly mop of sexy dirty blonde hair. "Todd is down there in the control room, I have to get back to my desk. If you need anything, just give me a call; my extension is 2356 on the internal system. Are you just here for the day and flying home or spending the night?" he asked, his intentions now crystal clear.

"I'm just here for the day, but I only live about half an hour away," I said, surveying his slim frame and the lightly muscled arms. He smiled even wider, gave me a light pat on the butt. "Have I seen you maybe at The Tool Box?" I said, naming a popular gay bar downtown. He smiled and looked at me more closely.

"Maybe, maybe indeed," he said and headed off. My cock had jumped in my pants at his touch. "Oh, just one thing," said Stu, turning back. "Watch out around Todd, he is such a heartbreaker," he grinned and walked away. Wow.

154

I guess a little explanation is in order here. I work as a freelance network consultant. I went to college for computers, but I always liked hardware much more than software (no pun intended there). Even in high school computer club, I had way more fun fixing computers than programming. As for sex, I always preferred guys, and in college and high school, I found that many of the smarter guys I met were much the same. We'd all been nerds in high school and never had a whole lot of luck or interest in the female department. Add to that some bad glasses, braces, and insecurity, on my part, and you had a pretty lousy shot at a conventional social life. But among my smart gay brothers, you would have been amazed at the mount of sex we managed to fit in after school in certain deserted areas of the silent building. Just thinking about certain rooms and what we used to do there still gives me a thrill.

In college I ditched the glasses for contacts, and lost the braces; started running and changed my hairstyle. I was now a nice looking guy with a nice tight body, a thick, eight-inch cock (though not quite the proverbial beer can) and a real taste for sex. I had several long-term relationships in and after college, but as of today, I was single and horny as hell. My last sexual encounter was a mellow little JO party at a friend's house the previous week. A nice looking black guy with a short but amazingly thick cock and I had really hit it off and spent some real quality time in a guest bedroom, but he hadn't called since. Oh well. He did have great hands though.

I walked down the hall, my cock half hard in my jeans and found the door to the control room wide open. The room was like something out of a sci-fi movie with server racks, switches, flat screens and miles of wires all neatly arranged around a horseshoe shaped central control desk. Sitting at the desk was, indeed, a heartbreaker. Todd was about my age, say late 20s with dark brown hair, a tight weightlifters body that was poured into khakis and a very well fitting red polo shirt with the company logo on the right breast. He heard me walk in and swiveled in his chair. He had mesmerizing green eyes and as he stood to his full six feet plus and held out his hand, my mouth went dry as I watched the muscles on his thick arms ripple.

"You must be Terry. You come highly recommended." We shook hands and my half hard cock went to full staff as his large, muscular hand almost swallowed mine in a warm, steady grip that made my mind reel. The picture of that paw wrapped around my cock immediately sprang into my mind, and it was everything I could do not to drop my pants for him. But, being a professional, I smiled and nodded as he described the problem he was having. I quickly attached my laptop to their main switch and found a number of issues with the routing tables and a few other technical issues. I showed him what I found while he stood very close to me as we stared down at my screen. I could feel the heat of his body and my erection, which had subsided while I was working, was back with a vengeance. I glanced down, and to my amazement, he had a huge bulge in his pants, too. I guess he liked me. Well, I hope he liked me.

We worked on the problem for a few more minutes and then he turned to me. "Terry, you obviously have this nailed. I'm going down the hall to my office to test a few things from the other side of the network while you finalize the changes. When you're done, why don't you come find me and we can make sure everything works." The way he said those last words and the glimmer of lust in his eye made me weak in the knees. He picked up a laptop and walked out, his tight ass swaying in a way that made my cock absolutely ache for release. I had half a mind to find a men's room and jerk off real quick, but something stopped me. I turned back to my computer and quickly adjusted the software in the switch. I ran several tests over the next hour and soon had things humming.

When I was completely sure the network was set up right, I unplugged my laptop and slipped it back in its case. I looked at my watch, and it was nearing 11:00 am. I walked down the quiet hall till I heard the soft tapping of computer keys. I walked into a large office with a huge leather couch against one wall and a big desk opposite. Todd was leaning back on the couch, the picture of relaxed confidence; his laptop sitting next to him as he tapped at a few keys. I looked at the screen and saw a small movie window open. As I got closer I heard soft moans from the computer and suddenly realized he was looking at a movie of two men having sex. They were both Latino, well hung and covered in sweat. One was on his back on a bed, the other stood next to it holding the first guy's legs high in the air as he pounded his ass with what had to be a ten-inch cock. I just love Internet porn.

Todd smiled up at me. "Just testing the Web filter. Can't have the employees watching stuff like this on company time. Guess I'll have to adjust it a little more so this sort of thing can't get through. Pity though. Don't you think people are more relaxed and work better after a good orgasm?" the bulge in his pants was massive, as was mine, and I could feel his eyes travel down my body and come to rest on my straining cock.

"Sounds like a good idea to me," I said, my voice just above a whisper. Then, as if in a dream, he stood and walked to me until he towered above me, my nose inches from his muscled chest. I looked up into his glittering eyes. "Uh, should we test your theory?" I asked, trying to be clever, but desperately wanting to touch him.

"Considering all the good work we just did, I think we really should." He placed a warm hand under my chin and leaned down. I smelled a light musk aftershave and mint on his breath as his lips met mine. The kiss was hot, wet and endless, before he pulled back, much to my disappointment. Wordlessly, he closed the office door, and then dropped all the blinds until we stood in semi-darkness in the middle of the room. "Why don't you show me the rest of your equipment," he said in a teasing tone, a lusty smile on his face. I didn't need to be asked twice. I unbuttoned my shirt and dropped it to the floor, kicked off my sneakers and then slid my jeans off. I wore no underwear and my cock and balls were waxed all the way back to my anus. I had just left a small tuft of brown curls above my shaft. I reached down to remove my small white ankle socks when I felt his hands on me.

"Leave the socks on, I think it looks really cute," he whispered as he moved behind me and ran his hands from my shoulders down to my nipples. He moved in front of me and began to suck and lick at my nipples while his hands moved down and cupped my ass, squeezing and massaging. Then he kissed his way down and began to slowly lick my huge, quivering boner. His touch was knowing, gentle and soon had me groaning in ecstasy. He kissed the head of my cock, licking away the salty precum that was now leaking freely. His hands continued to knead my ass cheeks, but his long fingers now began to slowly probe between them. He moved away from the head of my cock, dipping his head lower until I felt his warm mouth close around my balls, sucking and licking them while a finger began to tickle my sweat-covered anus.

"Mmmmm," I heard him say as he stood and quickly stripped. I wanted to unwrap him like some huge Christmas present, but he was way too quick for me. I looked at his incredible body and nearly passed out. His chest was like a chiseled sculpture with perfectly defined pecs and abs. His manhood was just gorgeous. He was fully waxed and smooth, not a hair in sight. His cock was perhaps an inch longer than mine, but slimmer (thank God!) so the thought of it sliding into me went from scary to I couldn't wait. His ass was beyond beautiful; with perfectly rounded cheeks and smooth, perfect skin. I was now so hot; I didn't know what to do first. He made the choice for me. "Top or bottom?" he asked.

"Both. I like to give and receive," I said, surprising him. I know many guys are into one or the other, but I've always liked to keep my options open. "How about you; what do you want?" I asked with a smile. I reached out and stroked his cock, which was hard and sticking way up.

"Well, normally I like to be on top, but in your case, I think I'll have one from column A and one from column B," he said with a laugh. He lay back on the couch and lifted his legs high in the air, exposing his perfect, brown hole to my hungry eyes. "There's some lube and condoms in the center desk drawer," he said. I went to the desk and grabbed both and then knelt on the couch between his wide-open legs. I leaned down and breathed in his manly scent and groaned in satisfaction. I began to lick him, starting with his heavy, soft sack, running my tongue over the skin and then taking his huge nuts into my mouth one at a time. He tasted salty and his musk aftershave lingered just enough.

"Oh yeah baby, that's the stuff!" he cried out as I moved downward and swirled my tongue over and around his tight little hole. Here, the earthy taste of skin was almost more than I could take. I licked and savored his luscious bud for long, endless minutes as his moans grew louder until I heard the magic words flow from his lips. "Oh, give it to me, fuck me," he groaned. I sat up and quickly rolled a condom down my aching shaft and then smoothed the oily lube into his hole and all over myself. I moved closer until my cock was inches from his glistening hole. He looked up at me as I positioned myself and our eyes locked. So much passed between us in those few seconds as my cock finally came in contact with his warm body that I became lost in sensation.

I felt his strong, long legs come to rest on my shoulders as my cock began to press into him. Warmth from his body suffused me, and I felt sweat break out all over. His anus was wonderfully tight, and I pushed steadily but slowly so as to not hurt him. I felt his muscles grasp and move around me as I slid inside his body. He moaned and pressed himself against me, driving my cock in until my naked balls came to rest against his tight, muscular ass. "So good," he whispered, his body shivering with pleasure. I began my thrusts very slowly, savoring his tightness and the velvety heat that surrounded my cock.

"Oh, faster," he groaned. I obliged. I began to move faster and just worked to keep myself from exploding too fast. I focused on his face as I felt my cock slide in and out of his steamy hole with ever increasing speed. His eyes were closed, and his mouth open wide as if in a silent scream as he gasped for breath. Sweat now poured freely from both of us, adding a slippery, sexy dimension to every inch of moving, touching skin. His arms were thrown back and around his head, and I was surprised that he wasn't jerking himself off. I looked down at his cock, and it was half hard with a growing pool of clear, glistening liquid gathering on his flat belly around the head. I reached down and began to stroke his cock, but he quickly grasped my wrist and pushed it away. "No, I'm saving it for your beautiful ass," he gasped. That thought; that image, ignited the last of my lust.

"Oh!" I cried out as I felt my nuts pull up tight against my body and the shivering, screaming ecstasy ripped through me at light speed. I cried out again and again as I emptied myself deep inside his churning, oily hole. My eyes closed and I watched as huge waves of green and blue rolled by. My whole body was on fire and I panted and gasped as the pleasure climaxed and then slowly ebbed. I slowed my movements until I came to rest, my chest heaving. He slipped his legs down from my shoulders and I crumpled forward onto his sweaty chest. His strong arms held me tightly and he kissed me hungrily.

I kissed him back between gasps for breath and felt my cock slowly soften and slide from his warm body. As it did, I became aware of his cock, trapped under me, as it grew and swelled rapidly as soon as his ass was empty. "How do you want me?" I moaned, coming shakily to my feet beside the couch. He reached to the floor and grabbed a condom package. As he unwrapped it and rolled it down his now solid shaft, he looked up at me through half lidded eyes.

"Standing up, bent over the desk," he said, his voice heavy with lust. I moved slowly to the large oak desk and stood in front of it. I lowered myself carefully until my chest and upper body rested on the cool, light wood. I spread my feet apart, fully exposing my bottom to him and took a deep breath as I felt his hands stroke my sweat covered ass cheeks. I crossed my hands behind my back and closed my eyes.

"Tie my hands, it's one of my favorite fantasies," I said.

"Mmm, I love a little kink." I heard him move to the front of the desk and rummage in a drawer then move back behind me. "Hope you like silk baby." I felt the soft touch as a strip of material, a tie I guess, was quickly wrapped around my wrists and then knotted, securely but not so tight as to hurt. My cock, now dangling between my legs, still inside the condom, began to harden. I loved the fantasy of being taken from behind by someone much bigger and stronger than myself. It was something I'd seen many years ago in a gay porno, and it still made me hot as hell anytime someone did it to me. After he tied me up, he quickly worked the lube deep into me with one, then two fingers. I moaned as his expert touch brought my half-hard cock to full attention.

"You look so hot like that," I heard him say as I felt his pole slide against my anus. That wonderful first contact when a new penis first slips into your body is like nothing else. The head was nice and wide and opened me up smoothly. I breathed in and out as I relaxed and welcomed him inside me. His cock was so wonderful, just the right length and thickness and he slipped quickly deep into my heated core. The pressure against my prostate was exquisite, and my cock was now rock hard. I felt him come to rest against me when he was fully inside and his hands moved underneath and carefully pulled the full condom off my cock. I groaned in pleasure as his lubed hand slid up and down my shaft.

"Sorry baby, but I don't think I'm going to last very long. Your ass is so tight and you fucked me so good."

"It's OK. I'm going to blow in no time," I moaned as he began to stroke my penis and fuck my hungry ass in perfect rhythm.

"Maybe I'll just have to leave you tied up and fuck you all afternoon," he said, tying into my fantasy as if he'd written it.

"I'm your fuck toy. You can fuck me till next year," I cried as his cock plunged inside me. I couldn't believe the level of pleasure he was bringing me. My whole body was like a giant nerve. His hand on my cock was stroking and getting me closer and closer to shooting all over the front of the desk while his cock stroked and massaged my insides as if it had been custom made for me. I closed my eyes and just focused on the sensations, sounds and smells as we climbed ever upwards together. The sweat from our bodies now wafted about the office like a cloud of pure sex and the slurping, squishing noises of his cock moving in and out of me and his hand on my cock were like a sensual song in my ears.

"Oh baby, I can't wait anymore," I heard him groan as his movements became jerky and hurried. "Come with me, please come with me!"

I did. With a soft groan of pure release, my body began shake and then spasm as huge wads of cum leapt from my cock as his hot cream began to jet inside my ass. We both were lost for an eternity as we swayed, sweated and came together. His orgasm was long and strong while mine was fast and so intense as to be almost painful. It was that knife-edge between tickling and unbounded orgasmic pleasure. Each time his hand slid over the super sensitive head of my cock, I cried out and came a little more and each time his cock hit my prostate, the pleasure inside me blossomed outwards and merged. I could actually feel the top of the condom inside me expand with his huge load and part of me wanted it to burst, so I could feel his hot juices slowly ooze from me. Perhaps later, after we got to know each other better.

Finally, with a groan, he released my penis and stopped moving, his cock still deeply embedded in my hole. I felt the sweat dripping from him onto my back as he stooped over me, his hands on either side of my body supporting him on the edge of the desk. I felt his soft lips brush the back of my neck in a tender kiss. "That was the best ever baby. Your ass was made for my cock. I am going to fuck you again as soon as I get hard." He kept kissing my neck and I moaned softly.

"Oh yes, please fuck me again and again," I groaned. "Your cock is the best." He slowly pulled himself from my body leaving me empty and suddenly close to tears for some stupid reason. I mean I'd just met this guy, and I had no idea if I'd ever see him again after this, yet I wanted him back inside me as if we'd been in love for years. This had never happened before. Maybe Stu was right. Todd was a heartbreaker. Then from out of nowhere a soft, sexy voice intruded.

"I warned you Terry." Both of us turned and standing in the doorway was Stu. He was naked, his small cock stuck out in front of him at full erection and he was smiling at us. "You know I almost came just watching you two," he said as he walked slowly inside, closing the door behind him. "You know Todd, I really wanted him for myself," said Stu.

"Sorry honey, he is mine; all mine," said Todd as he helped me down off the desk to kneel on the soft carpet, my hands still securely bound behind me. I studied Stu's nude form and liked what I saw. His cock was small, maybe only six inches and slender, but he had oddly huge balls and his penis was beautifully formed and classic with a heavy foreskin that he toyed with as he stood before us. My cock hung limply having just come twice inside half an hour, but having these two sexy naked men surround me and discuss me like I was so much meat was getting me hot again. The idea of a threesome was also one of my fantasies that I had yet to explore.

"Todd, I don't mind if you share me," I said, my voice obviously betraying my lust. Todd laughed and leaned down to kiss my lips.

"Terry, you should know that Stu and I have been friends with benefits for awhile now, but you and I are going to be so much more." He kissed me again and then walked into a small bathroom on the other side of the room and closed the door. I looked up at Stu as he stood in front of me, his hard cock inches from my mouth.

"Sweety, you have no idea how lucky you are," he said. Then he stroked his cock and slid it into my mouth. I looked up at him as I sucked and soon felt the welcome hands of Todd slide over my chest. They used me for the rest of the afternoon, and by the time I drove away, I could barely move I was so tired. It had been the ultimate day for fantasies. I think my favorite was when Todd was fucking my ass for about the fourth time while Stu and I did a really hot 69. The feeling of having a warm, loving mouth around your cock while an equally warm and loving cock fills you to the brim is just about impossible to describe.

But that was nothing compared to what Todd did to me the following weekend when he came over to my place, and we barely left the bedroom. It's been six months since then, and I'm still Todd's favorite fuck toy. But he's mine, too, and he loves getting tied to the bed now and again and being my toy now that we're living together. Oh, and Stu? He found a nice guy a few months ago and every once in awhile we all get together for a bareback foursome. Talk about good times.

# BECOMING
## Jim Clark

Dan tried to focus on the rows and rows of figures on the computer screen in front of him. But once again he failed, and his head slightly turned to the right, his eyes straying to the man in the white lab coat working behind him. Dan knew it had to be his own overactive imagination, but the way Joe's long fingers were running up and down the test tube and pipette it felt as if Joe knew Dan was watching and was deliberately teasing him. Dan swallowed hard at the thought. Joe had joined the research group a month ago, and Dan still hardly knew him. But he did know the contours of Joe's body very well. Now, as his eyes traveled over the familiar thin frame, the broad shoulders tapering into the narrow waist, he questioned yet again why he was so attracted to him. Dan's type was the bronzed muscle jocks he met at the gym, not a white skinny creature from work. But there was something about Joe that kept coming back to him and pushing everyone else out whenever Dan was wanking or fucking.

Dan coughed loudly. He had been messing around for long enough and that wasn't his style. Joe didn't even turn to look at him.

"Do you play chess?" Dan was surprised by the crack in his voice. He had been practicing this line for a long time, sneaking glances at Joe when he was on the computer and noting the non-work related sites he occasionally looked at.

There was no one else in the lab at this unearthly hour in the morning, the only reason Dan had been able to drag himself out of bed was the motivation that Joe would be there alone, but Joe looked around as if trying to find the person Dan had been addressing. Finally, he turned toward Dan and nodded. He looked so vulnerable and much younger than his years, Dan had a strong urge to take him in his arms right then and just hold him tightly against his chest. Somehow he managed to resist.

"Me too, I love chess, been a while since I've found a worthy opponent though."

Joe's whole face was transformed by a wide open smile, for a moment he looked like another man, one overflowing with confidence. "What's your rating?"

Dan paused. OK, he should have done more research. If he had ever played chess in his life what would his rating have been? He didn't even know how chess rating worked, was it straight numbers, or would it be something stranger, some weird code that would reveal when a man was pretending to be interested in chess just to strike up a conversation with a guy he was irrationally attracted to?

"Two thousand. And eleven."

"Wow. Wow." There was total awe on Joe's face.

Dan mentally praised himself on his lucky guess, and now that was over with, he could move onto the more interesting business of getting to know each other.

"You have to come to my chess club. You really have to come. I'm the highest rated, and I struggled to break eighteen hundred. It would be like having a real master amongst us."

And for some reason, maybe it was the way Joe's blue eyes were looking directly at him, or perhaps it was the fact that at that precise moment the sun shone through the window making Joe's hair look even blonder, but Dan found himself making a date with Joe to go to a chess club.

"C'mon, mate, you must have learnt everything about chess by now, you've been at it all week."

Dan didn't turn around. He knew his flat mate and sometime fuck buddy, Mike, would be standing naked in the doorway stroking his thick cock, and Dan knew that he wouldn't be able to resist the sight of that toned torso. He'd already stretched his willpower much further than he thought was possible.

"Aren't you supposed to be some sort of genius or something; how come it's taking you so long to learn a simple game? My kid sister can play chess and she's only eight."

"You aren't helping. And as I've told you before, it's not about learning it; I've got to master it. By tomorrow night."

"Do you realize how sad you sound? You'd rather shut yourself up alone with some dusty books to try and impress some geek than fuck me? Are you turning straight on me?"

"It isn't just some geek; it is a very particular special one."

"Whatever. Suit yourself. I'll phone Ed."

Dan was glad when Mike shut the door and returned to his own room. He was a couple of seconds away from breaking. As it was he had a night ahead of him of listening to Mike and Ed's loud fucking while he tried to absorb all the ridiculously small print in this book about endgame. And all the time he listened he would know that at any point he could join in and they would welcome him. There was no way he would be able to focus with those thoughts in his head. He hadn't had sex for a week. He picked up his books and hastily threw them and his newly purchased chess set into a bag and headed into work.

He had never been into work so late before, it was unnatural. He headed straight up to the lab's library, which was a dim place in the middle of the day, but somehow right now the duskiness that enveloped it seemed to suit his mood. All the tables were of course empty, Dan chose one in the corner and carefully got his books out and laid out his chess set in the move he'd been studying before Mike had distracted him.

It'd been a long time since Dan's uni days, and even then it had come so easily to him that when he remembered his time as a student it was the memory of sunshine, sickly sweet cocktails and a never ending succession of fresh faced beautiful boys. But now more than ten years later he was concentrating harder than it felt he ever had before to try and learn a game he had always connected with people who didn't have anything more exciting to do.

He was so intent reading the book and trying to memorize the moves that he didn't hear the person approaching him. A quiet cough made him jump and drop his book. He had never jumped at anything before in his life. He turned to see who was standing behind him with an embarrassed smile on his face. When he saw Joe's tall, thin body he first felt joy followed quickly by a deep shame at having been caught out.

"Hi, Dan," Joe said, sounding more relaxed than he ever had before. "Can I see what you are doing?"

Dan nodded, not knowing how else he could respond. As Joe looked over Dan's shoulder, Dan stared up at the other man's face, he had the most beautiful high cheek bones, they were almost mesmerizing on their own. Maybe the delicate facial features are what had attracted him to this quiet man.

"I see you are going over the basics. I do that, too, you know, to freshen up your brain a bit. I find that by stripping everything down it can be really invigorating. Is that what you feel like, too?"

Dan wasn't sure what the other man was really talking about, but when Joe's lips had parted and said the simple word 'stripping' something deep in his stomach had stirred. It had been too long since he'd had sex.

"I feel very invigorated," Dan said.

"Seeing, you know, how we are both here, would you like a game? It's been a long time since I played with a new person. It would be ..."

"Invigorating," Dan said.

Joe smiled warmly at him.

Dan slowly put his books back into his bag, there was no place for them anymore. He was on his own. He watched as Joe quickly laid the board out and pulled a chair up beside him. He wondered if it was merely coincidence that Joe's knee was touching his own. He didn't dare move his leg and risk losing the warm feeling that was rising inside him.

Joe took a white and black pawn in his hand. He swapped them round behind his back and then placed his closed fists in front of Dan. Dan put his hand lightly on top of Joe's right hand. He let it rest there for a long moment, feeling the softness of Joe's flesh, before reluctantly moving it away. All the time he was staring into Joe's blue eyes. Joe held his stare. All his usual downward staring and nervous glances had vanished. Joe opened his palm to reveal the black pawn. He replaced the pieces back on the board and turned it round so the black pieces were on Dan's side. Neither of them spoke. Finally Joe looked down and appeared to be contemplating his first move. Dan didn't know how it could take so long to decide which pawn or knight to move. It wasn't as if there were so many options. He hoped Joe was thinking about something else. The same thing he was thinking of. He pressed his knee slightly harder against Joe's leg. Joe responded by moving the king's pawn, and then looked up again at Dan. There was no mistaking the challenging look in his eyes. Dan stared back. Was this just Joe's 'chess face,' or was there something else going on?

Dan couldn't remember any of the many tactics he had spent the week cramming. Instead he reflected Joe's move and wondered how long he would be able to keep this man's interest? There was so much intelligence in Joe's eyes, not just in his eyes, in his whole face and bearing, a quiet knowledge and wisdom that he naturally emanated. And, Dan realized that is what had attracted him from the first moment he had met him, no, it was before he'd met him. When he had first read his CV and realized that this man with all his achievements and prizes was a hard working, serious rival to his own easy intellect.

The game progressed, and Dan watched as his pieces disappeared off the board and reappeared in a neat line by Joe until Joe made a decisive move that ended in him saying clearly, "Checkmate."

Dan didn't care. He had been watching hypnotized as Joe's fingers had held and moved the small pieces. He had been enamored by the look of intent concentration on the other man's face.

"I guess you were having an off day," Joe said with a small shrug. "It is kind of late."

Dan watched as the confident face of the chess player turned back into the insecurities of the man who skittered around work trying to avoid catching anyone's attention.

"Not for me," Dan said.

"You're an insomniac, too? We have so much in common. What do you do? I work as much as I can, and I wouldn't normally tell anyone this, but I collect comic books. If I'm feeling, you know, too lonely, and the night is too long, I just look at my collection. I don't even read them. I just look. Does that sound stupid?"

There was still a small voice inside of Dan that was saying, 'yep, that sounds fucking stupid,' but the voice that spoke was a gentle one, "I'm a Batman fan. Although I have to admit that I always wanted the Joker to win."

Joe laughed, and it was a beautiful sound, for a moment Dan felt like he was the wittiest man alive.

"Have you ever been to any cons?"

"Cons?"

"Sorry, conventions. I guess you haven't. But there's one in a couple of weeks not far away, and I think I read one of the artists from the latest Batman comic is going to be there, I can't remember his name right now, I have to be honest and say I haven't read Batman for a while, I tend to read stuff not many normal people have heard of. But anyway, maybe, if you like, we could go together?"

Dan wondered if he liked this man enough to go to a convention with him, and he was surprised that the answer was yes. But if he was at the stage where he was even thinking he could face a room filled with people who normally didn't venture beyond the safety of their bedroom then he was at the stage where he had to reveal himself. He smiled at the realization he was risking losing whatever connection he had with Joe, this man whom he was more attracted to than any other he remembered, by telling him he wasn't actually a geek, that he preferred playing sports than computer games. But it had to be done.

"I have to be honest as well, Joe. I haven't read any Batman comics for a while either. A long while. Since I was about fourteen. And then it was just because I was bored and my brother had tons of them lying about. Also, I'm not a chess master. In fact this is the first chess game I've ever played."

Joe's looked confused but didn't say anything.

"I've spent the week trying to work out the game. I don't stay up late because I can't sleep, but because I like fucking. Normally about this time, I would have my cock in someone's mouth. I'm only here right now because I was desperate to try and work out how to play chess, and I knew if I stayed at home, I would end up succumbing to my flat mate and not learning anything."

"Why would you lie to me and pretend you could play? I don't get it."

Dan put his hand on the back of Joe's neck and pulled the other man toward him. Their lips touched, and for a moment they stayed silently like that, then Dan pushed his tongue between Joe's lips. Joe remained still, not responding but not pulling away. Dan released his grip.

"I lied because I wanted to do that to you. And much, much more."

Joe was staring down at the ground, and Dan was scared he'd been too forward and impatient. Why hadn't he just gone to the convention and taken it from there? But then Joe looked up, and his blue eyes held that same challenging look they had had throughout the chess game. Just looking at this man made his cock begin to harden.

"I don't want you to miss out on anything because of me." Joe said slowly as if he was carefully choosing his words. "You said you'd normally have your cock in someone's mouth right now, is that right?"

Dan didn't have to reply. Joe was already dropping to his knees and had one hand on the zipper of Dan's jeans. There was nothing awkward about the blond man anymore, he slipped Dan's hardening prick out of his jeans and with a confident touch was stroking him to a full erection. Joe's lips were parted, and it was all that Dan could do not to grab the other man's head and force it onto his cock. He was desperate for sex. He was desperate for this man. He needed to concentrate to prevent himself from exploding all over Joe's face. But he had the image in his head of Joe's sweet face dripping with his cum now. Joe reacted to Dan's need. He sped the movements of his hand up and moved his face closer to Dan's cock. He pushed his tongue out and lapped up the drops of Dan's pre-cum, then he started to kiss Dan's cock. Pressing his lips around it, encircling it with his tongue. Dan couldn't hold back, he put his hands on the back of Joe's head and with two thrusts he had jetted down Joe's throat.

Dan stroked Joe's hair as he regained his composure. Maybe it was the week break from sex, but he couldn't recall ever having come harder.

"Now it's my turn," Joe said, pulling away from Dan and standing up.

Dan smiled. He'd spent a long time fantasizing about what Joe's cock would feel like. He began to rub his hand against Joe's groin and was satisfied to find a large bulge, but Joe shook his head.

"No, I want to teach you how to play chess."

Dan looked at the forgotten chess board, which still contained the remains of his earlier defeat.

"You won't find this in any of your books," Joe said. He picked up a pawn and placed it with a seductive balance of gentleness and firmness between Dan's lips.

Dan sucked on it. He opened his mouth wide and quickly flicked his tongue over the small hard head. Joe removed the pawn with a smile.

"Bend over," he ordered.

Dan obeyed, and as a reward, he had his jeans pulled down to his ankles and the pawn pushed hard into his ass. Joe fucked him with the chess piece before dropping it into the floor and picking up the next pawn.

Dan counted down as all sixteen pawns were placed first in his mouth and then pressed inside his tight orifice. After the pawns came the rooks, knights and bishops; each new piece was an increase in size and touched him in slightly different ways. Every part of his opening was being teased by the chessmen. Joe picked up both queens at once, he broke with his routine and did not put them into Dan's mouth, but thrust them straight away into his ass. It felt like he was being fucked at the same time by two small cocks. The effect made Dan gasp, but Joe did not pleasure him in this way for long. He let the queen follow the rest of their armies and fall to the floor. He picked up both kings, passing one to Dan to lick and pressing the other one hard into Dan's ass. He fucked him harder with the black king than he had with any of the other pieces. Dan pushed his ass out further wanting more, but Joe stopped, and Dan heard the clink as the piece fell to the floor. For a moment, the only sound was him slurping on the other king. Then the still air of the library was filled with Dan's moans as Joe rammed the full length of his cock inside him. Joe's cock was big; there was a slight pain, but the pleasure made every other feeling disappear. Joe was fucking him hard, pulling almost completely out then forcing Dan's ass to spread once again to take him all. Dan felt his body molding to the other man's. He tried to push his hips back into Joe's groin, but Joe had a firm grip on him and didn't allow him to move. He was much stronger than he looked. Dan felt pure excitement being held in the power of this clever, shy, but obviously dominant man. He wanted this feeling to never end, but when Joe gasped that he was about to come, the sensation was echoed in Dan's own body. As Joe filled Dan's ass up, Dan's own cream shot out over the now deserted chessboard.

They sat on the library floor their bodies entwined.

"So you think you'll come to the con then?" Joe casually asked.

"Yeah," Dan replied, "I think I will."

"Then maybe you should come back to my house, and you know, read a few comics to get a feel for it."

"Yeah, that sounds like a good idea, and you could show me a few more chess moves, too."

"I can do that right now," Joe said, leaning into kiss Dan. He reached his hand out to find the king amongst the pieces lying beneath them on the floor.

Dan felt an inner happiness in the knowledge that it was going to be a lot of fun becoming a nerd.

# THE GRAND DECEPTION
# Stephen Osborne

Something hit me hard in the square of my back, sending me stumbling forward. My textbooks and papers went flying. Totally off-balance, I slammed into a nearby locker, which caused a big enough bang that it seemed everyone in the hall stopped what they were doing to watch me. I groaned from the pain and pushed my glasses back up my nose, so I wouldn't suffer the further indignity of having them fall off. I knew before I even turned around that I'd been hit by none other than John Miller, our school's star basketball player.

Sure enough, Miller and his cronies were standing there, grinning like idiots. "Better watch your step, Puterbaugh," Miller said with a mocking laugh. He always pronounced my last name by drawing out the first syllable, like my moniker was something that could be smelled. "You might trip and fall and lose all your books."

Dennis Brewster, the gangly center of the team with the bad skin and huge, hooked nose, snorted loudly. "What a dweeb!"

Vicki Small broke away from the little gang that was assembled around the water fountains to come to my rescue. She glared at Miller and company as she helped me pick up my books and papers. "You idiots," she declared. "Graduation is only a few weeks away. You're supposed to be adults now, not little school bullies who have nothing better to do than pick on others."

"I wasn't picking on him," Miller claimed with mock indignation. "I may have accidentally brushed up against him ..."

"You shoved him!" There was venom in Vicki's tone. "I'm not blind. I saw what happened. You really need to grow up."

All traces of laughter left Miller's face. He and his friends began to move on, but Miller made sure he pressed up against me as he passed. I'm not short, but he still towered over me by a good five inches. He looked down at me in derision. "Maybe Puterbaugh here should grow some balls."

One of the other jocks guffawed as if this was the funniest thing he'd ever heard. "Yeah, and then one of his fag friends could suck on them!" I felt my cheeks redden as they continued on down the hall, jostling playfully with each other.

Vicki handed me the books she'd recovered. "Are you okay, Danny?"

Few people in the school referred to me by my first name, so it sounded odd to hear it spoken. It seemed to everyone in Jefferson High that I was Puterbaugh, the AV geek with the glasses that never stayed in place. I smiled at her. "I'm fine."

Her bright smile was like sunshine, and I found myself wishing that I knew her better. All I knew about Vicki was that she was on the cheerleading squad and that she was fairly smart. She was in my calculus class and always seemed to know the answers. She spared a final glance down the hall to where Miller and his friends were disappearing around a corner. "He thinks that just because he was a big shot on the basketball court that he can treat anyone however he wants. He's an ass." A faint glimmer of disappointment showed in her eyes. "I just wish he wasn't so good looking. It would make it easier to hate him."

"I don't have any trouble hating him," I said with a weak chuckle. "He's been pushing me around since we were freshmen."

"He's going to find out things are going to be very different in college," she said. "He won't be the big shot anymore." Vicki shook herself, as if banishing all thoughts of John Miller from her brain. "Hey, I'm having a party this weekend. Eighteenth birthday. Would you like to come?"

I nearly bit my tongue in surprise. AV geeks did not get invited to parties, especially parties thrown by the likes of Vicki

Small. I stammered for a moment before taking a deep breath and saying, in an embarrassingly squeaky voice, "Sure."

She smiled. "Good. I think it will be a lot of fun. Bring some of your friends, if you like." Vicki started to turn away, but paused as if she had just decided to make a confession to me. "You know," she said with an almost shy grin, "you're pretty cute."

What does one say to that? I swallowed hard and managed to eek out, "Thanks."

She tossed her blond hair. "See you Saturday night, then." She bounced off, rejoining her friends at the water fountains, leaving me stunned and shaken. Luckily the bell rang for the next period, and I forgot temporarily about Vicki Small and John Miller and pretty much everything as I rushed to get to class on time.

"This is stupid," Ellis said for what must have been the fifteenth time. Ellis was small and thin by nature, but seemed to be getting even smaller the closer we got to Vicki Small's house. An AV geek like myself, Ellis' shoulder length blond hair and androgynous features made him even more of a target for bullying than me. "People like us don't go to parties. We stay at home on Saturday nights and have Halo tournaments. We reread Tolkien or something. We don't go to parties."

"We don't go to parties," I informed him as I turned my car onto Vicki's street, "because we've never been invited before."

"We're not going to know anyone there," Ellis continued as if he hadn't even heard me. "I don't know why I let you talk me into this. What are we supposed to do when we get there? I don't participate in idle conversation, and I'm pretty sure no one at Vicki Small's party is going to want to have a long discourse over quantum theory. I don't drink. I don't dance. Good God, I'm not expected to dance, am I?"

"It's not mandatory," I told him. "Relax. Have fun. Meet new people. Actually, they won't even be new people. They'll mostly be people from our school, I imagine."

"I've been to that school for years and managed not to know most of them. We're mere weeks away from graduation, and now you want me to mingle with them? Why does she need a big party just because she's turning eighteen anyway? When you had your birthday a few weeks ago, all we did was rent all the Star Wars movies and eat potato chips until we puked. That's how birthdays should be celebrated."

He rambled on while I found a place to park, which ended up being nearly at the end of the block. Getting out of the car, we realized it would be impossible to miss the house. The sounds of the party could be heard even where we were. We began to walk, Ellis keeping up his litany.

"We're going to be laughed at. That's why she invited us. We're going to be the court jesters, there for everyone's amusement."

"She invited us because she likes me," I said. "As a friend, anyway."

"Cheerleaders don't like computer nerds." Ellis thought a moment before adding, "Nobody likes computer nerds."

The party was large enough that it had spilled out of the house and onto the large front porch. Dozens of people were scattered about, most of them with drinks in their hands. When we approached, someone let out a laugh, making Ellis stop in his tracks. I had to prod him to keep him moving. A dark figure bounded down the steps toward us, giggling like a hyena. As he stepped into the moonlight, I saw that it was Dennis Brewster. "Well, well, well, if it isn't Puterbaugh! And he's brought his little girlfriend with him." He was obviously intoxicated, swaying a little as he stood before us.

A light seemed to come into Ellis' eyes. "What's that you're drinking?" he asked, his tone almost accusatory.

"Beer," Brewster answered.

Ellis reached out and grabbed the cup from the basketball player. Both Brewster and I watched in shock as Ellis brought the cup up to his lips and downed the rest of the contents in a gulp. "Is there more?" he asked.

Brewster barked out a laugh and slapped Ellis hard on the shoulder. The blow made him rock a little, but Ellis just smiled as Brewster said, "You're cool, little dude. Let's go in and get you a cup of your own."

Ellis wiggled his eyebrows at me as Brewster led him up the stairs. "You told me to make friends," he said with a sly grin.

I followed them into the house but soon lost them in the crowd. It seemed that every available spot was taken up by someone, and the scene reminded me of the stateroom routine the Marx Brothers did in the movie *A Night at the Opera*. A few more people and the walls might burst, spilling party-goers out onto the lawn. Music was blasting but was so loud it was hard to tell exactly what was playing. The bass thudded, shaking my bones.

Somehow Vicki, standing near the kitchen doorway, managed to pick me out of the throng. It took her a minute to force her way through the revelers to get to me. When she did, she smiled. "I'm so glad you could come." She had to shout to be heard.

"I'm glad I did, too," I yelled back. "I came with Ellis. He came in with Brewster. Did you see where they went?" I didn't want to get separated from my friend for too long a time. Even though Brewster seemed okay (for the night, anyway), I still didn't trust him. He'd find some way to humiliate Ellis before the night was out.

A slight frown crossed Vicki's brow. "I think they passed me, going into the kitchen. The keg's in there."

I scanned the crowd. There wasn't an easy path to get through to the kitchen. I'd have to wiggle and shove my way, brushing up against people I didn't really know. Sure, most of them I recognized from school, but they had as little to do with me as I with them. I was sure that Ellis and I were the only ones of my crowd, usually dubbed 'The Geek Mob,' present. Looking at the dancing, intoxicated students gyrating around me, I suddenly felt that I'd made a mistake coming. This wasn't my crowd. I should find Ellis and leave. There wasn't anyone for me here.

I began to move through the throng and ran straight into John Miller. I mean that literally. I dodged other people, missing a stumbling Missy Cousins, obviously too drunk to dance and remain upright, but rammed right into John's chest. The collision made him slosh some beer out of his plastic cup. The beer splatted onto the carpeting, and I couldn't help but think, eighteenth birthday or not, that the Smalls weren't going to be too happy with their daughter once this party was over.

Miller didn't look too pleased himself. He looked from the spill back to me and glared. "You fucking jerk wad!" he shouted. "I'm going to teach you a fucking lesson!" Everyone around us suddenly got quiet, although the music continued to blare. He grabbed me by the collar and started walking, pulling me after him. The dancers and drinkers seemed to part, like he was Moses and they were the Red Sea. I struggled a little, but I didn't want to rip my shirt. My mother had just bought it for me, and she'd be pissed if I came home and it was torn.

He pulled me up a flight of stairs to a closed door, which I guessed was a bathroom. He tried the knob but it was locked. Miller pounded on the door and a voice answered, "Occupied!"

"Get the fuck out of there!" Miller yelled. "I've got me a fucking nerd who needs a swirly!"

A swirly. Great. The old stick-the-littler-guy's-head-into-the-toilet-and-flush routine. Miller obviously couldn't think of anything better. In his defense, he was a little on the drunk side and thinking on his feet wasn't something John did in the best of circumstances. But still, I thought he could come up with something better than a swirly.

The reedy voice inside the bathroom said, "There's another john down in the basement. Go shit down there." This was followed by some retching sounds. I recognized the voice as Paul Ott's. Poor guy. It wasn't even midnight, and already he was hugging the porcelain god.

Miller tightened his grip on my shirt and led the way back down the stairs. When we reached the bottom, there was an angry looking Vicki Small waiting for us.

Her arms were crossed. "John Miller," she said, "you let him go right now."

"He spilled my beer," he said, as if this explained everything. "I'm just going to give him a swirly. It's not like I'm going to kill him or anything."

She tried a different tactic, looking at John pleadingly. "Just let him go. I'll get you another beer."

Miller seemed to relent. "Fine," he said, letting go of my collar. The second Vicki turned her back, though, he threw his arm around my neck, pulling me against his side in a tight headlock. Under his breath he added, "I'll drink it after I take care of this fag."

He continued moving, pulling me along after him with my arms flailing. My cheek was jammed up against his bicep and I couldn't help but think of how hard it was. Before I knew it, Miller had found another set of stairs, these leading down to the basement. It didn't sound like anyone was down there. I caught sight of Dennis Brewster, who was loitering in the hallway with a beer in his hands. He laughed as he saw me in Miller's grip. There was no sign of Ellis. Before I had time to worry about where he'd gone, though, Miller dragged me down the stairs.

There was a single, shadeless light bulb illuminating the whole basement area, which consisted of a washer and dryer and a small but serviceable bathroom. John had shut the basement door behind us, cutting off most of the sounds of the party. The bass from the music still thumped in the rafters, though.

With a sigh he released me. Then with a quick movement he turned and wrapped his arms around me as his face met mine for a long, lingering kiss. I moaned slightly as his tongue slid softly into my mouth and began to explore. Suddenly the whole scenario seemed so laughable that I couldn't help but giggle, and I could feel his lips turn into a grin through our kiss. Finally we came up for air.

"What's so funny?" he asked.

"A swirly?" I kissed his neck "That was the best thing you could think of? A swirly?"

John's cheeks flushed. "Hey," he said, "it was the best way I could think of to get us some alone time." He pulled me tighter against him and kissed me again. I let my left hand explore his rock hard bicep. God, he was hot. I must have been too obvious in my admiration of his arm because suddenly the kiss sputtered and he broke away from my lips.

"Can't help it," I told him. "I love my big, tall jock."

He nuzzled the tip of my nose. "And I love my four-eyed nerd." He looked up at the rafters, obviously imagining the party-goers upstairs. "I just wish we didn't have to put up an act to fool those losers. I can't wait until we graduate and can be ourselves."

It was a conversation we'd had often, but I knew we were right to keep up our deception. After all, life would be hell for him if it came out that our basketball star liked to fuck boys, and while I had to put up with nearly the whole school calling me a geek or a fag, no one seemed to really believe that I was actually gay. And for now, that's how I wanted it.

"Keep on coming up with lame excuses like swirlies to get us alone, and you won't have to for long," I chided him.

"Hey," he protested, "I thought the headlock was pretty convincing. It really looked like I was hurting you there for a few minutes."

I laughed. "I could have got out of that, easy."

"You could not."

"Wanna wrestle" I asked, grinning up at him, "and find out?"

John suddenly lifted me up, smashing me against him in a bear hug. My feet dangled as he squeezed me. I continued to laugh even though the air was being forced out of my chest.

"You give?" he asked playfully.

"Uncle! Uncle!" He lowered me gently to the floor and we kissed again. With him pressed against me I could feel his dick growing hard in his jeans. His eyes were twinkling.

"Doesn't the winner get something?" he asked.

I glanced up at the door. "Do we have time?"

He shrugged. "We've got just a few weeks until graduation. Basketball season is long over. Who the hell cares if we get caught now? I mean, what the hell can they do now? Call us fags for a few weeks? Big deal. I'm getting tired of hiding the fact that my boyfriend is Danny Puterbaugh anyway."

He may have been a dumb jock, but John Miller was a sweetie. "So what do you want to do?" I asked, reaching down to stroke his hard-on.

"I don't care," he said, sucking in air as my attentions to his crotch brought shivers through his body.

I knew what I wanted to do, so I took off my glasses and stowed them in my breast pocket before sinking down onto my knees. John ran his hands through my hair as I unbuckled his belt and tugged down his jeans. John never wore underwear, so I didn't have to mess with anything else. His cock was stiff and hard and waiting for me. I closed my eyes and took his shaft into my mouth, tasting his familiar tang. I recalled the first time I'd sucked his dick. It had been in the front seat of his Corvette after a basketball game. He'd scored thirty-two points and wanted to celebrate. I'd wanted to suck his dick. I'd wanted to ever since I'd first clapped eyes on him. Luckily, it turned out that his way of celebrating was the same as mine. We'd driven out to the boondocks, with John worried all the time that one of his teammates might drive by and catch us. Afterwards, he'd told me how cute he thought I was. Me, cute. And that from the school basketball star. After that night we'd been secret lovers, coming up with elaborate ruses to ensure that no one found out. John became my bully at school, my lover when no one was watching.

"Oh, baby," he moaned as he began to move his hips, shoving his dick a little further into my mouth. John had a huge cock, but I'd learned how to handle it. I willed my throat to relax as he began to pick up the tempo. Soon he was face-fucking me like a madman, slamming his crotch rapidly forward until his pubic hairs tickled my nose and then pulling back, letting my lips slide along his shaft until I got to the head. I had my hands cupped onto his firm ass cheeks, and I could feel them tensing as he got closer to climax. I was ready to burst myself, so I reached down to unzip my jeans. I hated to take a hand off his hot, smooth ass, but some things just have to be done. My own cock sprang out as if gasping for air. I felt John's muscles tighten and his fists tightened, clenching tufts of my hair. "I'm coming, baby," he groaned. "I'm coming!"

He didn't have to tell me. I knew the signs. Still, I loved it when he called me his baby. My cock started shooting seconds after his juice began to fill my mouth. I swallowed hard, trying not to gag. I nearly succeeded.

Once we'd stopped shaking he helped me back to my feet, enveloping me in his arms. "You got some joy juice on your jeans."

I looked down. Sure enough, a few white globs had stained the denim. "Shit," I said.

John laughed. "There's a towel on the washing machine. And once we wet your hair, everyone will think that the wet spots are just from the swirly."

"Haven't we been gone an awfully long time for just a swirly?" I asked.

He shrugged. "You struggled."

I hugged him. Hard. Then we cleaned my jeans as best we could and headed into the bathroom, where I stuck my head down into the sink and he turned on the taps. We got my hair sopping wet. I thought it was in infantile subterfuge, but I couldn't go back on what John had said. But my God, a swirly? He was hot and a sweet lover, but no brain. Still, I loved him.

"Let's get back upstairs," he said, giving me one last kiss. "I'll see you later, okay?"

"Okay."

He bounded up the stairs, all jock energy, and burst through the door laughing. "You should see him," he yelled out to anyone who cared to listen. "He looks like a drowned rat!"

I put my glasses back on and went up the stairs myself, but with a slower, I've-just-been-tortured-by-a-jock gait. Out in the hall, I found Brewster still hovering. He had finished his beer and had a little smile on his face. There was no sign of John, who must have bounded back into the crowd to re-join the other basketball jocks.

Brewster cocked an eyebrow. "You're dripping."

"Yeah," I agreed sheepishly.

He nodded, as if in approval. "It looks convincing. Most people will probably believe you got soaked from a swirly."

I bit my lip. I started to try to think of some indignant reply, but then I chuckled. John was right. We only had a few weeks. Who cared if it got out that the school jock and the school nerd got it on? "You don't buy it, though?" I said.

Brewster made a face. "Dude, I figured out ages ago that you and John were screwing each other. Considering that he was supposed to hate you, he went out of his way to spend time with you. Plus, you guys aren't exactly Oscar winners when it comes to acting. Especially Miller. Don't worry, though. I haven't told anyone, and I'm not going to."

I couldn't think of anything to say except, "Thanks."

He'd been leaning against the wall, but now Brewster came closer to me with an almost conspiratorial air. "Can I ask you something?"

"Sure."

185

Amazingly, Dennis Brewster was actually blushing. "That friend of yours, Ellis," he said, "do you know if he's seeing anyone?"

# ADVENTURES OF JAKE #1
# Jeff Adams

"Labor Day weekend. Great for the bank account, sucks with the crowds. And could it have been more humid?" Jake muttered to no one as he entered the air-conditioned haven of the employee locker room. He'd spent most of the past 10 hours inside a Fire Force costume. He fought crime in the park and that meant he'd sweated the day away.

He tossed his goggles aside and his eyes adjusted to the florescent lights. Walking to the water cooler, he reached under his right arm to unzip the suit. The black outfit nearly cooked him on days like this. He loved wearing it though. Anything to turn into a superhero for the day was good by him. He freed his arm and pulled the top of the costume over his head and sideways so his chest was out of the hot lycra fabric.

He filled a cup with cold water and drank it down. Even though he had five minute water breaks every 20 minutes, it wasn't enough. He drew another cup of water and poured it over his chest. The short blonde hairs glistened with the sweat and cold water mix. The water felt good. It was time for a super cold shower to speed up the cool down.

He heard the water turn on in the showers, along with Tyler's familiar humming. Jake drank more water as he headed to the shower entrance. Tyler, working as Ice Force, had it good because he'd been in the Lair all day. He processed the bad guys and gave tours in air-conditioned comfort.

"Tyler!" Jake shouted as he arrived in the doorway. "Lucky you staying inside today. Whoa! Sorry dude." Jake caught Tyler working his hard on.

"Shit man. I didn't hear you come in." Tyler cupped his dick in his hands. Jake drank in the body he'd seen so many times before. Tyler was half-a-foot taller than Jake and was red haired

187

from head-to-toe, including a short buzz cut that Jake loved. Tyler and Jake had been an item for a month a year ago when they started working at the E-Force attraction, but they discovered they were better suited to being good friends than boyfriends. That didn't stop them from fooling around from time to time though.

"You might as well get in here and help me out now that you know I'm horned up."

"I'll take you up on that invitation."

Jake's cock grew stiff in his costume and it became uncomfortable fast. The costume's underwear was designed to keep private bits hidden at all costs. If you got the least bit aroused it could be quite painful. Park visitors were never the wiser, but the E-Force team long ago recognized why some team members looked pained.

"Gimmie a second to get out of this."

Back at his locker, Jake stepped out of the Fire Force get up. He tossed it on the bench, grabbed a towel and walked quickly back to the showers.

"I never get tired of seeing your hard cock," Tyler said. "It's been too long."

"Yeah," Jake said. He grabbed Tyler's cock and stroked it gently. "What's got you so worked up today?"

"This hunky guy was in the Lair. He didn't seem to be with anyone. Maybe just a solo tourist or a random E-Force geek. He was fucking hot though, man. Muscular arms like you wouldn't believe. The last hour has been rough."

Jake squeezed Tyler's cock in sympathy. "Let me take care of that for you." Jake dropped to his knees and flicked his tongue over the large mushroom-shaped head.

Tyler moaned. "Any idea how long we have?"

"Ten minutes or so, maybe." Jake slipped the hard cock between his lips and slowly worked his way toward Tyler's pubes.

"God, yes! You suck so good." Tyler stepped back against the shower wall for support. Jake moved with him, never letting the cock out of his mouth.

Jake drew Tyler deep, his tongue moving over the veiny shaft, caressing it as his suction increased. Tyler moaned and it echoed through the showers. The delicious, sweet pre-cum coming from Tyler's cock let Jake know he was pushing all the right buttons.

Jake kept the suction tight as he increased the up and down motion along the pulsating shaft. Tyler started thrusting too, shoving himself deeper in Jake's throat. Jake kept from gagging, happy to let his friend use him for a few minutes.

"Fuck man, It's gonna be a big load. I hope you're ready."

Jake gave a muffled "uhm-humpf." He ran his hand up Tyler's leg and pulled on his low-hanging balls. That put Tyler over the edge. He grunted loud, thrusting his hips against Jake's face as he unloaded streams of hot cum down Jake's throat.

Jake couldn't take it all. He had to release the cock. In return he got a face full of Tyler's white creamy load.

"Dude, when did you cum last? Are you trying to freakin' drown me?" Jake smiled up at Tyler, cum dripping off his chin.

"It's been a few days. My roomie is always around lately."

Jake stood and wiped cum from his face. "'Sokay. You tasted good as always." He licked his fingers.

Jake grabbed his cock and jerked it fiercely. He was good and slick from his own precum, so his hand moved easily over the hard rod.

"This will be quick. You got me worked up good." Jake jerked long strokes over his uncut cock, working the skin back and forth over the head for the perfect sensation. His body seized and he made short quick gasps as cum sprayed Tyler across the stomach.

Tyler laughed. "Looks like I'm not the only one that hasn't gotten off recently."

"This morning actually," Jake said, as his breathing clamed down. "But sucking cock got me goin' all over again."

The door to the locker room squeaked and they heard muffled voices.

"Shit," Jake said. He quickly turned on and stepped under a showerhead to rinse away the sticky mess. Tyler got back under his showerhead, too.

"Hey boys." It was Henry, a.k.a., Thunder Force. Jake turned and offered a wave as Henry passed the showers. "There is nothing worse than exit gate duty," Henry called out. "I'm jealous you guys are already getting cleaned up."

"Talk about cutting it close," Tyler whispered.

# # # # #

Jake stood in aisle three of World of Comics doing the evening sorting to clean up the mess from the after school crowd. He knew the stacks well after years as a customer and an employee, so it didn't take long to whip things in to shape.

"Excuse me, please. Can you help me?"

"Yes," Jake said, turning around. "What can I do for you?"

His heart skipped a beat as he stood face-to-face with Michael Hammond. Michael and Jake shared freshman lit last fall. Jake fell in lust the first day. How could he not? Michael had everything the perfect features: dark, thick, curly hair, perpetual five o'clock shadow and hairy, muscular legs. Jake thought about the legs all the time. Michael wore shorts most of the semester, and Jake looked forward to viewing those legs three times a week. Jake's preferred jerk off fantasy was stripping Michael to see how hairy he was other places.

"Wait. I know you, right?" Michael said. "Um, Jack, no. Josh ... No, it's Jake! Professor Williams, Advanced Lit, last fall. You did the paper on 'Prufrock.'"

Jake blushed, not only at being remembered, but he was overwhelmed by the enthusiasm Michael displayed.

"Um, yeah. You're Michael, right?" Jake's shyness was in overdrive. He spoke quietly, not looking Michael directly in the eye.

"Yup. Good to see you, man!" He clapped Jake on the shoulder.

"So, um, what were you looking for?" Jake tried to get back to business. What was Michael doing here? World of Comics didn't seem like a place he would hang out.

"Oh, right. So, my little brother's birthday is next week. He loves E-Force. I want to get him something really cool, but I think he's got virtually everything they make. Any ideas?"

Jake's confidence came back, presented with a question he could easily answer. "Is he into the comics or the TV show more?"

"Hmmm. I'd have to say the comics. But that probably edges out TV only by a little bit."

"Okay." Jake walked toward the E-Force comics. "In that case we can assume he's got most of the current ones." Jake pulled a comic from the rack and held it up. "Does he have the number one of the current series?"

"Oh yeah, definitely. I've seen that in the house."

Jake pondered for a moment and decided to go retro. "Does he have anything that goes back into the Elemental Force era?"

"I don't think so."

"It's a bit pricier, but you could drop back about 25 years." Jake moved over one rack and pulled another issue. "This is Elemental Force Number One. It's the definitive origin story and includes Typhoon Force, who didn't make it into the new series. They still write true to these origins today, even though they've never gone into details in the new series – comics or TV."

"Cool." Michael took the comic from Jake and carefully opened the plastic bag to look at it up close. "He will love this. I'm sure he doesn't have it. Are they any new action figures out? He's been collecting the new ones."

"Oh yeah, we just got new ones in yesterday. Come on upstairs." Jake was excited now, too. He'd already bought the two new Fire Force figures because they were awesome. Jake took the stairs two at a time, and noticed that Michael did the same. "Here we are." Jake pointed at the figures as he talked. "Two new Fire Force figures, one in his costume and one as his alter ego. Same thing for Gale Force, in costume and as her banker self. One new villain this week, too, with the release of Shocker."

"Perfect timing." Michael stepped up and took the two Fire Force figures off the wall. "He loves Fire Force, so I'll take these, too. Dude, thanks for the help."

"Glad I could," he said, idly straightening one of the displays.

"Later, man." Jake disappeared down the stairs.

Talk about jerk off material. He'd stood right next to Michael and got a good close look at him. He went back downstairs to get back to his straitening job. Luckily he'd be off work in a couple hours, so he could take care of his hard-on.

It'd been a while since Jake worked a birthday party that wasn't in the park. It was a great opportunity because it came with a hefty payday. Not only did it get him a few hundred dollars in his paycheck, it had the potential for a cash tip.

He grabbed his backpack as he got out of his car at the pizza place. He checked in with the hostess who went to get someone from the party. He was stunned when she returned with Michael.

"Dude. Twice within a week we run into each other."

"Weird, right? I didn't make the connection when I picked up the assignment last night."

"You can get changed in the office," the hostess said. "Follow me."

"Thanks." Jake went with her. Michael fell in step next to him.

"You didn't tell me you were Fire Force."

"It didn't exactly come up. I don't talk about it much, people usually find it weird I spend hours at a time dressed up like a superhero."

Michael shrugged. "Not so weird. Someone's got to be in those costumes."

"Here we are," the hostess said.

"Great. Thanks." Jake and Michael went in and closed the door.

"Hope you don't mind being stuck with me. I told my mom I'd take care of the hero, even before I knew it was you."

"It's cool." Did Michael plan to just sit here? Jake had to get changed, but Michael was right there. Jake took the costume out of his backpack and decided he didn't have a choice. He kept his back to Michael as he pulled his shirt off.

"So the semester start up good for you?" Michael asked.

"Yeah. I've already got a big exam in biology next week, but then it'll calm down for a couple weeks." He stripped off his jeans and took a deep breath as he dropped his boxers too.

Jake pulled on the briefs that went with the costume and worked to his adjust his cock and balls comfortably in the pouch.

Michael snickered behind him. "What the hell kind of underwear is that?"

Jake laughed. "Ridiculous right?" Shyness aside, he turned to face Michael. "It's designed to make sure there's no chance anyone can see any outlines in the suit."

"Dude," Michael said, shock in his voice, "you're built. I ... I didn't expect that."

Embarrassed, Jake turned around and pulled on the suit, bringing it up to his waist.

"Seriously, those baggy clothes you wear don't show you off right." Jake jumped as Michael's hands were suddenly on his shoulders, turning him around. "You look really good, Jake."

"It's, um, all part of the job. If I don't look right in the costume, I don't get to wear it."

"How long have you been Fire Force?"

"About a year and a half now." He had to reach into the underwear to adjust himself. Michael touching him gave him an instant erection, and it was straining in the briefs. He tried to be nonchalant, but he turned bright red with Michael just inches away, watching.

"Everything okay in there?" Michael gave him a mischievous grin.

"Um, yeah. It's gonna be a couple hours, gotta make sure everything's put away right." Jake pulled the suit across his chest and got his head through the hole so he could zip up.

"Wow. You are the perfect image of the action figure," Michael said as Jake zipped up the costume.

"Wait. Not done yet." Jake reached in his backpack for the hair gel and, using the small mirror he brought, he spiked his hair to match the Fire Force image. He added the orange-tinted goggles. "There. All done."

"Perfect I'd say."

They stood facing each other, practically touching noses. Jake's hard on crushed against the briefs. It was going to be a long party at this rate. An adorable smile broke across Michael's face. Before he could stop himself, Jake leaned in and put a soft kiss on Michael's lips.

"Shit, man. I'm sorry" Jake pulled away, took three steps back and ran into the desk.

Michael stepped forward. Jake cringed, waiting for the worst to happen.

"Dude, it's okay." Michael smiled again. "I got kissed by Fire Force. What's not to like?"

Michael leaned into Jake and returned the kiss. Jake eagerly kissed back. Their tongues met, pushing back and forth between their mouths. Jake's body vibrated from having this man push into him.

Jake gently pushed Michael back. "Wow." He smiled at Jake. "I can't believe I'm kissing you."

"I never thought I'd be kissing someone like you."

"Like me?" Jake grinned big, knowing where this was going.

"Yeah. Sorry, that's so ..."

"Shallow?"

"Um, yeah. I'm not used to geeks being this hot." Michael leaned in for more kissing.

"We'd better stop. I have to go dazzle your brother."

"I suppose you're right. He might not like me taking his hero. So, I'm supposed to be in charge of your visit. What does that mean anyway?"

"You just have to make sure I don't get mobbed. I can handle almost anything, but if I call for you, you'll need to help extract me from whatever is going on. It should be a pretty easy couple hours though."

"Okay. I'm here for you."

"Let's get this going then. Lead the way to the birthday boy."

# # # # #

"You're really good with kids. I think I would freak with that many 10-year-olds wanting something all the time."

"That's nothing," Jake said, stripping off the top of the costume. "Twenty kids versus thousands in the park during the summer. This was easy."

Jake screwed up his courage and stepped toward Michael. "I'm glad we're back in here alone." He backed Michael against the office door and kissed him again, this time taking the

Fred Towers

aggressive role. Jake grabbed Michael's hands, raised his arms over his head and pinned them against the door as he slid his tongue into Michael's mouth. Jake laid his full weight against Michael as his tongue moved deep. Michael moaned as the kiss broke off. Jake kept Michael pinned while looking into his brown eyes.

"You are fuckin' amazing dude. You can kiss me anytime. I don't suppose you'd want to come back to my place?"

Jake relaxed his hold on Michael, but still kept him in place. "I wish I could." He grabbed another quick kiss. "I have to go to work for the evening shift. We could, um, get together after if you want." Jake hated that it couldn't be right then, before Michael could reconsider.

"I'm in for that. What time do you finish up?"

"Around 11 by the time I get cleaned up and stuff." He peppered Michael's cheek with kisses.

"I'll wait it out." Michael kissed Jake on the chin.

Jake didn't know how to respond. Was Michael really going to wait until he got off work? "Sounds like we've got a date then," he said softly. He looked at the clock on the wall. "Shit, I gotta get going."

Jake hurriedly changed out of the suit and into his street clothes. He fished a baseball cap out of his backpack and put it on. He stuffed the suit into his pack and turned, ready to head out. Michael was grinning by the door.

"What?" Jake asked.

"You really have no idea how incredibly hot you are, do you?"

"I'm just me, man."

"It's an amazing transformation. You put on those baggy cargo shorts and the black T-shirt that's at least a size too big, and you're completely hidden away." Michael came forward to kiss Jake. He gently kissed Jake's lips. "You're trembling."

"I'm … I'm … um … not used to this."

"Just a minute ago you had me pinned to the door." He softly kissed Jake's lips again.

"I have to go." Jake gave a quick kiss to Michael and hurried out the door.

"Jake!"

Walking quickly from the restaurant, he got in his car and sped away, so he could get his thoughts together before he got to work. In his rear view mirror, he saw Michael standing at the restaurant entrance looking confused.

Jake didn't know what to think. He'd made out with Michael Hammond. Michael wanted to see him later. Was this some kind of elaborate gag? That must be it. Maybe Michael is just attracted to the Fire Force facade. Jake knew he was good at working the character, but he couldn't be Fire Force all the time.

Pulling into the parking lot, he had no answers and didn't think he was going to get any. If he was lucky Tyler would be working tonight and he could get some release with him.

# # # # #

"And I'm sure you all know Fire Force," said Thunder Force as he gave the Lair tour. Jake was glad to be in the Lair just manning master control, chatting with the guests and signing the occasional autograph. "He's helping the city stay safe by monitoring law enforcement channels. From here, he can also track where all team members are and dispatch them at a moment's notice."

Jake turned and gave a wave to the crowd. "Hello, everyone. It's great to see you all here. As you can see ..." An alarm went off and Jake, or Fire Force, went into alert mode. "Excuse me." He spun back to the control panel and saw that the bank was under siege. "Gale Force and Rock Force, this is E-Force control. The bank has issued an alert. This is a level 1 mission."

197

Everyone in the Lair was focused on Jake's station as the other tour groups all turned their attention to the large monitors Jake activated. Everyone could see the views inside and outside the bank.

"Copy that, FF," Rock Force said. "Will proceed with caution. What do you see?"

"Bank surveillance shows that it's a Sky Raiders party. There's five, three have weapons drawn covering civilians in the lobby. Two are in the vault, also with civilians."

"We are on the scene, FF, and patched into the feed."

"Copy that, I see you both."

Gale Force whipped up a storm inside the bank that had the wind and rain swirling inside the bank. The crowd in the Lair watched as the confusion gave Rock Force cover to bore up through the floor and knock out two of the Raiders in the chaos. The other Raider fired on him and the bullet bounced off and back at the Raider who fell down dead.

"Guys, the other two are closing up the fault," Fire Force said. "You've got seconds to get there before it's shut tight."

Rock Force was first on the scene and inserted himself between the door and the frame. When the door reached him it buckled and came off its large hinges. Meanwhile, Gale Force swept into the room and subdued the two Raiders.

"Looks like we're under control here, FF," Rock Force said. "The police will haul these guys away."

"Copy that. Good job guys." Jake pushed buttons on his control panel to reset the video screens and end the Lair's "alert" mode.

"Okay, we'll it looks like we can continue the tour now," Thunder Force said. "Let's move on to the vehicles area."

"Hey Fire Force, that was cool," a voice said behind Jake. "Could I maybe get your autograph for my brother?"

"Of course," Jake said. He turned and found Michael standing over him. He couldn't refuse an autograph request even if he wanted to. In this case he didn't want to refuse, but he was freaked out by it.

Michael handed over an autograph book and Jake opened it to the first page, trying to play this cool. A note was there: "You bolted so fast, I couldn't give you an address. I really want to see you after work. It's room 219 in Rose Hall."

Jake flipped to the next blank page and signed "Find the Fire in You. Fire Force!" Under that he wrote. "Will see you in 219 tonight."

He passed the book back with a smile.

"Thanks, Fire Force," Michael opened the book. His smile grew bigger as he read the message.

"You're welcome. You should catch up with the tour, otherwise Thunder Force might come looking for you, and you don't want that."

Michael nodded and kept smiling. "Will do. Thanks again!"

\# \# \# \# \#

Jake's inner voice nagged him on the walk over to Rose Hall. He parked at his dorm and used the walk across campus to clear his head. Ultimately, even if this was a big joke, it was still a good day since he'd been kissed and the guy showed up at work, too.

Rose's second floor was filled with noise. Not surprising for late on a Saturday night. Several doors were open, and people were milling around, going room to room. Jake was uneasy, as if he were being stared at. Did these people know he didn't really belong here? The inner voice tried to get him to bail out, but he stuck with it until he was in front of room 219.

He knocked.

"Hey," Michael said quietly as he opened the door. "I wasn't sure you'd show up, but I'm glad you did." Michael stepped aside for Jake to enter. "Come on in."

"I wasn't sure I was coming either. But after you turned up at the park, I couldn't bail out."

Michael stood in front of Jake. Jake worked to stay locked on Michael's eyes and keep his shyness at bay.

"It was worth the cost of admission. That was cool. Do you do that every day?"

"It depends. Some days I'm in the Lair, some days in the park."

"Cool. I gotta actually bring my brother out to see that sometime." Michael took Jake's baseball cap off and tossed it on the desk. "You're trembling again. I don't scare you do I?" Concern filled Michael's voice.

"No," Jake said. Yes. I don't know. I, um …" Jake was flustered. He hated when he got tongue tied, and the frustration only made it worse.

"You have been with a guy before, right?"

"Of course … I mean … well." Jake sighed. "I have had a couple boyfriends, but no one like you."

"Dude, I'm just a guy looking for a good guy to date and then see what happens."

"Really?" Michael took Jake's hand and gently pulled him closer until they stood toe-to-toe.

"Really."

Jake wrapped his arms around Michael, loosely holding him. He nibbled Michael's lips gently. Michael moaned softly, encouraging Jake to keep going. Jake ran his tongue along the soft lips and pushed his way inside Michael's mouth. Michael pulled Jake closer, and Jake responded by tightening the hug he had on Michael.

Jake hungrily explored Michael's mouth as his hands wandered over Michael's back and ass. Jake loved the rough feeling of stubble he kept running into on Michael's upper lip and chin. Michael steered them toward his bed and gently lowered them both down, so he ended up on top of Jake.

Their erections collided, straining against the fabric of jeans and shorts. Jake responded, grinding his hips into Michael's. Jake's cock pulsated in his shorts, sending wave after wave of pleasure through him. Michael, meanwhile, moaned with each gyration.

Suddenly Jake pushed Michael away from him, like he was bench-pressing Michael's body. "You know, you've seen me naked, and I haven't seen you yet. That needs to change." Jake found the confidence to take control of the situation as he had earlier in the day.

Michael supported himself on the bed as Jake reached behind him and pulled his T-shirt up. When he got to the shoulders, Michael finished the job by standing and pulling the shirt the rest of the way off and tossing it aside.

"Better than I ever imagined," Jake said. He sat on the edge of the bed and ran his hand across Michael's pecs and stomach. "So hairy," he whispered. He nuzzled the hair on Michael's stomach while his hands roamed over the lean chest muscles that were covered in hair. This was the hairiest guy he'd ever been with. The sensation of all those hairs moving across his face was intoxicating. It tickled, it scratched, it caressed. It was awesome.

"I've never had that reaction. Most people think it's too much, but I can't stand the idea of keeping it trimmed."

"Don't you dare." Jake placed little kisses all over Michael's stomach as he unbuttoned Michael's jeans. Michael's cock throbbed as he worked to release it. He slowly pulled down the jeans, making sure to caress the hairy legs he'd fallen in love with the previous year.

"You're making me crazy with how slow you're going," Michael said, barely above a whisper.

"Good." Jake found a wet spot just above the well-outlined head of Michael's cock and planted a kiss there. Michael made a sharp intake of breath as Jake sucked on Michael's cock head through the fabric. It tasted good, musky and sweet.

"My god. Will you please get me out of these?"

Jake looked up at Michael as he ran his mouth along the outline of the bulging cock. The pleasured agony on Michael's face didn't spur him to go any faster. He slowly tongued Michael's balls, which tightened up as his lips ran over them. Michael shuddered and grabbed Jake's head, using it to gently pull Jake into a standing position.

"Now it's my turn to see you up close." Michael pulled off Jake's T-shirt. As he did so, he buried his face in Jake's hairy armpit.

Jake squealed in laughter and tried to pull away, but only succeeded in falling back on the bed. Michael threw the T-shirt at Jake's head.

"Silly."

"Sorry," Jake said, tossing the T-shirt on the floor. "I'm very ticklish there."

"I can see that." Michael crashed down on the bed next to Jake. "Speaking of trim jobs." Michael brought his knees down on the bed and straddled Jake's legs. "This hair couldn't be much shorter." He ran his hands over Jake's chest, feeling the blond stubble.

"I have to keep it short, otherwise it looks bad when I'm in the suit."

"I'd love to see it grown out sometime." Michael ran his tongue over one of Jake's nipples. Jake's body quaked, and this time not from nervousness. Michael locked his lips around the instantly hard nub and rapidly flicked his tongue over the sensitive skin. Jake writhed under him and Michael played that up, sucking, pulling and nibbling on the nipple. Jake got nosier as the sensations flowed through him.

Jake wrapped his arms around Michael and smoothly flipped them over, so Jake was on top.

"Enough with the clothes." Jake bounced off the bed and quickly stepped out of his shoes and then got rid of his shorts and briefs.

"I have to say wow again," Michael said.

Jake smiled and went for Michael's underwear. Michael lifted his butt off the bed, so Jake could slide the boxer briefs down.

"Wow right back at you," Jake said. "I've fantasized about getting you naked from the first time I saw you." Jake ran his tongue along Michael's leg, starting just above the ankle. He crawled on top of Michael as he kept licking up past the kneecap and then along his inner thigh, which made Michael moan all over again. Michael tasted good, clean with just a hint of manliness.

At Michael's balls, he took one in his mouth and let his tongue explore its textures thoroughly before taking the other one and doing the same. The moaning was constant now. Jake licked up the shaft of the thick, throbbing cock, taking extra time at the head, so he could lick up all the juice. The sweet liquid was delicious and Jake coaxed Michael's cock to give up some more.

Jake lapped up the precum around Michael's bellybutton before continuing up to Michael's chest. He found a hair-covered nipple and tightened his lips around that, pulling on it.

"Fuck dude, you really know how to work a guy over."

Finally, Jake moved in one long lick from the nipple, up Michael's neck, over his chin and right onto his lips. Jake's tongue forced Michael's mouth open as Jake wrapped his arms around Michael, pressing their naked bodies closer.

As Jake grinded against Michael, his cock worked its way under Michael's balls.

"Oh yes," Michael said as Jake kept pressing in that perfect spot between balls and ass. Jake arched his back and worked his way more into that spot. Michael's expression intensified, complete with his eyes rolling back in his head.

"You like that, huh?" Michael nodded rapidly as he kept his body moving against Jake's cock. The head of Jake's cock dropped against the entrance to Michael's hole, and Michael gave his loudest moan yet.

"Condoms?" Jake asked, looking toward the nightstand to see if there were any sitting out. He wanted to take full advantage of Michael grinding against his cock.

"Drawer. Hurry. Need you inside me."

Jake stayed straddled over Michael as he crawled toward the drawer. Michael pulled and squeezed Jake's hard-on, sending chills through his body and making it hard for him to find what he was looking for. Then Michael swallowed Jake's cock, leaving Jake in an odd position over Michael with condoms and lube in one hand and the other hand supporting his weight.

"Oh man, oh yes, yes." Jake got loud now as Michael took his cock deep and rolled it around with his tongue. Jake froze, afraid if he moved he'd come crashing down on top of Michael. Michael increased his suction as he ran his tongue inside Jake's foreskin. Jake gave Michael a huge amount of precum as he worked on his cock.

"Dude, you're gonna make me shoot if you keep that up. You're hitting just the right spot." Michael immediately released some of the suction and let the cock slip from his mouth with a final kiss to the head.

"Can't have that, can we?" Michael winked at him.

Jake crawled his way back down Michael's body, letting his hardness caress Michael's chest and stomach and finally brush against Michael's own stiff rod. He sat up and grabbed both cocks in his hand. He slowly stroked them, using the combined pre-cum to lube them up.

"Please. You're killing me. Fuck me now," Michael said.

Jake grinned. "Killing you, huh? Doesn't feel like you're dying to me." He squeezed their combined cocks, which forced a long, low moan from Michael.

Jake ended the waiting game, ripping open the condom package and rolling the sheath over his rigid tool. Squirting a generous amount of lube in his hand, he put some on his cock.

Right on cue, Michael lifted his ass off the bed to give Jake access. Jake teased the tight pucker with his lubed fingers.

Michael pushed against the fingers, trying to force one inside. Jake willing helped out, slipping one in and slowly moving it deeper.

"More," Michael said.

Jake did as he was told, slipping a second finger in. "You're fuckin' tight man." Jake knew this was going to be amazing.

"It's been a while."

Jake moved his fingers against Michael's ass walls, working to loosen him up. Michael's grunts were a mix of pain and pleasure as Jake kept the finger massage going.

"You ready?"

"Yeah man. Do it."

Jake raised Michael's legs and guided himself to the entrance. He pushed in, watching the head of his cock disappear into the warm, tight muscle.

"Fuck, you're huge. Damn." Michael clamped his ass around Jake's cock head, sending shockwaves through Jake. It was even better than he expected. He grabbed Michael's hips and brought Michael closer to him, forcing his cock deeper. Jake's best JO fantasy had never been this good. He plunged his cock into Michael while holding on to hair-covered hips.

Jake entered slowly into Michael, so he could get used to him. As soon as Michael pushed back though, Jake moved with more aggression. Holding Michael's legs in the air, Jake slammed into Michael's tightness, striving each time to get a little deeper.

Michael moaned louder with every thrust. Jake suspected someone was going to barge into the room to find out what the noise was about. Michael showed no signs of caring. He gripped the sheets tight as beads of sweat formed on his chest making the hairs glisten in the light.

"Man, I'm getting close. I need to slow up a bit."

"Don't you dare," Michael said.

"Seriously, you want it that bad?" Jake gave Michael a wicked grin and started to slow up. Michael increased thrusting on his own. Jake laughed a bit. He liked how Michael went after what he wanted. "Okay then."

Jake released Michael's legs and let them fall next to him. He grabbed Michael's arms and pulled him up, making sure to keep his rod buried deep inside. He wrapped his arms around Michael, kissing him deep as he started to pound his ass again. Being able to hug and kiss Michael added fuel to the fire. Plus the new position allowed Jake's cock to find an even deeper position, they both moaned and writhed against each other as Jake kept hitting the new spot just right.

"That's it man. I'm gonna cum."

"Do it, Jake."

Keeping Michael close, Jake found the leverage to pound still harder as Michael tightened his ass.

"Cummin', man." Jake's body went rigid as he unloaded into the condom. The orgasmic sensation was intense. Every shot of cum seemed to send electricity through Jake. Both of them cried out as Jake's cock pulsated, discharging shot after shot of fluid. As his shudders subsided, Jake brought Michael close to him for a tender kiss. "My turn now." He gently dropped Michael to the bed and pulled out of his ass.

He pulled off the full condom, quickly tied it off and dropped it into the trashcan he'd seen by the nightstand.

"Did you see how full that was?" Michael said. "I'd love to feel that shoot into me."

"Maybe someday," Jake said as he grabbed another condom.

"What are you doing?"

"I said it was my turn." Jake quickly rolled the condom over Michael's cock.

"Oh, oh, um … I'm not going to last very long. Oh, damn. Not long at all."

"Okay by me." Jake grabbed the lube and slicked up his fingers to lube his hole. Jake positioned himself over Michael's cock. He reached behind and held it firm, sitting straight down on it.

"Fuck yes. Just what I needed after shooting that load," Jake said. Michael's cock filled him up perfectly, like it was made exactly for his ass.

"I can't believe you took it just like that," Michael said. Jake squeezed his hole tight. "That sensation alone almost made me cum."

"Good," Jake leaned over and kissed Michael. Jake started grinding on Michael's cock as they kissed. He pulled back from the kiss and started riding Michael fast and furious. Sweat dripped off his forehead as he moved up and down Michael, almost letting his cock pop out only to drive it deep in him.

"I'm gonna shoot, Jake."

"Good, give it to me." Michael let loose shot after shot. Again, both guys moaned, grunted and shouted in climax. Jake came again, too, letting loose a couple more shots of cum across Michael's chest.

Jake collapsed, completely spent, on top of Michael. "That was amazing. I'm glad you found me in the park today." He peppered Michael with kisses as he talked.

Michael stroked Jake's blond hair. "I'm glad I did, too. I'm glad I walked into the comic book store that day, and even more glad you ended up at the party. I wish we'd started talking last year."

"At least we are now."

"Yeah. You're pretty amazing, you know. You go from being inside that shy shell to taking charge and riding me like that. I like that range."

Jake smiled and felt himself blush. "So you're not going to try and change that? It's driven a couple people insane how I switch back and forth so fast."

"No way. I like you just the way you are."

"So maybe a real date sometime?" Jake asked, between kisses along Michael's jaw line.

"I'd like that."

"You'd be seen with me, out in public, in my baggy cargo shorts?"

Michael laughed. "Yeah, I would. We'll make an interesting case in contrasts. Preppy boy and geek boy."

"Sounds like a superhero pairing." Jake said, planting a kiss on the tip of Michael's nose.

"Leave it to geek boy to say that. Listen, you want to stay here tonight? I'd love to wake up next to you."

"I'd like that."

"Cool. Our first date can be breakfast then."

Jake rested his head on Michael shoulder. "Perfect."

# THE BULLY ON THE PLAYGROUND
# Helen E. H. Madden

Josh pulled up to the Shady Banks Municipal playground at sunset. The dying light of the end-of-summer day cast a burnt orange pall on the aging equipment. The swings creaked listlessly in the faint breeze. Overgrown weeds claimed the ball field stretched out in the distance. The mommies with their shrieking, hyperactive children had long since quit the place, leaving behind an empty, exhausted silence.

Josh climbed out of his car and wandered over to the swing set. He ran his hands along the cracked plastic cover of the chains before gripping them tightly and jumping lightly over the seat. He settled on the scarred rubber sling and with a gentle kick set himself in motion. He swung back and forth, back and forth, letting the years drop away from him until he could close his eyes and remember what it had been like to be a kid. Four years had passed since he'd last been here, four years since the day he'd officially left childhood behind, and the place still gave him the shivers. Not much had changed in that narrow span of time; a little more rust on the monkey bars, a little more graffiti scrawled on the big spiral slide. He swung up and then down, scuffed at the ground with his sneaker and sent a spray of shredded mulch flying.

Four years. Back then, he'd been a high school graduate, getting ready to leave for college. Back then, he'd been ready to escape from the purgatory of adolescent cliques, snobbery and popularity contests. He hadn't been Josh Stillman; he'd been the Freak, a name bestowed upon him by none other than Bradley Capps, better known as the Butcher or Butch. Butch hadn't been the most popular kid in Shady Banks. In fact, Josh had probably had more friends than he. But the Butcher was the biggest, toughest kid in the school, and so any name he gave always

209

stuck. Thus Josh had been the Freak for several long, tortuous years.

"What are you doing in my playground, freak?" That had been the question Butch had asked a terrified twelve-year-old Josh on the day he had first come under the bully's scrutiny.

"N-n-nothing!" A scrawny Josh huddled beneath the perforated metal steps that led up to the tower of the spiral slide. He felt like a rabbit cornered by a rabid dog.

"What's that in your hands?"

"A book ..."

"Give it here."

Josh remembered holding out the book like an inept zoo keeper offering a slab of raw meat to a snarling lion. Butch yanked the paperback volume from his grasp, flipped through the pages, and scowled.

"What's this crap?"

"Science fiction."

"What, aliens and rockets and shit?" Butch sneered. "Why ain't you playing football with the rest of us?"

"I don't ... I don't like football."

Butch had eyed him with cool disdain then, his gaze raking over Josh so savagely that the smaller boy thought he must be bleeding from it.

"Books, glasses, don't like football. Yeah, you're a freak all right." Butch hefted the book in his oversized mitt then pitched it into the distant parking lot. "Bull's eye!" he shouted as it landed with a splash in an oil-slicked puddle. He gave Josh another sneer before stalking away. "Stay out of my playground, Freak."

Josh waited, trembling, until the bully was a few yards away. Then he shouted before he could stop himself. "It's not your playground!"

"What?" Butch turned slowly, disbelief scrawled across his broad, square face. Every other kid on the playground froze and watched.

"I said ..." Josh swallowed hard. "It's not your playground."

It was at that moment that Josh first realized the sheer size of the Butcher. The bully advanced on him, a towering giant that eclipsed the very sun. His shadow fell on Josh like a hammer, and then the giant's fist seized Josh by the shirt and pulled him in close.

"Nobody," Butch whispered, "and I mean nobody, talks back to me!"

Josh shivered, but couldn't keep his mouth shut. "I do."

The look of shock on Butch's face almost made Josh laugh, but that would have been his death sentence. Instead, Josh managed to grimace appropriately as Butch dragged him across the playground, scattering the other kids from their path. When they reached the parking lot, Butch heaved Josh off the ground and dumped him in the same puddle with his book. Josh landed on his backside, but surprisingly only hard enough to wound his pride. As the oily water seeped through his corduroy pants to his underwear, he heard Butch snarl.

"Get out of here, Freak! And don't come back, unless you want more of the same!"

A smart person would have headed that advice. But then a smart person would never have challenged Butch in the first place. Over the next six years, Josh returned again and again to the playground to test the Butcher's threats. He couldn't say why. It was just something he had to do. He learned fast that he was safest in spring and early summer, when Little League ruled the neighboring ball field. The presence of so many over-protective parents hovering about the premises quelled even Butch's penchant for dominance. But it also ruined the thrill of their encounters. Josh got a kick out of mouthing off to the bully – again, something he didn't quite understand – and as the years passed, he grew more daring even as the punishments grew more severe.

"Why do you do it?" Arnie Hinkman had once asked Josh. "Why can't you just stay away and keep your big mouth shut?"

"Because," Josh said, extricating himself from one of the playground's trashcans. Bits of garbage clung to his clothing and hair. "Just because."

And that was as close as he could ever come to explaining his reasons to anyone, even himself.

By the time he entered high school, Josh had almost as much of a reputation as Butch. No one really liked the Freak, but no one bothered him either. He was Butch's property, his personal punching bag as they liked to say, and nobody dared to lay a finger on him. Not that Butch ever punched him. That wasn't his style. The bully liked to shove Josh, trip him in the hallway, dump him into garbage cans, or cram him into a locker. Sometimes he would sometimes sneak up from behind and yank up hard on the waistband of Josh's underwear, making his victim yelp with pain. That was his privilege, and his alone.

Tommy Sotto was the only person who ever made the mistake of violating that rule. Tommy was a newcomer Josh's sophomore year. He was a wanna-be in a leather jacket, a pretend tough guy who aped everything Butch did, all the while looking for a way to usurp his idol's place as King of the Hill. Tommy cornered Josh in the boy's locker room after gym class one afternoon.

"Hey Freak! I hear you like to play with the Butcher! How's about you and me playing some games, huh?"

Tommy's fist landed on Josh's mouth before he could even answer. He busted Josh's lower lip and knocked him to the ground then swung his foot back, ready to plant a wicked kick in Josh's midsection. The kick never landed. When Josh looked up through pain-fogged eyes, he saw Butch holding Tommy by the scruff of the neck.

"Whaddya think you're doing, Tommy?" Butch gave Tommy a little shake, the way a Terrier shakes a freshly caught rat.

"Nothing! Nothing, Butcher. Just taking care of some garbage for you ..."

Another shake. Tommy's head snapped back and forth. "I don't need anybody to take care of anything for me. You got that?"

"Yeah, I got it Butcher! I got ..."

Tommy's sentence ended in a loud crash as he collided with a row of lockers. Butch was kind enough to pull Tommy up to standing before shoving him inside one and spinning the combination lock. The bully didn't offer a hand to Josh.

"You're a freak," he growled. He stared down at Josh where he lay sprawled on the floor. "A goddamn freak. But you ain't garbage."

It was the nicest thing Butch ever said to anybody, and the words left Josh feeling dizzy the rest of the day. But Butch never let that compliment go to Josh's head. He stepped up his campaign of torment soon after that. He started catching Josh while he was alone, wrestling him to the ground and twisting his arms behind his back until Josh thought they might come out of their sockets. The matches were a challenge for Josh. He knew he could never win, so he didn't bother to try. But he never cried out either. He just grit his teeth in stony defiance and let the Butcher bend him this way and that until the bully got frustrated and dumped him into the nearest trashcan or locker.

On one particularly memorable occasion when Josh was seventeen, Butch jumped Josh on the playground and wrestled him to the ground. He pinned the slender boy beneath him and straddled his chest, then thrust his fingers under Josh's arms and started tickling. Josh couldn't keep silent this time. He shrieked and thrashed about, desperate to worm free. Butch grabbed his T-shirt to hold him still, and the garment ripped away in the bully's hands.

Butch knelt there, staring at the scrap that used to be part of Josh's shirt. He was breathing hard, his brows knitted together in confusion as though he didn't recognize what he was holding. When he looked up, Josh thought he seemed almost panicked.

Butch licked his lips. "Maybe I should take your pants too, huh? Maybe I should just leave you here on the playground with no clothes at all. What do you think of that, Freak?"

"Maybe you should," Josh answered back. He shivered as late afternoon breeze tickled his bare chest.

Butch stared at him hard then and pressed a broad hand down on Josh's bare chest. For one long, frightening moment, Josh thought he might actually do it. But then the bully threw down the rag and jumped to his feet.

"Stay the hell away from my playground, Freak. You come back here again, and you'll get more of the same."

Butch left Josh alone for a while after that, which was sort of disappointing. It was like spending years working to earn some great honor, only to have it evaporate once it was realized. Josh roamed the halls of the school, undisturbed. He raced his bike along the sidewalk in front of Butch's house. No one came out to chase him. He took to haunting the playground, but the bully seemed to have abandoned his precious territory. Then one day a rumor flew around the school. Butch Capps had a girl.

"Did ya hear?" Arnie Hinkman said at lunch. "Butch is making out with Louise Gellar in the school parking lot."

The words hit Josh the way Butch never had. "Like hell he is," he replied. "Butch doesn't even have a car."

"He got one last week," Arnie replied, digging into the ham and cheese sandwich his mother always made for him. "It's an old Corvette. Kind of beat up, though. I hear he got a part-time job at Black's garage just so he can fix it up."

"Bull. He doesn't have a car and he isn't screwing around with Louise Gellar."

"You don't believe me?" Arnie whined. "Go out into the parking lot and see for yourself. But don't blame me if Butch catches you and finally kills your sorry ass."

Josh waited until lunch was almost over and Arnie had left for his next class. Then he snuck past Vice Principle Vicar's and slipped out the back doors of the school. He crept through the small parking lot, searching the rows of cars until he came to a battered Corvette with peeling red paint. The car rocked from side to side, and a weird moaning came from within.

"Oooooooh ... Butcher ..."

The rocking continued. Josh slid closer. He spied a girl's foot hanging out one of the rear windows, a scuffed black pump dangling from the toes. A massive shadowy shape heaved to and fro inside the 'vette, a beast in full rutt. Josh slipped around to the other side of the car. He had to see, he had to know the truth. Just as the girl moaned again, Butch's head came up. His black eyes locked onto Josh's through the open window in a heated glare.

"Oh Butch! Butch! Don't stop! Hey, I said don't stop!"

Butch was out of the car in seconds. Josh barely had time to turn and run. He made it halfway across the parking lot, but was still miles away from the illusory safety of the school when a brutal hand clamped down on one of his shoulders.

Butch spun Josh around and slammed him against a car. "What are you doing out here, Freak? You spying on me?"

"Yeah, sure. Why not? I heard they were teaching biology class out here and today's lesson was on the mating habits of chimps. Or maybe it was pigs," he added as Louise Gellar's flushed and overly plump face popped out of the back window of the rusty Corvette.

"Butch, don't kill him!" she shrieked.

"He called you a pig, Louise."

"Oh, well fuck him then. Tear the little shit apart."

Louise settled back into the car and pulled a tube of lipstick out of her purse. She smeared it over her ample lips while she waited for Butch to finish with his business.

Butch slammed Josh against the car again. The door handle dug into Josh's back. "I asked you a question. What are you doing out here, Freak?"

Josh sneered. "Nothing. What the hell are you doing out here?"

"None of your fucking business."

"It's fucking business all right."

A third slam against the car. Josh was pretty sure if Butch did that again, something was going to break, either the car door or him. Most likely him.

"You want me to hurt you? You want me to turn you inside out?" Butch's face went from angry to sly and mean. "Or maybe you want me to do to you what I was doing to Louise over there."

"You wish."

For the first time since he'd known Butch, Josh fought back. He grabbed a thick ropy arm with one hand and shoved the heel of the other hand into the bully's face. Butch grunted and fell backwards, landing on the cracked asphalt. Josh threw himself on top of Butch, knowing his slight weight could never pin his opponent to the ground, knowing he'd probably end up crushed beneath Butch instead. And that was exactly what happened. As Josh came down, Butch thrust his hips up, bucking his opponent into the air. Then the bully rolled and folded Josh under him against the dirty black pavement. He dropped his entire bulk on top of Josh and drove the air from his lungs in a big whoosh.

"I wish ..." Butch growled in Josh's ear. "I wish. I wish you'd stay the fuck outta my way. I wish I'd never laid eyes on you, Freak. I wish you'd die and quit haunting me like some goddamn ghost."

Josh struggled beneath the bully. He got one hand free and tried to claw Butch's face. Butch grabbed it and yanked it over Josh's head. Then he caught the other and pinned it with the first. Josh kept struggling. He tried to duplicate Butch's earlier move, bucking his hips to force the bully off of him. Instead, he only ended up grinding his body against Butch's. Butch let out a low moan that sent chills down Josh's spine.

"I wish ..." Butch whispered again.

Josh felt something press against his pelvis, something that was a part of Butch, something that wanted to be a part of him. His breath caught in his chest. He pushed his hips against Butch's again, ever so slightly, and felt Butch stiffen and push back.

"I wish, too," Josh whispered back.

"You goddamn freak!" Butch jerked away. He rolled off Josh and sprang to his feet. Hands up in a defensive gesture, he backed away from the boy still sprawled on the ground. "Stay the hell away from me, Freak! Stay the hell away!" He edged back to his car, never taking his eyes off Josh, then slid into the driver's seat and gunned the engine. Louise shrieked as he peeled away in a cloud of dirt and gravel, leaving a startled Josh behind.

Butch dropped out of school soon after that. It wasn't a surprise. He wasn't much of an academic, but he was good with cars, and Mr. Black had offered him a full-time job at the garage. Louise Gellar made certain everyone at school knew how well Butch was doing, and how well she was doing, too.

"He got me a ring!" she shrilled to a pack of giggling classmates during lunch one winter afternoon. "Daddy won't let me wear it yet, but as soon as school is over ..."

The excited chattering that followed made Josh feel sick. He tossed his lunch into the trash can and stalked out of the school. He headed for the Municipal playground and shivered in the top of the tower of the spiral slide until long after dark. For the first time in his life, Josh actually hated Butch Capps.

Three more months passed after Louise's announcement. June breezed in, bringing with it final exams and graduation. The night Josh strode across the stage to accept his diploma was the first time in years that any of his classmates called him by his given name. The boys all slapped him on his back and shook his hand. Arnie Hinkman joylessly congratulated him on winning a full scholarship to State.

"Jesus, that fucker should have been mine for sure," Arnie groused. "You weren't supposed to survive high school, you prick."

But he had, and once the ceremonies were over and the parties had ended, a cold hollowness settled inside Josh's bones. What now? College. A degree, a job for sure. A wife and kids, too? Hell no. By now, Josh knew better than that.

June faded into July, with days of sun-burnt grass and dry, listless heat. Josh worked at the local library, earning enough money to buy a car. He bought one used from Black's garage. Butch wasn't in when he came to pay for it.

"Poor son-of-a-bitch is all caught up in wedding plans," Mr. Black drawled. "Most days he comes in here looking like a goddamn deer in the headlights. He made a mistake proposing to that Gellar girl. She got her hooks into him now and ain't letting go for shit."

August came hot and heavy on the heels of July. Josh stayed indoors during the day, either working at the library or locked in his bedroom at home. At nights, he slipped out and roamed the town, visiting all the places that used to belong to Butch – the ball field, the old vacant lot, the swimming hole out in the woods, the Municipal playground. Places where Butch had tormented him without mercy. Josh spent long evenings in the tower of the spiral slide, watching the sun go down, watching the day end. Watching for the Butcher, who never came.

Until one evening he did.

The Corvette pulled into the playground parking lot just as the sun started to go down. The paint job was new. So were the tires. The young man behind the wheel looked old though, old and worn out. He stepped out of the driver's seat, slouched over to the passenger's side and held open the door like an obedient servant. Louise Gellar stepped out, fluffing her bottled blonde hair.

"Come on, Bradley. Let's find someplace nice."

She handed him a blanket and a picnic basket and set off across the empty playground. Butch followed like a whipped dog. Louise sniffed about, looking for the perfect spot, before pointing to a patch of bare earth beneath a tree that grew about ten yards away from the spiral slide where Josh hid. Without a word, Butch spread the blanket and dropped the basket on top of it. Louise frowned.

"Sit down, Bradley, and quit moping. We're getting married next weekend. You're supposed to be happy, you big jerk."

Butch sat, but didn't look happy. He reached for the basket, but Louise pulled it away.

"Forget the food. I know what'll put a smile on your face." She gave him a sly smile and started to unbutton her blouse.

"For crissake, Louise! Not here. What if somebody comes along and sees?"

Josh heard the pout in Louise's voice. "Well what if they do? The whole town knows we're getting married. What's the harm in starting the honeymoon a little early?"

"I'm not in the mood, okay?"

"Oh fuck you. You're never in the mood anymore. What's wrong with you? You're not supposed to start this shit until after we've been married!"

Butch didn't answer. He turned away from her, pulled his knees up and wrapped his arms around them, then rested his head on top of that. Louise's hands fluttered in a sort of panicked frustration.

"Oh baby, I'm so sorry! I didn't mean to start in on you like that. I know you've been working hard, trying to save up money for the honeymoon. You just need some rest, that's all ..."

She prattled on like that for several minutes, all the while edging closer to Butch. She came up behind him and started kneading his shoulders. Butch seemed not to notice.

"Maybe I can get you in the mood, huh baby? I know what you like."

She pulled on his shoulders, and Butch finally capitulated. He lay back on the blanket, staring up into the tree while Louise went to work on his belt buckle. Josh watched, fascinated, as she unzipped Butch's fly and eased down his jeans and shorts. He could see Butch's flaccid penis resting against the bully's thigh.

"You just need a little tender loving care, that's all," Josh heard Louise murmur. Then she leaned over and blocked his view of Butch's cock. Her head bobbed up and down. Butch continued to stare up at the trees as though lost in thought.

Josh thought, too. He thought about Butch and what Louise was doing to him. He wondered if she was having any luck. He didn't think so. Butch seemed too distracted, and Louise seemed to be doing more work than would have been necessary had Butch been hard. He thought about the brief glimpse he'd just had of Butch's cock. It seemed to be the wrong cock for the bully. It should have been hard, just like the rest of him. Just like Josh's cock was hard now.

Louise gave up the head bobbing and stretched out by Butch's side. She wrapped a hand around his still soft penis and stroked it. The head peeked in and out of her grasp as she pulled on it. Josh bit back a groan. He shifted about in the cramped space of the tower, carefully so as to not make a noise, and unbuckled his belt. He freed his erect cock from his briefs and started stroking it out of synch with Louise's efforts. She was doing it wrong, fumbling around with Butch's cock like she thought it might break when instead she should have just grabbed it and squeezed hard. Butch liked things rough. He liked to wrestle. He liked to be challenged. He liked.

Josh's car keys dangled from the front pocket of his jeans. Dislodged by Josh's frantic masturbation, they slid out, hit the metal surface of the spiral slide with a sharp clink and slid all the way down with an audible **shush**.

Butch sat up, knocking Louise away. "What was that?"

220

"What?" She looked about, confused.

"That noise. I heard something. I think there's somebody here."

"Oh bull. We're alone, Bradley!"

Butch ignored her and stood up. He did up his fly and stalked toward the slide. Josh huddled in the tower, unable to even breathe. He heard the muffled crunch of Butch's feet on the shredded mulch, the sound growing louder until it stopped at the foot of the slide.

"What's this?"

Josh looked down. He could see Butch's feet, then his knees and hands as the bully knelt and picked up something from the ground. Josh's keys. Butch jingled them then stood.

"What is it?" Louise called out.

"Nothing. Somebody lost their keys. Pack up the basket and head back to the car ..."

"But I wanna make out here!"

"Just do as I say Louise!"

Butch turned and walked away. Josh closed his eyes and let out a shaky breath. He listened to his racing heartbeat. Everything else was silent.

"Enjoying yourself up here, Freak?"

Josh's eyes flew open. Butch crouched at the top step leading up to the tower. He dangled Josh's keys in his right hand.

"Where's your car, Freak? I didn't see it in the lot."

Josh couldn't speak. Butch slipped into the tower, and hissed.

"I said where's your fucking car?!"

"B-b-behind the ball field."

"What are you doing on my playground?"

"It's not your ..."

"Fuck that! What are you doing here? Where you watching us, Freak? You get off on watching my girl give me a blowjob?"

"No. She sucks at it."

Butch gaped at him. "That supposed to be a joke, Freak?"

"No, but it was pretty fun …"

Butch's hand shot out and grabbed Josh by the hair. He yanked Josh toward him.

"You were watching us." His whisper was ice cold. "You were jerking off. You want Louise."

"No," Josh whispered back. "I don't. And neither do you."

The grip on Josh's neck tightened. "You got your pants pulled down, Freak, and your dick hanging out. I could strip you naked right now, take your clothes and just leave you here. Would you like that?"

"If you did it, yeah."

Josh's heart pounded. He was more frightened than he had ever been in his entire life, but he was also hard. In the tiny space of the tower, Butch pressed up against him. Josh felt his cock rub against the bully's leg.

"You want me to do it?" Butch asked. He brought his face to Josh's until their foreheads were almost touching. "You really want me to do it?"

"Sure. Unless you're too scared to do it."

"I'm not the one who should be scared. Take off your shirt, bitch."

Butch let go of Josh's neck long enough to let Josh pull his T-shirt up over his head. Then the bully clamped down him again with a steel grip.

"Now your jeans. Underwear, too."

With shaking hands, Josh reached for his jeans.

"Bradley!" Louise's cry split the air, making Josh freeze. "What the hell are you doing up there? I thought we were leaving!"

"Get back in the car," Butch shouted back. "I'll be there in a minute." He gave Josh a sly smile. "Take off the pants, Freak, and give 'em to me."

Josh pulled down his jeans. He had to struggle to get them over his hips without falling out of the tower and down the slide. His shoes and socks came off with them. He handed everything to Butch, who tucked the bundled clothing under his arm.

"You scared, Freak?"

Josh nodded. His chest was too tight to let him speak.

"Good. I'm gonna take your things now and leave. You're gonna stay here until I come back for you. And when I do, I'm gonna show you what happens to freaks like you when they spy on people like me."

Butch crawled back out of the tower and descended the steps. Josh huddled as far back in the little shelter as he could and watched Butch stride across the playground and through the parking lot.

"Where are you going now?" Louise demanded as he walked past the car.

"Trashcan. Some asshole left a bunch of dirty clothes up in the slide. I'm getting rid of them."

"Bradley, don't do that!" she called after him. "What if somebody's looking for that stuff? You should take it to a lost and found."

Butch reached the trashcan and dumped Josh's clothing inside. "You see a lost and found around here? Forget it." He strode back to the Corvette, no longer old and weary, but young and full of cocky pride. He flashed a wicked grin at Josh's hiding place before sliding into the driver's seat and taking off.

Josh waited. He had no choice. It was still light out, and his clothing was over 200 yards away in a trash can on the other side of the parking lot. He wrapped his arms around his naked body and shivered. He wondered what would happen when Butch came back. When would he come back? Or was it if he would come back? Josh didn't know.

The sunset faded into evening. The parking lot lights flickered on, bathing the asphalt with their hot yellow glow. Josh sweated in the tower, slapping at the mosquitoes that feasted on his bare flesh. After what seemed like an eternity, he heard the sound of sirens fast approaching. His heart beat like a trip hammer. He started to hyperventilate. Butch had called the police, told them there was a pervert lurking in the playground. The sirens grew louder. Their keening shattered the night. Josh began to sob. Through his tears, he saw blue and red lights race toward the playground and then speed past it. More sirens, more lights followed. A fire engine and an ambulance roared by. None of them stopped at the playground. Still weeping, Josh slumped inside the tower, relieved.

He waited, and then waited some more. The occasional car drove by, but never stopped. The mosquitoes ravaged his flesh. Eventually Josh's fear turned to boredom then to annoyance. Midnight came and went. The lights in the parking lot flickered and died. Darkness shrouded the playground. Josh slapped at the mosquitoes and fumed.

"Where the hell are you already?" he whispered in the dark. But no one was there to answer.

The night stretched on and Josh grew angry. He climbed out of the tower, naked and itching like crazy. The barest sliver of moon lighted his way as he ran across the parking lot to the trash can. He fished out his clothes and pulled them on. They reeked of half-eaten sandwiches and spilled soda. A cloud of flies joined the mosquitoes and harassed him as he picked through the garbage looking for his keys. When he found them, he noticed the car key was gone.

"You mother fucker!" he shouted into the empty night. He threw the keys onto the ground. "You goddamned mother fucker!"

He kicked at the garbage can and bruised his foot. Then he picked up the keys and limped home. Nobody saw him; nobody came driving after him demanding to know where the hell he was going. It was a long, lonely walk. When he got home, he tossed his clothes in the wash and went to bed.

Josh woke up to the strident alarm of the phone. The glare of the mid-day sun streamed through his bedroom window, blinding him. He swore and fumbled for the receiver on the nightstand and dragged it under the covers with him.

"Hello?" he mumbled.

"Josh, is that you? It's me, Arnie!"

"What the hell do you want?"

"Jesus, you sound like shit. What's wrong with you?"

"I'm tired. What the hell do you want?"

"What'd you do? Stay out late on a hot date? Wow, the Freak graduates from high school and all of a sudden he's got a girlfriend."

"Fuck you, asshole!"

Josh slammed down the phone. Arnie called back. Josh let it ring until his mother shouted at him to get out of bed and pick up the phone.

"What?!" he snapped into the receiver.

"Look, don't be mad at me if your date didn't work out last night."

"Fuck you, Arnie."

"Yeah, we've been through that already. Look, I called to tell you something. Your arch-nemesis is dead."

"What?"

"The Butcher. Butch Capps. You didn't hear yet? He bought the big one last night. I thought you'd wanna know since you two were so close and everything."

Josh sat up in bed. "What did you just say?"

"I said Butch Capps is dead. What's the matter, you can't hear me? You want me to call back on another line?"

Josh started to shake. "What ... happened? How ...?"

Arnie chuckled. "The big ape smeared himself all over the highway. Apparently he had a huge fight with his fiancé and they broke up. My dad's a golfing buddy with Sheriff Riggs. Riggs said Butch was probably going 90 miles an hour when he hit that hairpin curve on Route 13, headed toward Municipal Park. He's not certain yet, but he's betting Butch's blood alcohol level was way over the legal limit. So there you go. Ding dong the asshole is dead and all that ... Hey Josh? You still there? Josh?"

Josh let the phone slip from his fingers. It hit the floor with a heavy thud. He curled up on the bed while Arnie whined at him to pick up. He cried the rest of the day.

Butch was buried two days later. Louise Gellar showed up at the funeral dressed all in black, wearing the small diamond Butch had given to her when he proposed. She wailed through the service and had to be half-carried out of the church when it was over. Josh sat at the back of the church, alone. A few of his former classmates glanced at him and frowned, but didn't bother him.

A week later, Josh went to Black's garage to get a new key made for his car.

"That's gonna cost," Mr. Black muttered. "What did you do with the last one?"

"Lost it."

"Well I figured that, boy. But how did you lose it?"

Josh didn't answer. Mr. Black shook his head.

"You might want to call Sheriff Riggs and tell him not to tow your car. I can't get to this today. With Butch gone, I'm backed up on work. That damned fool. Why did he have to go and get himself killed?"

Josh didn't answer that either.

He got his new key a week before the end of August. He picked up his car from the ball field, taking the long way around instead of walking through the playground. He didn't want to set foot in that place. It was Butch's place. It always had been. It always would be. He got his car, drove it home, and loaded it up. Then next morning he drove away from Shady Banks and didn't come back for four years.

And now he was back. Josh leaned back in the swing one last time and rose up high into the air. He had never done this as a kid, had never actually played on the playground. He had just hid hear, waiting for Butch to show up and shove him around. But there was no more Butch, no reason left to wait. Josh came back down and dragged his feet through the mulch, coming to a halt. Where had Butch been headed that night? Back to the playground to fulfill his promise to Josh? Or had he been headed out of town, unable to live with the lie his life had become but too scared to face the truth?

Josh would never know. He was home for one week, much to his mother's surprised delight. Even his dad was happy to see him, and his dad hadn't been happy about much of anything since Josh came out two years ago. Arnie was hoping to see him, too.

"I uh ... I hear you bat for the other team," he said when he called the day before.

"Yeah. So what?"

"So. You wanna go out, maybe?"

Maybe. Maybe not. Josh was out, but he wasn't interested. He'd gone as cold as ice since the day Butch died. Nothing stirred him anymore. Nobody touched him. He had been Butch's property, just like the playground, and he was just as empty and useless with no one to put him in his place.

"Fuck this," Josh muttered. "What am I doing here anyway?"

He moved to stand up and froze as a cold, steel grip caught him by the back of the neck.

"I thought I told you to wait for me, Freak."

Josh spun around to see who was behind him, but the hand that held him gave him a vicious shake.

"I didn't tell you to look around, Freak. I didn't tell you to do anything but wait. So why didn't you wait?"

The voice was barely a whisper, but it sent a chill down Josh's spine. "Who are you?"

His captor gave him another shake. "Who the hell do you think, Freak?"

"Butch? But that's not ... you died ..."

A mouth breathed in his ear. "Does this feel dead to you?"

A body, cold as the grave, pushed up against Josh's back. He felt the stranger's pelvis ground against his buttocks. Even through his jeans he could feel the erection.

"Get off of me you son-of-a-bitch!"

Josh made a grab for the hand on his neck, only to be pushed to the ground. A heavy weight settled on top of him.

"Get off of me! Get the fuck off!"

"Go ahead. Fight me all you want. I like it when you fight. Don't you remember? I tell you what to do, you fight me, and then I get to punish your freak ass. Just like I punished you for spying on me and Louise."

That stopped Josh cold. "How did you ...? I never told anybody!"

"I was there Freak. I was the one you were spying on."

Josh craned his neck, trying to see over his shoulder. The hand around his neck tightened even more.

"No peeking, Freak. Tonight you do what I say, when I say, and maybe, just maybe, I'll let you go when I'm done. Got it?"

Josh swallowed hard and nodded.

"Good. Now we're gonna get up and go over to that slide you like so damn much. Don't turn around and don't try to run off."

The weight lifted from Josh's back. The hand on his neck plucked him off the ground and set him on his feet. Josh and the stranger moved together toward the spiral slide and then behind it, putting the slide between the parking lot and them.

"Thought maybe you'd like a little privacy for what I've got in mind tonight." The hand pushed Josh's face against the smooth metal surface of the slide. "Now, take off your clothes, starting with your shoes and socks."

"No, I don't want to."

"Liar. Take 'em off."

"You're not Butch. You can't be. He's dead."

"Take off your clothes or I'll take 'em off for you. And if I have to do it, I won't leave them in the trash this time. I'll rip 'em to shreds and make you walk home naked. I'll take your car keys again, too. Toss them in the weeds of the ball field where you'll never find them. Now take off your clothes."

Whimpering, Josh kicked off his shoes. When he stripped off his socks, a hand reached around to take them from him. The hand was big, like Butch's used to be, but it was so pale it glowed in the dying light.

"Now your jeans," the voice whispered.

Josh unzipped his fly and pulled down his jeans. Before they reached his ankles, the pale hand snaked around to tug at the waistband of his briefs.

"What have you got in there, Freak? A hard-on? You gonna get hard for me?" The hand slipped inside the waistband to wrap around Josh's cock. The frigid touch made him gasp. "You were playing with this thing last time I saw you. Had your eyes closed and everything. What were you thinking about, Freak? Were you thinking about me? Were you thinking about how nice it'd feel if it were my hand playing with your dick instead of your own?"

"Oh god ..." Josh groaned. The hand squeezed and his cock grew hard.

"Pull off your underwear, Freak."

Josh did as he was told. He was rewarded with another squeeze of his cock.

"Good boy. Now all we've got left is your shirt. I tore your shirt once. You remember that? We were screwing around on the playground and the damn thing just tore in my hands, just like this."

The rip was sudden and violent, starting at the back of Josh's neck and going straight down the back. His T-shirt fell open and slipped down his arms.

"Grab it and tear a strip off," the stranger ordered. "Tie it around your eyes."

The cold hand stroked his cock, urging him to obey. Josh tore a long strip from his shirt and fastened it around his head.

"Perfect," the voice said. "Now we're ready to play."

The grip on his eased while the one on his cock tightened. The stranger pulled him around by the dick and led him slowly across the playground.

"Where are we going?" he demanded.

"Not far. Just a few more steps. Here. Reach overhead and grab."

Josh lifted up his arms. His hands banged against cold metal. The monkey bars. He nearly screamed. The bars were set in the middle of the playground. He was standing naked and blindfolded, with a stranger's hand around his cock, in the most exposed area of the entire place.

"What are you doing? Let me go!"

The hand came back to the back of his neck. The other hand grabbed his balls and pulled up, bringing Josh up onto his toes. "I said reach up and grab hold, Freak!"

"Ah! Please!" Josh fumbled for the bar overhead.

"That's right. Beg. You mouthed off to me enough; it's about time you begged." The cold hand released Josh's balls and went back to squeezing his cock. "Beg. Say pretty please. Tell me exactly what you want."

"I want to go home!"

"Liar. You want what you got right here. You've been wanting it for years."

Josh felt the stranger lean closer. His body pressed up against Josh's. It was cold, so damned cold even through his clothing. A mouth, just as cold as the rest of him, came down on Josh's. It kissed him, soft at first, then rough.

"You're hard, Freak, and you're leaking." A cold finger trailed over the tip of Josh's cock, smearing a drop of cum. "Tell me again how you want to go home."

Josh moaned. The sound was cut off by another kiss. The hands moved to his chest, plucking his nipples to frozen points.

"You're pretty, you know that Freak? Prettier than any girl. Prettier than Louise Gellar."

Josh pushed his hips against the stranger. His cock brushed against rough denim. He held onto the monkey bar and ground himself against the stranger's thigh.

"Say my name, Freak. Say it and beg."

"Butch," Josh managed to gasp. "Butch, please! I'll do anything you want."

"That's right. You will."

The hands abandoned Josh's nipples and pushed away from him. Josh stood there, whimpering. He heard the sound of a zipper opening. When the hands came back, they grabbed him by the buttocks and pulled him close. A cock, thick and hard, rubbed against Josh's. It was so cold it burned.

"You want my cock, Freak?"

"Yes!"

"Would you go down on it and suck it better than Louise ever did?"

"I'll do anything you want."

The hands pushed Josh to his knees. He slid against the cold body, feeling the hard cock rub against him all the way down until it bounced in his face. Josh put his lips around it and for one hysterical moment thought of Arnie Hinkman and the time he licked a frozen flagpole on a dare and got stuck there. Then the hands wrapped in Josh's hair and urged him forward, and his mouth was too full of cock for him to think of Arnie anymore.

"Play with yourself, Freak. I want to watch you jerk off while you suck me."

Josh dropped his hands to his waist and began to stroke himself. He timed his strokes to the thrusts of the cock into his mouth. The pace was steady, pounding, relentless. Josh had blown a few guys in college, but memories paled in comparison to what he was doing now. He shifted on his knees to straddle the stranger's denim-clad leg. He humped the leg and let his hands wrap around the base of the cock that drove into his mouth.

"That's right. Harder. Suck as hard as you can."

Josh humped and sucked faster. His jaw ached. Fear mingled with lust coursed through his veins. Any minute now, somebody was going to pull into the parking lot and see him. And then they'd know the truth, that he really was a freak, had been all his life. He hadn't mouthed off to Butch Capps because he'd been too stupid or too brave for his own good. He did it because he knew Butch would punish him, and the Freak liked being punished.

The fingers wrapped in Josh's hair pulled back. Josh released the cock, felt it slide out of his mouth. He wanted to protest, but before he could he was thrown back on the ground and the stranger landed on top of him.

"Tell me what you want, Freak!"

"I want you, Butch!"

"Scream for me. I want to hear you scream my name."

So he did. He screamed and he thrust his naked cock against the icy cold body that lay on top of him. He shrieked Butch's name as cruel fingers twisted his nipples and a rough mouth attacked his neck. He screamed and screamed, and then screamed some more as he came and then the stranger came, spurting frozen come all over his belly.

"We're done. Get up."

The dead weight lifted off his body. Josh struggled to his feet. He felt dizzy, disoriented.

"Take off the blindfold, Freak."

Fear seized Josh's body. "Why?"

"Just do it."

He lifted the blindfold, eased it off his head. The stranger stood in front of him, glowing faintly in the dusk. His face was as pale and cold as the moon. Dark blood clotted at the temple. More blood stained his shirt and jeans.

"You were right, Freak. I am dead. But you aren't. Now put your clothes back on and quit waiting for me. And get the hell off my playground. If I ever catch you here again ..."

He faded away before he finished the threat. Josh dropped to his knees, cold and confused. After a while, he crawled over to the spiral slide and found his clothing. He put everything back on except the torn shirt. When he picked it up to throw it away, a car key fell out. He picked it up. It was a match to the one on his key ring.

Josh stumbled away from the slide, past the swings, and back toward the parking lot. As he reached the curb, he heard Butch whisper one last time.

"Get the hell off my playground. If I ever catch you here again, you'll get more of the same."

Josh got into his car and started the engine. Before he left, he shouted out the window.

"It's not your playground!"

But still, he never came back.

# AUTHORS

**JEFF ADAMS** has published short stories in *The First Line*, a magazine he co-edited from 1999-2006. He's currently working on more short stories, as well as a novel. Jeff is based in New York City with his husband, Will. You can find out more at www.jeffandwill.com.

**JIM CLARK** is by daytime a normal scientist, but by night he is Geek Supreme, enjoying and being obsessed with virtually everything that is remotely geeky. But somehow he still gets time to write stories and spend fun nights with his closest friend, who Jim is currently on a mission to convert to the joys of geek hood.

**DALTON** is a writer and sexual adventurer who lives in the Northeast with two longtime companions and a Chihuahua with major attitude.

**LANDON DIXON's** writing credits include *Options, Beau, In Touch/Indulge, Three Pillows, Mandate, Torso, Honcho, Men, Freshmen,* and stories in the anthologies *Straight? Volume 2, Friction 7, Working Stiff, Sex by the Book,* and *Ultimate Gay Erotica 2005* and *2007.*

**AUGUSTA LI** is the author of several short stories, novellas, novels, and yaoi manga scripts, created either on her own or with her partner in crime, Eon de Beaumont. Gus and Eon are also artists and are currently hard at work on many manga and prose projects. They would love nothing more than to see the yaoi/BL genre flourish in the West. Visit Gus at www.yaoimagic.com, or just watch for her at anime conventions and Goth clubs around the East Coast.

**HELEN E. H. MADDEN** is a writer whose published works have appeared in *CREAM: The Best of the Erotica Readers and Writers Association* and in the charity anthology *Coming Together: With Pride.* Helen writes and produces *Heat Flash,* a free weekly podcast of erotic speculative fiction. When not working, Helen thinks about sex. A lot. Web www.helenehmadden.com, Podcast: www.heatflash.libsyn.com.

**WAYNE MANSFIELD** was born in rural Western Australia and now lives in the capital, Perth. He is university educated and has written many erotic gay short stories, most of which have been or are about to be published by STARbooks.

A bit about me... my name is **DAVID MULLER**, and I am an Israeli author. In 2003 I wrote a fictional series called *Peachtree Passions* for *David Atlanta Magazine* under the pen name "Day-Day Los Angeles" and in 2004, my story "Driving Around with Dad" appeared under my real name online at *Mirsky's Golems*. In 2006 many of my stories were published in English: "I Met God Once" appeared in *Shevet: New Voices from Israel*, (published by the Bar Ilan University CW program); and "Renata's Three Statements" in *Jane Doe Buys a Challah*, (published by AngLit Press). Last year my story "The Galilee" appeared in *Gay Travels in the Muslim World*, published by Hawthorn Press and another story entitled "The Beekeeper" appeared in *Love in a Lock-Up* published by STARbooks Press.

**STEPHEN OSBORNE** has had stories published in many anthologies, including *Ride Me Cowboy, Unmasked, Ultimate Gay Erotica 2008, Best Gay Love Stories: Summer Flings, Frat Sex 2, Dorm Porn 2,* and *Best Date Ever.* He is also the author of *South Bend Ghosts and Other Northern Indiana Haunts.* He lives in Indianapolis and is single but taking applications.

**ROB ROSEN** is the author of *Sparkle: The Queerest Book You'll Ever Love* and *Divas Las Vegas*, and has contributed to more than fifty anthologies, most notably for STARbooks: *Ride Me Cowboy, Service with a Smile, Boys Caught in the Act,* and *Pretty Boys and Roughnecks.* See him at www.therobrosen.com.

Published in dozens of gay erotic anthologies, **JAY STARRE** pumps out fiction from his home in Vancouver,

Canada. He has written regularly for such hot magazines as *Torso, Mandate* and *Men*. His work can be found in titles like *Love in a Lock-Up, Don't Ask, Don't Tie Me Up*, and *Unmasked: Erotic Tales of Gay Superheroes*. His steamy gay novel *Erotic Tales of the Knights Templar* came out in late 2007. His latest erotic book is *Lusty Adventures of the Prince of Knossos* in the spring of 2009.

A Little about **BRYL TYNE** … A combination of Cherokee Indian and Bukovinian Gypsy, Bryl's a wrangler by nature and a writer by choice. Raised to believe little seen and nothing heard, Bryl's pastimes have evolved from years of hands on research and discreet observation.

**J. D WATERS** loves red wine, good pasta, hot men and porn. But not necessarily in that order. The ocean, good books, uninterrupted writing time and ice cream are also appreciated.

# EDITOR

**FRED TOWERS** lives in Indiana with his husband of 10 years, Mel. *Nerdvana* is his first time to edit an erotica collection. He was published in *Bearotica* from Alyson Publications, *Muscle Worshipers* from STARbooks Press, *Ultimate Gay Erotica 2008* from Alyson, and *Flesh to Flesh* from Strebor Books. He decided to write his story in *Bearotica* to inspire his best bear friend, J. Michael Mills to publish his stories. Unfortunately, Michael died of a heart attack before Fred convinced him to try sending out his stories. His friend is his inspiration for a lot of his stories. It's his way to memorialize his best friend.

He wrote book reviews for gay fiction for Rainbow Reviews.com. He hopes to write and edit more. Visit him at http://fredtowers.blogspot.com.

ing any underwear. "Excuse me," I said, having a hard time lookin

ded by that bulge in his crotch, "but don't I know you?" "Maybe,"

l of t                                                         bout a n

h Ray                                                         God, you

oser?                                                         in?" he a

. "Lik                                                        s stronge

body                                                          e on Gre

, he l                                                        s I ever s

p to t                                                        any idea

aking                                                         ne same

coul                                                          ery long

d raci                                                        ne swel

g with                                                        e in sto

e go                                                          behind

see                                                           in pub

?" he                                                         vent to 1

vacy.                                                         grabbe

rd. I

traci                                                         t, so fir

it, ha

ith m                                                         bing di

ing, I                                                        n cock,

sound of unzipping filled the small space. I don't know who's ha

ut before I knew it, I had his rod in my hand, and mine was in his

to do?" he asked, his tone challenging. I knew exactly, and sank t